I0699043

Praise for *Gringolandia*
by Lyn Miller-Lachmann:

★ 2010 YALSA Best Books for Young Adults list

★ 2010 Bank Street College Best Children's Books list, grades 9–12

★ 2010 Americas Award Honor Book

★ 2010 ALAN Pick

★ 2010 IPPY Gold Medal, Children's Multicultural Fiction

★ 2011 Texas Library Association Tayshas High School Reading List

"[T]he overarching exploration of injustice and its costs gives the novel memorable heft."

—The Horn Book Magazine

"This impressive novel . . . skillfully incorporates elements of family drama, teen romance, and political thriller. . . . [A] rare reading experience that both touches the heart and opens the mind."

—School Library Journal

"Heartfelt and strong, with an in-your-face immediacy, this novel is revelatory in its portrayal of repressive regimes, immigrants, and familial relationships."

—VOYA

"This poignant, often surprising and essential novel illuminates too-often ignored political aspects of many South Americans' migration to the United States."

—Kirkus Reviews

"This action-packed story is a wonderful work of historical fiction that is a must-have for any library or personal collection."

—Children's Literature

SURVIVING
Santiago

by Lyn Miller-Lachmann

RP|TEENS
PHILADELPHIA · LONDON

Copyright © 2015 by Lyn Miller-Lachmann

All rights reserved under the Pan-American
and International Copyright Conventions

Printed in the United States

*This book may not be reproduced in whole or in part, in any form or by any
means, electronic or mechanical, including photocopying, recording, or by any
information storage and retrieval system now known or hereafter invented,
without written permission from the publisher.*

Books published by Running Press are available at special discounts for
bulk purchases in the United States by corporations, institutions, and
other organizations. For more information, please contact the Special
Markets Department at the Perseus Books Group, 2300 Chestnut Street,
Suite 200, Philadelphia, PA 19103, or call (800) 810-4145, ext. 5000, or
e-mail special.markets@perseusbooks.com.

ISBN 978-0-7624-5633-8

Library of Congress Control Number: 2014954486
E-book ISBN 978-0-7624-5635-2

9 8 7 6 5 4 3 2 1
Digit on the right indicates the number of this printing

Cover and interior design by T.L. Bonaddio
Edited by Lisa Cheng
Typography: Scala, Maxwell Slab, Special Elite,
Filmotype Lucky, and Good Foot

Published by Running Press Teens
An Imprint of Running Press Book Publishers
A Member of the Perseus Books Group
2300 Chestnut Street
Philadelphia, PA 19103–4371

Visit us on the web!
www.runningpress.com/rpkids

For Aunt Ruth

CHAPTER 1

I'm not going to cry.

My crew surrounds me, all of us in our stuffy clothes, fanning ourselves with our invitations—my best friend, Petra, and a bunch of my other friends who've come to see Mamá and Evan get married. They shield me from sniffling adults, and if I do cry they'll rag on me and tell me that turning sixteen has made me old and no longer cool.

Adults cry when they're happy. I know that because Mamá's eyes are shiny as she stands in front of the judge. And she blinks a lot.

I'm happy for her . . . I think.

She has Evan—an awesome guy who loves her.

But Evan is not my father. Not the guy Mamá means when she says, *half of you is him.* My father lives at the ends of the earth, and I'm getting shipped there tomorrow—a pawn in a kicked-over chess set.

Mamá may not be skinny anymore, but her lacy wedding dress makes her look like she's still twenty-one, the bride from the album she brought with her when we moved to Madison from Santiago in 1981, eight years ago. Nearly nine years after soldiers arrested my father. Papá had wire-rim glasses and a beard like Evan, but he also had shaggy hair. Evan is going bald.

Peludo como un oso, Mamá used to say. Whenever I paged through the album, she would look over my shoulder, her teardrops splashing onto the plastic that kept the photos dry. I would imagine Papá flying out of that prison and laughing at her. A big, laughing bear with a beard that covered half his face and wild chestnut hair that blazed in the sunlight.

When I was your age, I didn't cry for the whole year, he said on my seventh birthday after Daniel, my older brother, ripped the arm off my brand-new doll. *You can be brave, too. Not like your mother who cries over every little thing.* Papá twisted the doll's arm back into its socket and stitched the torn shoulder as if he were a surgeon instead of a taxi driver.

I didn't cry for a whole month after that. Not even when I tripped on broken pavement and scraped my knee. Papá loved me, and his love made me brave.

I had no idea it would be my last birthday with him, the way he used to be.

Beside me, Petra uses her set of colored pencils to decorate the black-and-white Victorian house on the invitation. Evan bought the house from the city of Madison for back taxes two years ago. His sketch for the

8

invitation doesn't show the real story—the boarded-up windows, collapsed porch, and sagging roof. He calls fixing up houses his *mitzvah*, which is a Jewish way of saying "good deed." I was supposed to help him finish this *mitzvah* house over the summer so our new family could move there in September.

Now I'm going to Chile.

"Dropped your purple," I whisper to Petra. Trying to fetch her pencil from underneath my wooden folding chair, I rock on the inn's bumpy lawn, which slopes down to the lake and nearly pitches me into her. I slide my left foot from my sandal and kick the pencil forward so I can grab it. The damp grass tickles my toes.

"Thanks," Petra says as she taps the invitation with the eraser end. Two rows in front of us, Evan's mother's chair sinks into the ground. My real grandparents, Mamá's parents, aren't here. They refused to come from Chile for the wedding because they consider divorce a sin—even though they also consider my father a subversive and a criminal who destroyed his family and deserved everything that happened to him.

The last time I saw Papá was three years ago, after they let him out of prison. He stayed with us in Madison for six months I wish I could forget. He no longer had a beard. His hair hung limp and stringy, and an eyelid and the corner of his mouth sagged. He sat in our apartment drinking wine like it was water. When he left for Chile to work underground against the dictatorship, I thought I would never see him alive again.

As the judge officially turns my mother into Mrs. Evan Feldman, I focus on Petra's invitation. Mint-green siding. Light and dark purple trim. Gray roof. Bright blue front door.

The first bars of "Mellow Yellow" float in the air while Mamá and Evan are still kissing—not a restrained peck but a madly in love newlyweds' smooch in front of a hundred people that goes from cute to embarrassing by the end of the first verse. Petra holds up her invitation and raises her voice above the psychedelic music and the buzz from sappy comments around us. "I'm giving this to Evan."

Mamá and Evan walk arm in arm down the aisle, Donovan crooning from the speakers behind them. The top of Evan's head shines in the sunlight. His skin is starting to go pink, so I make a mental note to tell him: *sunscreen*. I reach for the rose petals in my purse and toss them over Petra's head toward my mother. A couple land in Petra's blonde hair, and their scent mixes with her Herbal Essences berry shampoo. After the song fades and everyone stands, my friends and I hug each other.

Max asks, "Do you really have to leave tomorrow?"

"Yeah. They wanted me out so I wouldn't have a party with fifty people in our itty-bitty apartment while they're gone."

"So does the water really go down the drain the opposite way there?" Petra says.

"Don't remember." I wriggle my foot back into my sandal. "How about if I do an experiment? I'll flush my summer down the drain and see which way it goes." A few of my friends laugh. In my mind summer dissolves into yellow and green paint circling clockwise instead of counterclockwise.

"Will it be snowing?"

"Do you have to go to school?"

"Are you gone the whole vacation?"

"They can't make you, can they?"

I sigh. "Guys, we wouldn't be having this wedding if I didn't agree to go. They don't allow divorce in Chile, so my father let it happen here in exchange for visitation rights."

"That sounds like he's taking you prisoner," says Max.

Prisoner. That's the exact wrong word. "It was my decision. . . ." My voice comes out funny. I clear my throat.

Mamá wouldn't have gotten to marry Evan unless she divorced Papá. And if Papá demanded visitation rights, it means that he wants to see me, that maybe he still loves me. Me, his little Tina. Not just Daniel.

Petra clutches my wrist and drags me away from the others, toward the food table. Silently, I thank her. "You can come back sooner, right? When your mother gets home from her honeymoon?"

I lower my voice. "It depends." On whether he's my old *papá* again.

My old *papá* drove us to the beach in his beat-up green taxi. We ran into the ocean and let the waves chase us back to shore. But I was too small, so he lifted me onto his shoulders. My hands squeezed his hair like a horse's mane.

"Would he, like, get really mad if you left early?"

I shrug. Petra never met Papá. Never knew what he was like before. Or after.

"You said every time he and your mother talked on the phone during the divorce, he acted like a jerk and she ended up crying. Maybe she can use that as evidence."

I run the back of my hand across my eyes. One teardrop. Doesn't count.

"Or remember that short story we read freshman year?" Her voice rises. "'Ransom of Red Chief' or something."

"Yeah, I could totally act up so he sends her money to get rid of me." Or he could yell at me and slap me. And so could my aunt, Tía Ileana, who lives with him. She doesn't have kids of her own, and even though she never spanked Daniel and me when we were little, she often yelled at us for making noise and running around too much.

Petra pivots toward our friends, but her spiked heel slides into a mole hole. She trips and crashes into Evan.

"Oh, sorry, Ev—, uh, Mr. Feldman." She lifts her foot from the hole, brushes her hair back, and hands him her invitation. "Look, I picked out some colors for the house."

Stroking his beard, Evan studies Petra's artwork and smiles.

"We can use a stencil when we do the inside. Tina can hold it up while I paint. You know I cut my own." Petra taps the card, and I bite my lip to keep from laughing. Her signature stencil is a marijuana leaf. "You guys will have the most amazing house in Madison."

That's why Petra's my best friend. It'll suck not getting to hang out with her this summer.

I'm not going to cry.

CHAPTER 2

"*P*asaporte.*" The uniformed customs officer holds out his hand. I can't tell how old he is because of his military cap and lack of a mustache or beard, but his hand is callused and wrinkled. His other hand rests on the automatic pistol in his holster. I hand him my dark red Chilean passport and the notarized permission forms, which I already showed the soldier at the immigration window. "Cristina Isabel Aguilar Fuentes," the officer reads. *"¿Nombre de padre?"*

"Marcelo Leonardo Aguilar Gaetani."

"Marcelo Leonardo Aguilar Gaetani." The officer's lip curls into a sneer as he says, *"alias Nino."*

I nod slowly. The name Papá used when he worked underground is no secret to the dictator's people now. After all, Papá calls his daily radio show *Oye, Nino.* And my brother said it's one of the most popular talk shows in the country.

"¿Madre?"

"María Victoria." I hesitate, because her name changed only two days ago. "Fuentes Rubio . . . de Feldman." I

15

never liked the *de* part, which makes it sound like women are the property of their husbands.

He switches to heavily accented English. "What is the purpose of your trip?"

"Visiting my father. My parents are divorced."

I shift from one foot to the other. People on the lines next to me pass straight through while the guy examines my passport and the letters from my parents that prove I'm not a runaway or a sex slave. Then he uses a two-way radio to call someone else.

Sweat tickles my neck and chest, though my hands are ice-cold. I remind myself to be careful and say as little as possible. *He* is still in power—Pinochet, the dictator who led a violent military coup that brought down our elected president just three months after I was born. Unlike Daniel, I didn't know what it was like to live in a democracy until I moved to Wisconsin.

People think a little kid doesn't notice the difference, but I did. Even if I didn't know who told the tanks and soldiers to be there, it was hard to miss them. A bunch of times, I saw soldiers—like the one in front of me right now—beat people up in the street. Daniel would try to cover my eyes while Mamá would grab Papá's arms and beg—*think of your kids, Chelo*—so he wouldn't run to help the people. Daniel saw Papá get beaten and arrested in our apartment in Santiago while I was asleep. It's not something my brother talks about, but before he left for college, his bedroom and mine shared a wall, and whenever he cranked up his music in the middle of the night, I knew he was thinking about it.

And when I think about what they did to Papá in that prison—torturing him so he'd name his sources and associates, beating him into a coma when he refused, sticking him into solitary confinement, even though the left half of his body didn't work. . . . It's like our whole family got twisted around this man with his military uniform, his gray mustache, and his pompous smile.

Two more men show up. One looks young and carries a machine gun. The other one has wrinkles around his eyes and a gray mustache clipped the same way as the general's. He wears a special uniform.

"Open the bag," the man in the special uniform says. He has almost no accent in English.

I unzip my duffel. The man paws through my stuff and pulls out the plastic bag with the medicine my mother sent for Papá. After exchanging smiles and nods with the customs official that make my insides clench, he takes out the pill bottles one by one. He and the customs official count them out, all twenty-five of them, and examine their labels. He tells the other two to wait while he gets a camera.

Sweat drips down my back. My knees go weak.

I'm screwed. How do I get the next plane home?

The special uniform guy returns with a Polaroid camera. "Why are you bringing all these pills in?" he barks. "Are you planning to sell them?" The man with the machine gun writes something in a small note pad, using the gun's stock as his surface.

"They're for my father. The prescription's there, too."

The customs officer takes a piece of paper from the bag. "Here it is." He hands the prescription to the guy with the camera, who I guess is his boss.

"What does *he* need them for?" the boss asks me in English.

I stare at my sneakers and mumble, "He has seizures."

Because of what you people did to him. This I cannot say out loud. Rule number one: no discussing politics with anyone besides Papá, Tía Ileana, and their friends. Even though Papá's side won the plebiscite, the election to decide whether or not Pinochet would rule for another ten years, the general is still around until next March and a lot of his supporters are mad that they lost.

Daniel said I'd be safe if I followed this rule. I'm not so sure. A month ago I overheard Mamá on the phone, arguing with Papá about a musician who got beaten up in the street. The government media called it a drug deal gone bad. Papá thought it was a political attack and wanted to investigate, but Mamá told him to let it go until after my visit.

The customs official steps toward his boss and says in hurried Spanish, "I need a picture of his kid, too."

I step backward and cover my face. *Why?*

"Hands at your sides, please," the boss orders in English. He gives the customs official a quick glance, then takes one photo of me standing alone and one holding the pill bottles and the prescription. Like I'm a mule for a drug cartel. And after sixteen hours on three separate planes and zero sleep, I wonder if I look like those grim-faced, glassy-eyed people in police mug shots. The boss shakes the two photos dry, but I don't get to see them.

The customs guy returns the bottles to my bag and hands me my passport. "Have a nice trip . . . Cristina," he says. His smirk makes me shiver.

///////////////////

After I escape the evil threesome, the only one waiting for me in the airport lobby is my aunt. She wears a dark blue business suit and a pinstriped shirt, as if she's on her way to the office.

"*¿Donde está mi papá?*" I ask. My voice trembles.

"He had to go to work early, *amorcita*. But he promised he'll come home to eat after his show." She kisses me on both cheeks, then takes a few steps backward. "I can't believe how much you've grown."

"You're still taller," I say.

"You grew out your hair, too. It looks nice."

I push my airplane-matted hair back from my face,

19

twist it around my finger, and tuck it under the hood of my sweatshirt.

Tía Ileana lifts my duffel over her shoulder and starts toward the exit. She's six years older than my father, which makes her forty-seven, but she doesn't look much different from when I saw her last. She's cut her hair short, like my brother's, but added red highlights. She wears gold hoop earrings and a stud at the top of her left ear. Her face is smooth, except for a few wrinkles around her eyes.

She asks me about my flight. I don't answer, chewing on my disappointment instead. Now I have to wait for *la comida*, the main meal of the day. That's not for another four hours.

Tía Ileana keeps looking at me, so I finally say, "They showed two movies. And I saw the sun rise over Lima." Though I worried that my Spanish would be rusty, I have no problem finding the right words—or understanding everything my aunt says to me.

"That must have been beautiful." She doesn't ask me which movies I watched, so I assume she's not a movie person.

Outside, it's a clear day, though the sky has a purple tint and my eyes sting after a few minutes.

Tía Ileana puts her free arm around my shoulders. "Smog bothering you?" she asks.

"A little."

"It's bad in winter. A lot worse than when you lived here."

The aromas of my childhood come back to me. Wood smoke. Exhaust fumes. Dirt and vegetation. Palm trees border the parking lot, blue-green fronds spreading out from their smooth trunks like sparklers. Pollution aside, it feels more like a damp early fall at home, with leaves still on trees, sun heating the pavement, and just a bite of cold in each wind gust. By the time we reach her little gray car at the back end of the lot, I'm over-heated in my sweatshirt.

We get in the car. I slam the door. "I didn't want to say anything in the airport, but the customs people treated me like a *narcotraficante*."

"They give everyone a hard time." Tía Ileana pats my knee, like I'm still the little kid who left years ago. Where the palm trees end, two khaki-and-olive-uniformed sol-diers with machine guns guard a rusted white metal gate.

"A bunch of people went through on the other lines while they searched my bag. I thought they were going to take the medicine away."

"They didn't, did they?" There's a trace of panic in my aunt's voice. I shake my head.

The road from the airport takes us through a neighbor-hood of shanties with tin roofs and walls of scrap wood and metal, each shanty connected to the other in a crooked three-dimensional patchwork. Graffiti covers many of the walls, mostly initials in red and black. Tía Ileana says the graffiti stands for the various political parties that have come together in opposition to Pinochet's candidates in the upcoming October election.

When we stop at a traffic light, I point to a wall with at least three different party tags, a hammer and sickle, and stenciled portraits of Che Guevara in red, black, blue, and green. They look like the picture of Che that we wear on T-shirts at home. My T-shirt has him in black on an olive green background, but Mamá wouldn't let me pack it.

"Aren't these people afraid of getting arrested?" I ask.

"Not anymore." My aunt turns to face me. "All the parties are legal now, and people can't be arrested for taking part in the campaign."

"Really?"

"Yes. I know it's hard to believe, *amorcita*. But your father and a lot of other people worked hard to make it happen."

She smiles. I sure hope she's right, especially since she's the one Mamá is counting on to watch out for me.

The light changes, and Tía Ileana drives past more shanties. Some blocks have identical one-story brick houses with sturdier corrugated metal roofs. Most of these look new and don't have graffiti on the walls, or if they do, it's a different set of letters. According to my aunt, they're for the Alliance whose presidential candidate likes the dictator. I guess that's how the people got the better houses. Ragged children play in ditches beside the road, and packs of scrawny dogs wander through the scrub. The kids and the dogs ignore each other. A military jeep passing in the other direction ignores the kids skipping school.

I remember the *poblaciones*, shantytowns, and the kids who never went to school or who begged for money in front of the shopping centers and cafés where my *mamá* and *abuelos* used to take me. *People shouldn't have to live like that,* Papá used to say—words that could get a person beaten up and arrested on the street or in their home in those days.

Smog hides the mountaintops, but I see two large hills in the middle of the city and a lot of modern highrise buildings near one of them.

I point to the tallest of the steel-and-glass buildings. "Is this one new?"

"Brand-new. The one under construction will be a condominium." The booms of a pair of cranes kiss an unfinished building's steel frame—twelve—fifteen stories high.

Even the highways are modern, just like the ones in Chicago or Milwaukee, but most of the cars and buses here are a lot older. Their tailpipes spew smoke.

"This might look more like Madison, from what your father says." Exiting the highway, my aunt drives along tree-lined streets through a neighborhood of tidy one- and two-story brick and stucco houses, with a few small apartment buildings. The streets are clean, the yards have trees and flowers, and many of the houses are painted in delicious pastels—blue, green, pink, and yellow. It does look like home, except the houses are closer together, and many, even in this nice neighborhood, have bars on the windows or walls and gates around them.

"Love the colors. Is this where you guys live?" I ask. The apartment building where we lived before Papá's arrest was nowhere near this nice.

"No, but here's where I used to live before your father bought his place." My aunt waves her hand toward a modern four-story building with lots of balconies.

"I was supposed to be fixing up a house."

"Your mother said something about it."

"Yeah, Evan, my stepfather—"

"Don't mention him to your father." Tía Ileana's voice is hushed.

"I'm not that dumb." I push my hair from my face. "We're doing a good deed by saving an old house and making the neighborhood nicer."

"We tear down the old houses when we can," Tía Ileana says. "And build office and apartment towers to take their place."

I repeat my stepfather's words. "There's history in an old house. Once it's gone, you never get it back."

"I like that." She taps the steering wheel. "But the city's

growing, and the new buildings are safer in earthquakes."

She turns onto a one-way street so narrow that at home it would be considered an alleyway. She stops in the middle of a block of split-level stucco duplexes with shingle roofs. I'm surprised because most houses here seem to have either corrugated metal or orange terra-cotta roofs.

"This is it," she says. She takes a gray transmitter from the glove box and opens the automatic gate and garage door for the house on the left side. Metal numbers on a low cement wall read 52-50, and the wrought-iron fence above the wall matches the design and height of the automatic gate. Both sides of the duplex are painted white.

"Bright blue," I say.

"What?" She cuts the engine.

"We should paint the house bright blue. Like in that other neighborhood." I think of Petra's plan to turn our house in Madison into an upside-down eggplant.

Tía Ileana laughs. "Are you a bright blue person?"

"Actually, red's my favorite color, but I haven't seen a house painted red so far. Maybe it's against the law. You know, troublemakers' color."

"Troublemaker," she repeats with a smile. "That was the one thing your father and mother agreed on about you." The way she says it makes me think she's cool with the way I am, but then her smile fades. She hits the button to close the garage door. "Your father wanted white."

Inside, Tía Ileana introduces me to Graciela, who cleans the house and cooks the midday meal. Graciela is short, with a round face and salt-and-pepper hair in a single braid almost to her waist. She gives me a big hug. "Your father is so happy you're here," she says in Spanish, but with a different accent, like she's from another part of the country.

I'm too stunned to answer. We never had a housekeeper or nanny growing up, except for the eight months we lived with Mamá's family after Papá's arrest. Almost no one has them in Wisconsin—at least no one over the age of two because all the little kids go to preschool. But I remember my *abuelos* offering to pay for a *nana* when Papá drove the taxi, and Mamá telling them we didn't need one because our apartment was too small and Daniel looked out for me. Years later, Daniel told me our parents didn't want anyone coming in and finding out that Papá worked for the resistance.

After we carry my stuff upstairs, Tía Ileana lifts the duffel onto a wooden trunk at the foot of my new bed. I stare at the brightly colored three-dimensional tapestries that decorate my walls. Slightly larger than a picture book, each one has tiny dolls and scraps of fabric in the shape of animals sewn into scenes of the countryside and the mountains.

"I thought you guys didn't believe in servants," I say to my aunt as soon as Graciela goes downstairs.

"Your father believes in equality. No masters, no servants. So Graciela may cook and keep the house clean, but she and her husband are also people he worked with underground." Tía Ileana unzips the duffel. "We all agreed it was the best way to go, with both of us working and him not being able to do a lot of things for himself."

Flooding into my mind is an image of a twisted man with stubble and stringy hair. One of his arms dangles useless, but the other can lash out in an instant.

Then the fog of sixteen hours on an airplane descends upon me. I run the toe of my sneaker along the shiny hardwood floor, thinking that I might fall asleep standing up while Tía Ileana unpacks for me. A couple of open-mouthed yawns, and she gets the message.

CHAPTER 3

I awaken to the sound of my father's voice. A little slower than the typical machine-gun pace of Chilean *castellano*, with a slightly odd inflection. I crawl deeper under the covers.

Give him a chance, Tina.

I climb out of bed and pull on my jeans and sweatshirt.

When I reach the top of the stairs, I freeze and stare down at Papá. Thick, wavy hair falls to the middle of his neck, parted so it hangs over his glasses and covers his bad eye. He has a mustache, too—mostly gray like his hair. No beard. He's still skinny, but he looks good. Washed. Dressed. Apparently sober. He has a crooked smile. He beckons to me from the bottom of the stairs. "Come, *m'ija*. Don't be a *coneja*."

I force my legs to take me downstairs. My arms circle his waist, but his sweater is a force field keeping me from touching his body. My old *papá* would have picked me up, lifted me over his head, and spun me around. But when he came back from prison, he cringed at my touch.

My father grips me tightly with his good arm. The pressure on my shoulders inches me forward, toward his sweater. It smells like cigarettes. My throat closes, but I squeeze him tighter into a real hug. His body is warm, and through his sweater and shirt I feel his ribs. I hold on to him for a superlong time so he won't keep calling me girl-rabbit because he thinks I'm trying to run away from him.

He lets his arm drop. "Did you have a good flight?"

I step backward and take a deep breath to get rid of the cigarette smell. A black wrist splint pokes out from his shirtsleeve on his bad side. "Yes. I watched two movies on the plane."

"Which ones?"

"*Big* and *Bill and Ted's Excellent Adventure.*"

"Haven't seen them."

"*Big* is about a thirteen-year-old kid who wakes up as a thirty-year-old guy, and the other—"

Papá taps my shoulder, interrupting me. "How do you like the house?"

"It's . . . nice."

"I got one with an extra bedroom so you and your brother could visit." One side of his mouth turns up while the other side doesn't move at all.

Say you love the house. I think that's what he wants me to do. But I don't love it. It's cold. White. New.

I draw in my breath. "I love the house, Papá. You did a good job."

"Come outside. I want to show you the best part."

He walks stiff-legged through the kitchen into what looks like his office, with bookshelves, a desk, and a daybed piled with papers. He opens a sliding door to a small brick patio with a round metal table painted pea green, two matching chairs, and a brick–and–cinder block barbecue. Beyond the patio is a garden surrounded by a high wall covered with vines. A huge tree in back takes up about a third of the space in the yard. Along the left side wall stretching all the way to the back there's a wire-fenced area like a dog run, but with trees and vines inside.

He unhooks the clasp of the wire fence's gate, reaches into the narrow opening, and comes out with a small parrot on his finger. "Pablo, this is Tina," he says to the bird. And to me, "Do you want to hold him?"

"Will he bite?" I ask. Papá shakes his head, so I hold out my finger. The bird hops on and stares at me with yellow eyes. His claws feel like two sticks wrapped around my fingers. I stroke the dark gray feathers on his back. "How'd you get him?"

"I rescued him. His wing was dislocated, so he can't fly." Papá rests his hand on my shoulder. "I have another one named Víctor. Graciela's husband brought him to me last month because he had chewed part of his foot off. I think he can still perch, but he doesn't trust me yet."

"Does that one fly?"

"Yes," Papá says.

"Why'd he chew his foot off?"

31

"He could have injured the foot or got it caught. Or he could have been abused. These birds are very sensitive, and if they're miserable, they harm themselves." Papá takes Pablo from me and holds him at eye level. "This one plucked out all his feathers. But they grew back, didn't they, Pablo?" He stands still for a while as if waiting for a response, sets the bird on a branch inside the cage, and closes the wire door.

"Remember when you used to fix our broken toys?" I ask.

He nods. "But birds aren't toys, *m'ija*. They're living things. It's different."

I stare at Pablo and imagine him *desplomado*. Featherless.

Back inside, Papá washes his hands, sits at the head of the table, and pours himself a glass of mineral water. That must be some kind of signal, because my aunt sits on his left. I wash my hands like he tells me to and take the chair opposite hers, where Graciela has set a place for me.

"How's your brother?" he asks me.

You mean, the favorite? The one who worked with you at the radio station all last summer? But I don't want to make Papá mad on the very first day. And I have other methods. I give my father a sly smile. "Fine. But he brought his backpack to the wedding. It was truly embarrassing."

Tía Ileana's mouth opens wide before she covers it with her hand. Still, a giggle escapes. Papá closes his eyes and laughs out loud.

Score one point for the little sister.

Papá stops laughing and leans toward me, his good arm on the table. "Did your mother send the pills?"

"Yes. I'll get them. They're upstairs in my bag." I stand.

Papá motions for me to sit. "In my house, we don't get up and walk around during meals."

The pills. That's why Daniel had the backpack. Take the sister's point away.

Papá digs into his *pastel de choclo*. I dismantle mine—pile the ground corn on one side, mash the potatoes with my fork, push the olives around the plate, and nibble the ground beef and hard-boiled eggs.

For the rest of the meal I keep my mouth shut while my father and aunt discuss the election in October and the candidate that he just interviewed on his radio show. After dessert—vanilla ice cream with chocolate syrup—Papá stands, rubs his stomach, and stretches. "*Bueno*, back to work," he says, then asks Tía Ileana for a ride.

"Didn't you promise you'd stay this afternoon for Tina?"

Tell him, Tía Ileana. Would he have ditched Daniel the same way? Or would he have invited my brother to the station?

"I have to edit that interview for the evening news. And I'm going out with the campaign staff tonight." Papá pats me on the back. I force myself to smile, lips pressed tightly together. "Get some rest, *m'ija*. You've had a long trip."

///////////////////

Night comes early in the middle of winter, and after dark the house turns cold. My aunt reheats the leftover *pastel de choclo* for supper. It has even less appeal the second time around. I curl up on the sofa under a wool blanket and watch a stupid game show on TV. It's good practice for my Spanish, if nothing else.

The TV set is like a shameful secret in the room, small and tucked into a corner of the floor-to-ceiling bookcase that covers the wall next to the stairs. It's an hour earlier in Madison, and on a Monday night like tonight my friends and I would get together at Petra's house, cook marijuana brownies, and eat them while watching reruns of *St. Elsewhere* on her big TV. We'd try not to drool over Boomer, who suddenly became a single father after his wife tripped and hit her head in the shower. Poor Boomer. All of us girls wished we could give him a hug.

Tía Ileana sits on the sofa next to me. I pull my legs up to make room for her. She holds a folder with lots of pictures, front and back. "Remember the condominium we saw driving here?" I nod. She says, "I put together the publicity for the company that's building it."

I flip the folder, glance at the drawing of a tower with balconies. There are even pots with flowers. Surrounding the drawing are photos of living rooms, kitchens, bedrooms, and a bathroom. "Where did these rooms come from? I thought the place wasn't built yet," I say.

"They're from my company's other condo in the same neighborhood."

"Do you like working for them?"

"I like that things are happening. Your father calls me Material Girl, but I like the new malls and restaurants. And the fact that people are going out again."

I stretch and yawn. Material Girl—Madonna. I'm amazed Papá even knows about her. And Tía Ileana has turned out to be a lot cooler than I remember her from when I was a little kid. "So no more curfews late at night?" I ask her. We used to have to stay indoors or risk getting shot, but sometimes when people needed help or a ride, my old *papá* would go out anyway.

"No. And people aren't as afraid as they used to be. Even though *he's* still in power."

Around midnight, a couple of hours after I get to bed, I awaken to talking and laughing downstairs. I put my clothes back on and creep to the top of the stairs. The living room is full of men. They eventually leave in groups of twos and threes. Papá and one other guy stay. I hear something about the political campaign, but since their words all run together and I'm tired, I can't make out most of what they're saying. A cloud of cigarette smoke hovers just below the ceiling. And they match each other—shots and beer chasers—littering the coffee table with their butts, ashes, and empty bottles. Finally, the other guy passes out sitting in a corner of the sofa, snoring so loudly that I can hear him from upstairs. Papá raises a fist in triumph, announces, "Journalist outdrinks politician any day," and turns off the light.

My old *papá* wouldn't have won a drinking contest. He wouldn't have even tried.

I decide to count the days until I go home.

Chapter 4

Tuesday, June 13: 69 days until I go home

I expect Papá to drag himself around the house hung over the entire next day, but he's gone to work by the time I wake up. Also gone are Tía Ileana and the politician who crashed on the sofa.

At least Tía Ileana returns for *la comida*.

After she leaves, I decide to explore the neighborhood. I figure it's hard to get lost because the mountains on the eastern edge of the city always tell you which direction you're headed, even if clouds cover their peaks. Still, I recheck the number in front of Papá's house because the duplexes on his street look exactly the same behind their cement walls and high fences, and I don't want to try the gate key on every house.

By the middle of the second block the sky turns dark and huge raindrops pelt me. I pull my hood up and turn back. I don't know what I'll do for the rest of the day until Papá and Tía Ileana get home from work. A motorcycle speeds past, its rider's jacket a flash of orange in my

37

peripheral vision. When it's gone, I realize the bottoms of my jeans are soaking wet. I break into a run.

Graciela meets me at the door. "Would you like me to wash your clothes?" she asks.

Mumbling *gracias*, I strip off my soggy sweatshirt and hand it to her, but I don't want to take off my pants in front of her. I did it all the time for my *nana* when I lived with Mamá's family, but I was younger then, and my *nana* wasn't part of an underground resistance along with the person she worked for.

I change clothes in my room, take my waterlogged jeans downstairs to Graciela, and write a letter to Petra, telling her about the flight and the movies I saw on the plane. I ask her to fill me in on last night's *St. Elsewhere* even though it's a summer rerun and I've probably seen it already. Ten episodes—that's how many I'm missing while stuck at the ends of the earth.

At seven thirty, Papá and Tía Ileana return. The first thing Papá does when he gets home is feed his birds. Then he brings Pablo into the house for a conversation, downing a shot of whiskey and a beer chaser while Pablo sprays drops of water all over the kitchen and squawks, "*Curado!*" This new *papá* thinks it's funny that his parrot calls him a drunk. After he takes Pablo back to the cage outside, he wipes the kitchen cabinets and counters while my aunt reheats leftovers in the microwave for her and me. She pops two slices of bread into the toaster and mashes an avocado with lemon for Papá. He eats with no appetite, only the need to line his stomach for the tumbler of straight whiskey he drinks before he goes to sleep.

We have about an hour and a half before he's glassy-eyed and drooling and Tía Ileana has to help him upstairs to bed.

It rains again on Wednesday. I sleep on and off throughout the day, and while lying in bed, I think of things to do with Papá at night. Maybe he'll let me read to him. Or we can work on a jigsaw puzzle or play board games. I saw a couple of puzzle boxes on top of the bookshelf in the living room and Clue and Jenga on the mantle above the fireplace.

I remember how my old *papá* used to read to me before bedtime. He drank only a glass of red wine with supper because sometimes he'd have to go back to work at night. Even then, he would wake me up and kiss me on the head as soon as he came home, letting me know that he made it back all right. *I'm here,* he would say. *I hope you dream of something nice.*

Tía Ileana returns at seven to eat with me, but Papá doesn't even come home until I'm asleep, and then he and his friends wake me up with their drinking games. I don't bother to get up and find out who won.

Thursday is dry but still cloudy and the coldest day since I arrived. And since Papá's house has a washing machine but no dryer, my sweatshirt is still damp, which means I'm stuck inside another day. The good news is that I find *The House of the Spirits* in the original Spanish and discover that I understand nearly everything. I make a small pile of other books I'd like to read and bring them upstairs to my room. In one of them, I learn about the tapestries on my walls. They're called *arpilleras* and have been made by women whose family members were killed or disappeared under the dictatorship.

After supper, I sit with Papá in the dining room because it's my only chance all day to see him. Tía Ileana is upstairs in the master bedroom looking over plans for a shopping center that her company is building.

I sort through the pieces of one of the jigsaw puzzles. No one has opened it before, and a bunch of pieces are stuck together. I go into the kitchen for a paring knife to separate them, but I can't find any knives in the drawers or on the drying rack.

"Papá?"

My father looks up from the magazine he's reading. "Yes?"

"Do you know where they keep the knives around here?"

"No." He takes a long drag from his cigarette and stares at the stream of smoke he blows out. I'm not surprised. At home Evan and my mother cook together all the time, but I never saw Papá or Daniel as good for anything more than boiling water.

"I'll ask Tía Ileana." I start toward the stairs.

"If her door is closed, she doesn't want to be bothered," he tells me before returning to his magazine.

The door to the master bedroom is shut, so I go across the hall to my room and get a deck of cards for solitaire. I think about writing some of my other friends besides Petra, but there'll be time after my father and aunt go to sleep. And tomorrow. And the day after that.

I slip inside the half-opened door to Papá's bedroom. It's hardly big enough for a bed, a chair, and a dresser. On top of the dresser are a small TV and a boom box. The chair faces the dresser but sits under an open closet door where there is a flimsy-looking pulley, the same kind Papá used to exercise his bad arm in Madison. His bed has a black, brown, and tan woven blanket that matches the one on mine. Unframed posters of rallies and concerts cover the walls. The bareness of the space and the faint disinfectant smell make me think of the nursing home where Petra and I did a community service project last fall.

"Tía Ileana was busy," I say when I get downstairs.

Papá nods. His splinted left arm rests on the table and he squeezes an orange ball while counting out a rhythm. A few rounds of solitaire later, he asks me, "What do you think about your aunt?" He has trouble pronouncing his words. Less than a quarter of the glass of whiskey remains.

"I like her. She's nice." I flip over the first three cards
to start a new round.

"You know she never married."

I shrug and place the nine of clubs under the ten
of diamonds. I didn't know that, though I could have
guessed, seeing as she was available to move in with
Papá when he needed someone to help take care of him.

"Do you know why she never married?"

I'm not thinking of an answer because I'm thinking
of her name. Ileana Aguilar Gaetani. *De* Nobody. Belongs
to herself and herself only. Not like Mamá, who used to
be Victoria Fuentes de Aguilar and is now officially Mrs.
Evan Feldman everywhere but at work.

"*Es tortillera.*" He pauses, then spits the next word out
as if it's a bad taste in his mouth. "*Maricona.*"

Pretending not to hear him, I lay the two of hearts
over the ace. Lovers of the same gender. Fine with me.
Obviously not fine with him.

Papá swallows the rest of his drink and slams the
glass on the table. I jump.

"What do you think about that?" he slurs.

I flip three cards from the pile to reveal an eight of
diamonds. I add it to the row under the nine of clubs,
and move three cards from another row underneath. "I
don't think anything about it," I say, wanting to remind
him that Tía Ileana has at least bothered to come home
in the middle of the day to keep me company.

42

"You get what I'm talking about?"

I think of Max's cousin, whose mother and stepfather threw him out because he was gay, and how Max's family took him in, even though they live in a tiny apartment. Putting the kid out really sucked, and I hated those parents even though I never met them. I sweep the cards into a ragged pile, destroying my game. "Sure, I get it. I go to an alternative high school. Half the girls at my school are lesbians." I glare at him. "How do you know I'm not?"

That's right. He hardly knows me and hasn't made much effort in the past four days to change that situation. I hardly know him, either, but what I'm finding out, I really don't like.

"I didn't hear this," Papá says. He slaps the ball from the table with his wrist splint. His strong right hand clenches into a fist. He never hit me like that in Madison, only with his open hand, but I'm not taking any chances. I push away the cards, ready to make a fast break for upstairs. He scrapes his chair back, but instead of going at me, he lurches out of the room.

//////////////////////

The next day I pretend to nap upstairs while Graciela blasts *Oye, Nino*, which she listens to every day between noon and one while she cooks. I don't want to hear his voice again. Last night's encounter still creeps me out, but I'm proud of myself for sticking up for my aunt and letting my father know he was acting like a jerk.

A few minutes after the show ends, Tía Ileana comes home from work. She wants to take a walk before eating, which sounds good to me because I'm not hungry. I still haven't gotten used to eating a big meal in the middle of the day and nothing before bed except a few tasteless leftovers.

"What happened last night between you and your father?" she asks as soon as the gate clangs shut behind us. She speaks in a hushed voice, even though there's no one on our narrow street.

"Did he say anything to you?" I ask, tugging the hood of my finally dry sweatshirt over my head. The air is damp and heavy, again threatening rain.

"He had a bad night. I'm surprised you didn't hear him."

"I had my headphones on. I was writing letters. To my *friends*." I recall the times in Wisconsin when my father woke up screaming. "Did he have a nightmare?"

She shakes her head. "He told me he said something to you that he probably shouldn't have."

I kick a stone farther up the street. It crashes against the low wall in front of a house on the corner. The graffiti in black on the wall reads "*nunca más*"—never again. Next to it is a sketch of the blue, white, and red Chilean flag outlined in black. Another one for our side.

"Did he say what it was?" I ask my aunt.

44

"No."

In the middle of the next block of duplexes, a medium-size dog with matted black hair and no collar trots up to me. It's a lot less skinny than the dogs I saw on the way here from the airport, but it reeks of rotten fish and poop. Tía Ileana claps loudly and hisses to shoo the beast away.

"Could you tell me what he said, Tina?" she asks stiffly as soon as the dog slinks off.

"He called you a lesbian. But not nice words." I hope she isn't mad at me for telling her.

She grunts, as if she's heard it before. "And then?"

I tell her exactly what I said back to him, expecting her to find it amusing. When she doesn't laugh, I say, "I chased him from the room."

My aunt presses her lips together. "This isn't a joke." I send another rock flying into a cinder block wall with red-and-black graffiti and a stenciled portrait of Che in blue. The rock pings on Che's nose.

At the next corner a boy in his late teens with olive skin and short dark brown hair adjusts something on the back of his motorcycle—closer up, I see it's a grimy plastic milk crate attached with a bungee cord to the silver and black *moto*. He wears an orange rain jacket with the logo of a sneaker.

Was he the guy who splashed me on Tuesday when I got caught in the rain? He gives me a slight nod, as if he's seen me before.

Tía Ileana turns right and crosses into a different neighborhood, one that has sprawling one-story houses with terra-cotta roofs and huge yards that separate each house from the one next to it. The block ends in a cul-de-sac of thick-bladed grass, flowers in a rainbow of colors, and palm trees. Wild parrots fly free beneath the purplish smog clouds.

We're long out of our neighborhood and the sight and earshot of Motorcycle Boy when Tía Ileana speaks up again. "I don't like that you're around your father when he's drinking. Neither does he. He said to take the TV from his room, put it in yours, and for you to go there after supper."

I dig my clenched fists into the front pocket of my sweatshirt. "Why are you guys punishing me? He started it." It will be a long boring summer—except that it's winter—ahead of me, full of cheesy war movies, *telenovelas*, and variety shows because they don't have *St. Elsewhere* and *Hill Street Blues* here.

"One of these days you're going to set him off," Tía Ileana says, nudging me forward.

I turn from my aunt and gaze at a red, yellow, and black bird with a pointy beak perched on a palm frond. "He never hit me when I was little."

Tía Ileana lays her arm across my shoulders. "I'm sorry, *amorcita*," she says, like someone died and will never come back.

I consider asking her to enroll me in school so I could meet kids my age and have something to do. Like homework when I'm stuck in my room. And something to help me forget about my new *papá*—like some decent weed if I'm lucky enough to find a source. Mamá gave me the choice, but I couldn't see going to school for three months now and then having nine more months at home. Even at my alternative school there are papers and tests and having to wake up early.

School's an option for when I get truly desperate, but I'm not there yet.

Before returning to our neighborhood, I ask Tía Ileana, "Why do you put up with this anyway?"

She squeezes my shoulder. "What do you mean?"

"You moved in with him and do all this stuff for him, and he hates everything that you are."

Tía Ileana quickly puts her finger to her lips to shush me, though I don't think I was talking that loud. Anyway, the boy with the motorcycle is now gone. "You have to be careful. There's even more prejudice here than in your country. Sometimes there's violence, too, which the police do nothing to stop." Her jaw clenches, and I see the veins pulsing in her neck.

"Have you ever been attacked?" I ask.

She shakes her head. "It's worse for men. For us women, it's, 'How cute, they're best friends holding hands' when you're younger. Then when you're twenty, the same people tell you it's time to get married and make babies."

"And if you don't? Do they kick you out?"

"You're the maiden aunt expected to devote the rest of your life to any family member who needs help." She presses her lips together for a moment. "Of course it bothers me that my brother's the way he is. But ever since your grandmother died, he's the only family I have."

My grandmother died while Papá was in prison. Mamá said Nonni Rosa died of a broken heart, knowing what the government was doing to her baby. And there was a sister between Ileana and Papá, who would have been my Tía Cecilia, except she and her boyfriend were killed in a car crash when she was nineteen.

Tía Ileana continues, "And because you and Daniel are so far away, I'm the only family he has. You take care of family."

"Have you told him how you feel?"

"He knows prejudice is wrong. He just doesn't apply it to himself."

The cold concrete of my father's neighborhood closes in on me. Even if he isn't my old *papá*, someone has to tell him that it makes no sense. Just like it makes no sense that he'd demand visitation rights for the summer and then never be around. Or that when he is around, he'd rather drink than spend time with me.

CHAPTER 5

Friday, June 16: 66 days until I go home

Before she returns to her office, Tía Ileana gives me a grocery list and directions to a nearby shopping center. I take the same route, but instead of turning at the corner and going through the fancy neighborhood, I walk straight one more block to a major street and turn left. The trip is about a kilometer, which is six-tenths of a mile, and I'm not used to walking that far, breathing so much pollution, or making my way through hordes of people who push past me. At the first block of apartments above repair shops and hair-and-nail salons, the sun comes out and the temperature rises. By the time I get to the shopping center, I'm out of breath and sweaty. Then the wind picks up and I shiver.

The entrance is narrow, crowded, and shabby, with faded paint, dirty windows, and papers blowing all over. It doesn't look at all like the one my aunt said her company is building—more like what I remember from when I used to live here. Inside are two levels of stores around an open plaza. The supermarket, about a quarter the size of the average one at home, is at the back end.

First I buy the items on my list—heavy things like condensed milk and tomato sauce. Tía Ileana said I could spend the money left over on whatever I want. I bypass the packages of cookies and lug the two plastic grocery bags through the Friday afternoon crowds upstairs to the bookstore listed in the directory I saw on the way in. Like most of the stores in the plaza, it has a small, hand-lettered sign and sun-bleached merchandise in the window.

I don't know what I'm looking for. Papá and Tía Ileana own a ton of books, and this store seems to have little besides Spanish translations of Stephen King, Anne Rice, and other writers I can get cheaper at home and in English.

After backing out the door, I notice a record store tucked between the bookstore and a children's clothing store. I hoist the bags higher on my arms because the plastic handles are cutting off the circulation in my fingers.

"Want some help?"

A boy leans against the rusted railing, smoking a cigarette. Although he has a black leather jacket rather than an orange rain jacket, I think he's the kid with the motorcycle who I saw before. He wears tight jeans and black Converse high-top sneakers. Close up, I notice his razor-sharp hairline and solid lower jaw, his long lashes and dark brown eyes. He gives me a wide smile that reveals a small gap between his upper front teeth. On his lip is the trace of a mustache.

My mouth dries up. *Quick—think of something smart.*

"Are you going to walk off with my groceries?" I say. *Um, okay.*

He shrugs. "Depends on what you have. Steak, maybe. Books, no way."

I glance back at the bookstore. "No way is right. Those books sucked."

"The record store." He points with his half-finished cigarette. "Much better."

I hold a bag out toward him. He throws away the cigarette and takes both bags.

"I'm Frankie. Frankie Zamora. And you?" His first name doesn't sound Spanish, but he speaks *castellano* like a local.

"Tina Aguilar."

"Is Tina short for Cristina?"

"Yes." I've never known a Tina who wasn't Cristina, but I guess they do exist.

"I haven't seen you around, Cristina Aguilar. Did you just get here?"

I let his deep voice echo in my head. Everything about this Frankie says *older, more mature.* I rub my forearms, where the plastic handles have left unsightly red dents. "I'm visiting my father. I live with my mother in the United States."

Frankie's eyes get a faraway look. "The United States of America. That's my dream. Can I go back with you?"

My mouth gapes. "I just met you!"

"Okay, see ya," he says in accented English while pretending to hand back the groceries. "I find the American girl to marry with me."

I laugh. He winks at me. I don't tell him I have permanent residency but won't get my U.S. citizenship until I turn eighteen. Instead, I say in Spanish, "How about we get to know each other first?"

"A deal." Still gripping the bags, he pushes the door of the record store open, holds it with his foot, and follows me inside.

I flip through the first bin of cassettes, labeled ROCK CHILENO, but recognize none of the groups. "Oh, you don't want those," Frankie says.

"Why not?"

"They're no good."

He nods toward a bin labeled ROCK INTERNACIONAL. I spot the huge section devoted to Metallica—not only . . . *And Justice for All*, *Master of Puppets*, and their other releases, but also scuffed cassette boxes with crude black-and-white artwork and some variant of the title *en vivo*. I paw through them, looking for my favorite songs.

"They sell bootleg Metallica here," Frankie says. He

sets down one of the bags and picks up a cassette that reads *Metallica, en vivo, Osaka, 8/88,* the title printed over a dark, blurry photo of the band. "This is a concert they played in Japan last year. *La raja.*"

I take the cassette from him. I'm disappointed he can't recommend any local bands, but Metallica is definitely on my top-ten list. I can't believe I've traveled to the opposite end of the world and found someone—a fine-looking guy, too—who likes the exact same music I do.

"Have you heard them live?" Frankie asks.

"Last November. With some friends from school."

"Was it the most incredible experience of your life?" That gap-tooth smile again.

"Yeah, it was cool." I repeat his word for "the coolest"— *la raja.* Then I think of the other kids from school at the Metallica concert with me—Petra, her boyfriend, and Max. Even after I broke up with Max last fall, we've stayed really good friends. Max is nowhere near as cute as Frankie— more like a little kid compared to him.

Frankie edges closer to me. "They're never going to come here. No good bands ever do," he says.

"Maybe now that there's . . ." I catch myself before saying "democracy," remembering my mother and brother's warning about political discussions with strangers. "I guess it's too far away."

I pay for the cassette. Frankie offers me a ride home. I think about it for a half second. Hot guy. Motorcycle.

Long walk. Heavy bags. Dusk. He arranges the bags in the plastic crate, wedging them in place with a rolled-up orange jacket. Definitely the kid I saw before. I climb onto the seat, and when he hops on in front of me, Frankie squeezes me into the space between him and the crate. He hands back his helmet for me to put on.

"What about you?" I ask.

He knocks the top of his head. "Hard as a rock."

The helmet is big for me and smells like boy sweat and hair gel. Its heaviness strains my neck. I tighten the strap and wrap my arms around Frankie's waist. He's solid underneath the leather jacket—all muscles, no flab or bones. I think about when I hugged my father around the waist earlier this week, feeling his ribs and the places where his ribs had been broken and hadn't healed quite right.

I like holding on to something that's solid and not broken.

Frankie guns the engine, and we speed off. The chilly, damp wind whips my hair against my neck and the chin strap. I shout my address to him.

He pulls up in front of my father's house and cuts the engine. "Nice place," he says. He kicks the stand in place, slides off the seat, and holds out a hand to help me off.

I unstrap the helmet and hand it to him. "Do you live around here?"

Frankie starts to shake his head then quickly says, "Yes. No. My grandmother lives in one of the apartment buildings near here, and I sometimes stay with her."

I did see him in the middle of the day—twice. Maybe he's one of those vocational education kids who only takes classes in the morning. "Are you in school?" I ask.

"No, I graduated last year. I'm working to earn money before I go into the army in September." Frankie taps the crate with his helmet. "I deliver things."

I swallow and almost choke. "The army? Are you into the military?"

He laughs. "It's required here. When you turn eighteen." Frankie switches to English. "I hope go to university of United States after."

My sigh of relief is way too audible. "You speak well, Frankie."

"I need . . . *practicar*."

"Maybe I can help you practice." I smile at the prospect of seeing this Metallica-loving Chilean hunk again. And having someone around my age to talk to at night.

"Tomorrow night. Eight thirty."

"*Perfecto.*" I flash him a wide-open grin. "See you tomorrow."

I expect Frankie to ride off, but he says, "I'll wait while you ask your father."

"No, it's fine."

"You live with him, don't you?" Frankie squints as if confused.

"Yes. But I don't need his permission."

Before putting on his helmet, Frankie shakes his head. At home, we make plans without our parents all the time. With half my friends, the parents aren't even there.

Like Papá.

Papá doesn't come home for supper, and my aunt doesn't know where he is. But after we eat, I get the idea to practice teaching English, with his parrot as my student. I assume parrots can learn to speak any language.

I carry Pablo into the kitchen on my finger. Inside, the greenish-gray bird seems bigger than he did in the garden. Pablo's almost as long as my outstretched arm, though most of that length is tail.

The moment I set Pablo down, he fluffs his tail and takes a dump on the counter. Tía Ileana yells at me. She hasn't yelled at me since I got here, but I guess I'd yell too if a bird pooped where I sort of cooked.

"*¡Pégame un tiro ya!*" Pablo screams back.

"It's okay. I'm not going to hurt you," I murmur, stroking his head.

He keeps screeching, "Just shoot me," in Spanish. The poor thing's previous owner must have seriously abused him.

A frowning Tía Ileana hands me a wet towel and powdered bleach to wipe up the mess. Afterward, I cover the counter with newspaper. I take a package of salted crackers from one of the cabinets.

When the parrot quiets, I say, "Hello. How are you?"

"*¡Alfonso, conch'e tu madre!*" the parrot squawks at me.

I don't reward him for calling someone named Alfonso his mother's private parts. Instead, I repeat, "Hello. How are you?"

This time, the bird squawks, "*Vamos, pajero dormilón.*"

Laughing, I say, "I did get my lazy ass out of bed." I'm surprised Graciela hasn't brought Pablo to me, since I've slept until noon every day since I got here.

An hour later, I've discovered that Pablo also knows his name and about a half-dozen other swear words. But he still doesn't speak a word of English.

When Papá comes home, he stumbles into the kitchen, whacking his left shoulder on the doorframe. Pablo flaps his one good wing and makes tutting noises with his gray beak.

"Yeah, get me a beer," Papá says. He backs out of the kitchen into the dining area and falls into a chair. Pablo and I stare at each other.

I lift the bird onto my finger. "I'm going outside," I announce. My father can get his own beer. I'm not supposed to be around him when he's drinking anyway.

"Pablo tell you my secrets?" Papá asks as he lights the cigarette dangling from his mouth.

"Yes. Who's Alfonso?"

"The bird torturer I took him from. The one who

broke his wing." Papá takes a puff and coughs. "I taught Pablo to express his anger in words."

When I return from putting Pablo in the cage, I see Tía Ileana with my father and two bottles of Cristal beer—his and hers—with their now familiar yellow-and-green labels. Papá tells her that he's covering the weekend News Director's shift tomorrow and Sunday and needs to be up early. If he's working tomorrow, this will be my only chance to let him know about Frankie. I take a deep breath and step toward the table. "Papá, Tía Ileana, I met this boy at the shopping mall. He wants to learn English, so I'm going to teach him tomorrow night."

"What's his name?" my father asks.

"Frankie Zamora."

"Absolutely not," Tía Ileana says. "You just met the boy."

I hold her gaze. "He came home with me today and carried my bags. He was nice."

Papá takes a long drag from his cigarette. "How old is he?"

"Eighteen. He said he graduated last year."

"And you're . . . ?" Papá asks.

"Sixteen. My birthday was June third." *And guess who missed it?*

"Chelo," my aunt says, using his childhood nickname, "this is not a good idea. We know nothing about him. He could hurt her."

"He's a boy." My father stabs his cigarette into the

ashtray and glares at my aunt. "Get it? A boy. She's meeting him, and that's final."

Tía Ileana flushes. "Cecilia. Remember what happened to her?" My aunt's voice breaks at the mention of their sister. She stalks out of the room.

"*Gracias*, Papá," I whisper as soon as I hear her footsteps above us. Then I realize I just thanked him for being a bigot and a jerk, and I feel like crap.

He finishes his beer and looks around the room. "Where's Ileana?"

"You pissed her off, so she ditched you."

He shrugs one shoulder. "She'll come back."

"Don't count on it." I shudder and reach for his hand. "I'll help you upstairs."

CHAPTER 6

Saturday, June 17: 65 days until I go home

At eight thirty, Tía Ileana and her girlfriend, Berta, are at the house baking empanadas for a party. Frankie doesn't show up as he promised. I pace between the door and the living room window until the waxed floorboards turn dull. My aunt pops out of the kitchen, her pale hands covered in flour. "Calm down, *amorcita*. He'll be here," she says.

Berta steps into the room. She's the same height but about twice the width of my aunt. Her hair is short and gray and her skin almost as light as Tía Ileana's. "She's your brother's kid." Berta shakes her head. "No damn patience."

"Tina doesn't understand. She's lived half her life in the United States, and there it's all hurry, hurry," my aunt replies. She explains to me that thirty minutes late is the custom here. But it doesn't stop me from pacing for the forty-five minutes until Frankie arrives.

I hear the buzzer for the gate and grab my purse. "*Chao*," I call out.

"Not so fast. I meet this boy first," Tía Ileana says.

Berta stays in the kitchen. Tía Ileana goes over the rules one last time. No physical contact, except for holding hands. No drugs. No drinking. She raises her voice when she says, "Do not get into a car with him if he's been drinking," leaving little doubt in my mind how the crash happened that killed Tía Cecilia. She doesn't say anything about a motorcycle because I don't tell her Frankie has one. She's almost out of breath from reciting the list by the time she says, "Home at midnight— no excuses."

"Do I get a thirty-minute grace period for Chilean Standard Time?"

She presses her lips together and frowns. No sense of humor. "Your father called from the station and expects you back." She gives me the number at the place where she and Berta are going with their empanadas.

At the door, a smiling Frankie bows. "I'm sorry I'm late. Bad traffic." He hands me a small bouquet of windblown purple flowers. I pass them to my aunt. She'll probably put them in a vase, but I'd like her to give them to Berta, to make this a romantic evening for all.

Frankie wears his leather jacket, but underneath is a freshly pressed button-down shirt instead of the T-shirt he had on yesterday. Even his jeans are pressed. "I'm Francisco Zamora," he says to my aunt.

"Ileana Aguilar de Gaetani," she answers him, inserting the "de" where there isn't supposed to be one, pretending to be married. And straight. They shake hands. She asks him where we're going.

"I thought we'd see a movie," Frankie answers.

"That's good. I told Tina no nightclubs."

"I don't drink," Frankie says.

My aunt's eyes meet mine. "I'd like to speak with Francisco alone for a few minutes."

"He goes by Frankie," I tell her.

She leads him into the living room, as if she were the master of an obedient big dog. I take the opportunity to refresh my makeup, which got smudged during my long wait. My chest is tight, not from worry about Frankie passing Tía Ileana's test, but me passing Frankie's.

On my way downstairs, I see Tía Ileana giving Frankie an approving nod. "Tina needs to be home by midnight," she says.

"Yes, ma'am." They shake hands, thus sealing my on-time return.

Frankie has chained his motorcycle to a streetlamp all the way up at the corner, which strikes me as a bit strange, though I'm glad my aunt can't see it and take back her nod of approval. The crate on the back is gone, and two helmets are attached to the bungee cord. The lights in the living room flicker off, but I suspect Tía Ileana is still spying on us.

"What did she say to you that was so private?" I ask him, my voice barely more than a whisper.

"The usual. Making sure I won't get you drunk and take advantage of you." He smiles, and his teeth shine white under the streetlamp. He pulls a folded copy of *El Mercurio* from the inside of his leather jacket. "*Die Hard* is playing near here. I've seen it, but I'd like to see it again. Unless you have another idea."

I take the paper from him. He points to the theater's ad, which he has circled in pen. His aftershave smells like pine needles. Below *Duro de matar* I see *Gorilas en la niebla*. I missed *Gorillas in the Mist* when it came to Madison. None of my friends would go with me to see what Max called a science class flick. I couldn't even get Mamá to take me because someone at work told her she'd end up depressed, though she wouldn't tell me why. "Can we see this one?"

"It's your night. But in return, speak to me in English." Frankie flashes me another smile.

On the way, I squeeze him extra tightly to feel his muscles. Despite what he said at the house, there's little traffic, and it takes only a few minutes get to the theater, a triplex next door to a different shopping plaza. Though the stores are now all shuttered with metal gates, the plaza looks like the one where I met him yesterday, only a bit newer, with shinier signs and less trash strewn around. Even the supermarket is from the same chain. A line snakes down the block, but when we get closer, it turns out to be for *Duro de matar*. There's only the stump of a line at the ticket window for *Gorilas en la niebla*.

"See the long line I spared you," I say.

He doesn't answer me in English, but I hear him mutter in Spanish, "Because everybody wants to see the other one." I don't think he's angry, though, because he puts his arm around my waist.

I love the movie, but it leaves me in tears. Not just because Dian Fossey gets killed in the end like her gorillas, but also because she sacrifices everything—family, friends, comfort, and safety—for them. She starts to go crazy because of what happens to the gorillas and the fact that the world doesn't care.

It's like when Papá lived with us in Madison. He'd write articles or give speeches about his time in prison, which left him with horrible nightmares afterward, but no one would publish the articles and hardly anyone showed up to hear him speak. That's when he started drinking—because of the nightmares, Mamá said—and now he can't stop. And now I know why Mamá didn't want to take me to the movie or see it herself.

When the lights go on in the theater, Frankie lays his arm across my shoulder and pulls me to him. His long fingers stroke my upper arm. The warmth from his fingers spreads through my body. "I'm sorry," I say. "We should have seen *Die Hard*."

"Es okay." He kisses my cheek. His lips are moist.

"And we only have twenty minutes."

"We'll get dessert. Five minutes."

I don't know whether he means it's five minutes to my house or he expects to spend five minutes getting dessert. But there's an ice-cream place a block away from the theater.

"Do you always cry at movies?" he asks while we wait in line for our cones. Actually, in three lines. One to pay for the ice cream, one to choose our flavors—I pick chocolate, Frankie *manjar*, which our Argentine friends in Madison call *dulce de leche*—and one to pick up our order. It's major-league inefficient, and I'm amazed if we get out in anywhere near five minutes.

"No." I don't want to tell him my life story, especially in this crowded place, but I don't want him to think I boo-hoo every time a movie character dies. "The gorillas getting killed was pretty awful. They're just animals—they don't understand. And then they killed her, too."

Frankie takes the two cones and hands me mine. He pushes a strand of hair from my forehead. "That woman I meet. She is . . . how you say *madrasta*?" The way he says the Spanish word for "stepmother," I think "wicked stepmother." I imagine myself as Cinderella at the ball forced to come home at midnight, though I know Tía Ileana is nowhere near that evil.

"My aunt. She lives with my father. He's disabled."
With these words, I feel as if I'm letting go of my old
papá forever.

"What's that?"

I've gone way beyond Frankie's English vocabulary,
but I hate the Spanish word, *minusválido*, even more
than *madrasta*. I mean, take it apart. *Minus.* "Minus."
"Less." *Válido.* It too is a cognate, "valid," with the same
definition in Spanish. So *minusválido* makes it seem as
if someone like Papá has less worth, less reason even to
live. I explain the translation to Frankie.

"You know, you're right," Frankie says as he throws
open the door for us to go outside. "They should save
the word for the rats that drink and don't work."

He spits out the word *"ratones,"* then hurls his unfinished cone into a trash can and rips the chain from around
his motorcycle wheel.

I recoil from him. "I . . . I'm sorry."

Frankie presses his hands to the side of his head and
mutters, "Old man, he'll wreck my life."

His father? Just like mine? I nod. "I know how you feel."

Frankie grunts and shakes his head, like he doesn't
think I'll ever understand. Like I'm a little kid who couldn't
get past the first date without picking a movie he hated, crying during the show, and then saying something incredibly
stupid. My heart puddles in my stomach along with the
chocolate ice cream. I climb on the motorcycle behind him.

Frankie gets me back to the house three minutes before midnight. The light is on in the living room. A car is parked next to the wall, two tires on the sidewalk and two in the street.

"Looks like you have guests," Frankie calls back to me. He makes a sudden U-turn. I grab two fistfuls of leather jacket to keep from flying off.

"Careful, Frankie!"

He stops at the corner and turns back to me. "I'm sorry," he says. "I'm not used to taking riders. Only packages."

My heartbeat returns to normal. I lift off the helmet and slide down, for the first time relieved to be on solid ground.

"Well, uh, good night," I say.

Frankie jumps down beside me and asks, "We can meet again?"

Wow. Maybe I was wrong when I thought he didn't have that good a time. I don't want to seem too eager by suggesting tomorrow, even though Papá's working all day. "Is Monday good for you?"

He looks away. "Monday, no. Tuesday at eight? We go eat and speak more English."

"Yes!" I pump my fist. He bends down and kisses me on the cheek. His breath is sweet, like caramel. He waits while I fumble with the keys, dropping them twice. As soon as I open the gate, he rides away.

My head swirling, I unlock the door and skip up the few steps from the entryway to the living room. A man

I've never seen before—I guess late twenties, with horn-rim glasses, dark wavy hair, and a beard—sprawls in one of the chairs. He's reading a book. Papá lies face-down on the sofa, his left arm and leg hanging, his leg brace on the floor next to his boots. On the coffee table are his glasses, ten crushed Coke cans, and an empty bottle of pisco.

"What's going on?" I ask.

Papá lifts his head and slurs, "I'm being a responsible parent and waiting up for you." He props his head on his good arm. "Be sure to tell your mother."

I glance over at the other guy. "And who's he?"

The bearded man sets down his book—something about musicians reflecting on their lives—stands and stretches. "I'm leaving."

"That's your name? 'I'm leaving'?" I can't help being flip when my mind is somewhere else—especially somewhere happier than this scene.

The man laughs and holds out a pudgy hand. "Ernesto Moya. I'm your father's producer." After shaking my hand, he slaps Papá on the back. "See you tomorrow, Nino." He walks to the door in a straight line and lets himself out, leading me to wonder if Papá finished off all ten cans of *piscola* by himself.

"How was your date?" my father asks as soon as the front door clicks shut. His head is still propped on his arm. He stares open-mouthed at the cushion in front of him as if it were about to roll toward him and swat him in the face.

"I had a good time."

"Wha'cha do?"

"We saw a movie. *Gorilas en la niebla.*"

"Great film. I had someone on my show to talk about it when it first opened." In slow motion, he struggles to a sitting position, squeezes his eyes shut, and rubs his forehead. "Listen, could you help me to the bathroom? I gotta take a piss."

"Where's Tía Ileana?" Taking care of my wasted father is the last thing I want to do. I almost barfed when I had to brush his teeth last night.

"At her old place. Staying over with that other one."

I lift his bad arm over my shoulders and grab him around the waist. My fingernails dig into his side underneath his rib cage, but I don't think he feels a thing. He teeters. Without his brace, he can only bear his full weight on one leg, and he's way past any ability to balance himself. He drapes himself over my shoulder, his wrist splint chafing my neck and his warm pisco breath—bitter and sour with a touch of salt—in my face. I tell him when to step.

In the kitchen, he reaches blindly toward the wall. "I'm working tomorrow."

Another step. "I know."

"Ernesto's picking me up at nine."

"I can set your alarm." *Better set two alarm clocks.*

"No worry. Birds'll wake me."

Instead of taking him upstairs or to the downstairs bathroom, I guide Papá down a few steps and through his office to the backyard. The minute he gets out into the clammy night, his body stiffens. "Where am I?" His voice trembles.

"The yard."

"Why am I here?"

"To pee. Your aim is terrible when you get like this." I slide him off the patio and onto the dirt. "I'm not stepping around it like I did in Wisconsin."

"*Puta la güeá*, you sound like Vicky." He tries to imitate me, but trips over his words. He's right, though. That's exactly what my mother said. Except in the apartment complex where we used to live, she couldn't take him outdoors as if he were a dog, so we had months of stepping around and cleaning up disgusting accidents.

I wedge his body into the corner of the barbecue and the wall separating our garden from the neighbors. While he unzips his jeans and waters the bushes with what's probably pure poison, I stare into the birds' cage. I can't find either of the little parrots; they're camouflaged in the darkness.

"Hey, Pablo and Víctor. How are you?" I murmur in English but get no answer. "Don't look, okay. Wish I didn't have to look at him, either."

When Papá is done, I help him inside. Figuring his crooked and broken teeth won't rot out any further from one night of not being brushed, I move the papers from the daybed in his office, lay him down, and pull a blanket over him. He shivers, so I bring a second blanket from the living room. "Fine, set an alarm for seven thirty," is the last thing he says to me. After that, he mumbles to himself, but I can't make out a single word.

While I pick up the cans and bottle from the living room, I think of Frankie, of the way he held me when I was crying at the movie. Then I remember his rage outside the ice-cream shop. Could he have returned to a similar scene at his house?

The thought of seeing Frankie again makes me feel less alone, as if there's someone else in this country who could possibly understand my life here, between the *minusválidos* and the *ratones* that drink and don't work.

CHAPTER 7

Sunday, June 18: 64 days until I go home

Someone's banging on my bedroom door. It pulls me from my dream of Frankie in his leather jacket, but in the dream he's leaning back in his desk chair in my classroom in Madison, snoring. Like Max always does. I burrow under the covers and pull the pillow over my head.

"Tina, wake up." Papá's hoarse voice slices through pillow, sheets, and blankets.

"In a minute," I say in Spanish, but I want to shout, *why are you banging on my door and screaming at the crack of dawn?* Then I realize this could be an emergency. Last night I put my father to bed piss drunk. I throw off the covers and stumble to the door.

Outside in the hall Papá leans on his wooden cane. He clutches a gray sweater and his leg brace in his bad hand, his elbow bent at what appears to be a painful angle. His boots are unlaced and he's buttoned his shirt crooked.

"*Chuta*, you're a mess," I say. "What time is it?"

"Eight fifteen. Can you help me?"

"How did you get upstairs?"

"Slowly, with great difficulty, and the whole time cursing myself for buying a two-story house." I laugh. At least Papá finds humor in his purchase of a house with grab bars in the bathroom and stairs all over the place. He coughs and clears his throat. His face has a gray-green tint like the smog-filtered daylight.

I rebutton his shirt from the bottom up and the cuff of his right sleeve, too. His aftershave smells like VapoRub. My fingers stumble over each other, and not just because I'm half-asleep. I shouldn't have to get my own father dressed for work. I yank the sweater and brace from his clawlike grip and maneuver the sweater over his head while holding up the dead weight of his bad arm. The sweater's neck is stretched out and fraying. I roll Papá's jeans leg above his knee to reveal a pale, skinny limb with curls of fine hair the color of rust. I snap on his brace and tighten the Velcro straps over his knee, ankle, and foot.

"Okay. I'm going back to bed," I tell him when I'm done lacing his boots.

"You're coming with me. I told you last night." He squeezes his eyes shut. Hung over.

"No, you didn't. You passed out." He has to be kidding. It's at least four hours before my normal wake-up time. I'd planned to spend the day writing my friends to tell them about the awesomeness of Frankie. And separating the pieces to start the jigsaw puzzle because I won't get to see him again until Tuesday. Besides, I want my dream back, the one Papá interrupted for nothing more than a clothing problem.

"Graciela's off, Ileana's away, and you're not staying here alone."

"I can take care of myself."

"I'm not up to arguing today. Be ready and downstairs in half an hour."

I cross the hall to the bathroom and slam the door. "Not up to arguing. Whose fault is that?" I say, loud enough so he can hear me through the thin wall. He doesn't answer.

I shower, dress, and go downstairs to the kitchen. Papá stands at the counter, sipping a mug of tea. "Where's breakfast?" I ask him. Having Graciela around has already spoiled me.

"Get your own. I'm not hungry." He sorts different-colored pills from a bottle and swallows them one by one.

"So you're just going to eat pills?"

He turns his back to me. "Don't give me a hard time."

I carry a bowl of cold cereal to the dining table and flip through the morning newspaper. The front section has stories on the election campaign, along with car crashes, armed robberies, and a single page of international news.

Back home, I won a school essay contest on the protests in Tiananmen Square, but here they don't even get a mention—as if people have enough of their own problems and can't worry about the rest of the world.

I close my eyes and imagine riding on the back of Frankie's motorcycle, my body pressed against his, taking in the smell of oil and leather and pine-scented aftershave.

Ernesto arrives half an hour late in a dinged-up little blue Fiat—the car I saw last night, though it was too dark to notice the color, or the dents. Papá opens the passenger door and slides the seat forward for me to climb in the back. He hands me his backpack. Then he drops into the front seat, kicks his bad leg inside, and slams the door. "Where the hell were you? I've been up for hours," he says.

Ernesto shakes his head. "It's Sunday morning. Nothing ever happens on Sunday morning, except the Cardinal's sermon." He merges onto the wide avenue. I unzip the main pouch of Papá's pack and search for liquor bottles while Ernesto keeps talking. "Do you know why the Cardinal gives his sermon on Sunday morning, Nino? So we can sleep late."

"Well, I have things to do."

"*Oye, huevón*, you're way too intense to be News Director. The minute you take over, there's going to be an uprising." Ernesto turns to me at the next light. I hug the pack to my chest. "You should be proud of your *papá*, Tina. When our News Director retires next year, he's getting the job."

My father interrupts. "And the news department meeting will start at eight sharp."

Ernesto winks at me. "That means nine around here."

"Eight."

We pull up to the curb in front of a tall Victorian house. It looks more like the house I was supposed to help Evan and Mamá restore than something I'd see in the middle of a Latin American city. They've painted the siding dark purple and the gingerbread trim white. I will have to tell Petra in my next letter and suggest the color combo to Evan.

Papá asks me to bring his backpack inside. It contains no liquor bottles, but an agenda book, five well-stuffed manila folders, and a pad of lined yellow paper with writing. The thermos clipped to the daisy chain is filled with hot water. Unspiked. I tasted it when no one was looking.

My brother was right last year when he said Papá doesn't bring alcohol to work—except what may still be in him from the night before.

Lifting the pack from my hand, Papá turns to Ernesto. "I have a couple of articles to finish for the newspapers. Give her the tour and meet me in the News Director's office."

Ernesto leads me to the basement control room, where a napping engineer babysits the live feed from the Metropolitan Cathedral. Ernesto taps on the window to the adjacent darkened control room for music programming, where he'll be spinning records after the Mass. On

Saturdays and Sundays, he says, the station mainly plays music, so the weekend News Director's job consists of editing the UPI newswire to five minutes, giving it to the music programmer to read on the hour, and being available to assemble coverage in case of a big story.

I am at home in this tall old house. And I'm starting to like Ernesto, the way I'd like a young, cool teacher. While he shows me the meeting rooms and the kitchen, I notice a wedding band.

"So are you really going on strike when my father becomes News Director?" I ask.

Ernesto laughs. "Not a chance. We worship him. He taught us everything we know about investigative journalism." He holds out his hand in front of a framed black-and-white photo on the wall next to the refrigerator. I recognize Papá sitting on a stool behind a microphone, wearing headphones and holding a stack of papers. "During the plebiscite, he was on the air for thirty-five hours straight. Said he couldn't sleep until he knew the bastard was going down so he might as well work, but I'm sure it's an on-air record."

"Cool," I say.

"Check out these." On the opposite wall are three more framed photos. In the largest one Papá stands at a microphone on an outdoor stage, facing a tightly packed crowd of people holding posters for the "NO" vote in the plebiscite. I imagine him finally getting to describe what happened to him in prison to people who cared, people who would then go and vote to make Pinochet leave office in eighteen months rather than ten years. In the photo, my father has a huge smile. He's smiling in the next photo as well, where he leans against a news van with a tape recorder and cables slung across his body. In the third one, he sits on a stack of boxes hand-labeled TESTIMONIOS and gives the photographer a thumbs-up sign.

"He looks happy," I say.

"We've had some great times together. Made history." Ernesto takes a can of nutritional supplement from the fridge, dumps it into a blender along with two scoops of vanilla ice cream, and hits the button. "Nino's mid-morning snack," he explains. It looks like the stuff one of my friends had to drink when she came back from rehab for anorexia. *And all Papá ate this morning for breakfast was pills.* After pouring the shake into a tall glass, Ernesto puts his hand on my shoulder and guides me up the stairs.

Papá stands in front of the clacking teletype machine on the landing outside the News Director's office. He smokes a cigarette while he tears off strips of paper.

"Anything good?" Ernesto asks.

Papá takes a pen from the back pocket of his jeans and writes on the top sheet. "Big story," he says without looking up. "One of the lions in the zoo died last night."

Ernesto sets the glass on the table next to the machine, a zookeeper dropping off the eleven o'clock feeding. Papá ignores it. Strands of dull gray hair cover half his face. I want to know what it was like to be on the air for thirty-five hours straight as the election results were coming in, but instead, I silently watch him work while the ice cream melts in his neglected shake.

Papá hands the edited pages to Ernesto and tells him to take me with him. I wonder if they'll let me read the news on the air, just like Papá did in the photo. That would be amazing. I ask him as Ernesto and I are leaving.

My father's sharp "no" hits me like a gunshot. Even Ernesto freezes for a moment. *Then why did you bring me here?*

"Nino's full of cheer today," Ernesto remarks on our way downstairs.

"He's super hungover," I answer. "Why'd you let him get so drunk?" My friends and I do it because we like watching people make complete fools of themselves, but that didn't look like Ernesto's plan last night. Especially since he bailed the minute I got home.

Ernesto grunts and shrugs. I follow him into the music control room. He flips the light switch and describes all the electronic equipment—a soundboard, microphones, two turntables, a bank of cassette players, a reel-to-reel player, and shelves filled with LPs on every wall.

"That's awesome," I say.

"We had to build this station from scratch, since we were banned for so many years." Ernesto pulls three records from the shelf and hands them to me. While he goes on about where the collection came from and adds more albums to my stack, I think about Frankie, and maybe requesting a Metallica song for him in case he's listening. Then I notice a razor blade next to the reel-to-reel player. I lean the records against the tape player and pick up the metal blade.

"Where did you get that?" Ernesto's tone is accusing.

"Here." I point to the counter in front of the tape player. "Why?"

"These aren't supposed to leave the editing room. Ever."

"I didn't take it. I just found it."

He holds out his hand, like I'm supposed to give the blade to him.

I run my finger along the edge, not hard enough to slice skin or draw blood. I don't want to give up the blade; it would be way better than a knife for the puzzle.

"Hand it over," Ernesto says. His voice is low, almost a growl.

Even if the equipment and records are secondhand, I don't believe that this radio station is so poor it can't afford to lose even one teeny razor blade. But I drop it into his hand anyway. He selects a key from the ring on his belt, strides out into the hallway, and unlocks the door next to a handwritten sign that reads *Sala de*

Edición No. 1. After leaving the blade on a table full of electronic equipment, he locks the door and rattles the knob to make sure it's shut tight. Then he goes into the other control room. He doesn't ask me to come along, so I open the door a crack to listen.

"I know you're new," Ernesto tells the engineer. "Just don't do it again. There are people around here who shouldn't be near those things."

Then it hits me who he's talking about.

Why did they all make me come here? And what does anyone expect me to do with a father I barely know and can't help?

Despite layers of clothing, I can't stop shivering. I wedge my body into a corner and pull the hood of my sweatshirt over my head, then over my face.

But Ernesto notices when he comes out. Like a favorite teacher, he seems to know that something bad has happened. But I don't think a teacher would ever tell a kid what he says next. About Papá's drinking, which got even worse after the plebiscite. About his writing for all those newspapers and magazines on top of his regular job with the radio station, to pay off the house. About the gun he tried to get, supposedly for self-defense.

"I never saw a gun."

"That's because we never gave him one." Ernesto leans against the doorframe next to me. "We set up a security detail so he's pretty much never alone and never with anything that can do serious damage. He thinks we're protecting him from his enemies, but really it's himself."

Before Papá got home from work every day, Graciela counted out his pills and moved them from bottle to bottle. I never thought anything of it before. "I guess that security detail means me, too."

"We have it under control. You just be yourself."

///////////////////

That night at home, I slip into the kitchen as soon as Tía Ileana brings my semiconscious father upstairs to bed. I check all the drawers and cabinets again. I still find only butter knives and round dull-bladed dinner knives. But under the sink, there's a heavy lockbox, and when I rattle it, I hear metal scrape against metal.

The harsh, hollow sound echoes inside me and stays until sometime in the early morning hours I finally fall asleep. I don't dream of Frankie.

CHAPTER 8

Tuesday, June 20: 62 days until I go home

Dear Mamá,

I hope you and Evan are having fun on your honeymoon. Things are really weird here. Like 24-hour-suicide-watch weird. Why didn't you tell me Papá has threatened to kill himself?

I want to come home early. Half the time I'm bored and half the time I'm scared I'll do the wrong thing and something bad will happen. I hardly ever see Papá because he's either working at the radio station or getting completely wasted. Tía Ileana's pretty cool, but she and Papá don't get along because . . .

I erase the last line and try again.

The only good thing that's happened is that I met this boy. His name is Frankie Zamora, and he's 18. I erase and write *16.* There are things I don't want my mother to worry about.

I check my watch. Just one hour until Frankie picks me up. I fold the paper in half, slide it under the letter I just received from Petra, and stack books on top so no one can see it's there. I weave my hair in front into small braids like Petra does. Then I shake out the braids because they look better with long natural-blonde hair than they do with layered dark brown hair. I think a ponytail would be more practical for riding Frankie's motorcycle, but it takes me three tries to get rid of the lumps.

Picking an outfit is even harder, and by the time Frankie rings the bell at the gate, rejected T-shirts and sweaters cover my floor. I kick them under my bed in case Tía Ileana looks in my room. I don't want her poking around my stuff.

Downstairs, Papá's already seated at the table, and Tía Ileana's putting two fish fillets in the microwave. I give my aunt a quick hug, then my father.

"Do I get to meet this boy?" Papá asks.

I sniff alcohol on his breath. "Maybe another day. We're rushing to catch a movie."

Papá scrapes his chair back. "I'd like to ask him a few questions." He starts to stand, but his face goes pale and he collapses back into his seat. "Leg spasms," he says, his voice brittle. Tía Ileana rushes to him.

"I already talked to him, Chelo," she says as she unsnaps his leg brace and massages his calf. He groans and writhes in his chair. My aunt turns to me. "Bring me his pills."

The bell rings again. I grab the bottle that Graciela prepared that afternoon and hand it to Tía Ileana on my way to the front door. I poke my head out. "Just a minute, Frankie. We have a little problem."

"Totally understand," he responds.

86

When I get back to the dining area, Tía Ileana holds the bottle in front of my father's face. "It says take with food. If you go drinking with the guys after work, eat something or the new medicine isn't as effective."

"I can't. My—" He sucks in his breath with a moan, then grabs his leg with his good hand.

"Chelo, I don't know what to do with you." My aunt places a pill on his tongue and tips a water glass toward him. "Your stomach hurts because you drink and don't eat. You need to start taking responsibility for your own health."

I clasp my hands in front of me. "Guys, Frankie's waiting. Can I go now?"

"It's all right." Tía Ileana crouches in front of Papá. "Francisco said his parents voted for the 'NO.' His father's PS," she says, referring to the initials of the Socialist Party. "But not active because he's sick."

Sick like Papá's sick?

Papá grips my forearm. "Fine, go. Home by midnight."

Tía Ileana watches me leave. I know those same eyes will be on me when I walk back through the door tonight.

Outside under the streetlamp, Frankie kisses my cheek. "I'm sorry I'm late," I say and switch to English. "My father had, like, this small seizure."

"Es okay. You look beautiful." Tonight he wears a green-and-white striped scarf over his leather jacket, and a white shirt underneath with a brown tie. Instead of his usual blue jeans, he has on dark brown corduroy pants. My insides relax and my jaw falls slack. I didn't expect him to dress up this nice for me. And I don't feel like a kid in high school anymore.

I slip on my helmet. "Where are we going?"

"I know a good restaurant in Providencia."

The Providencia neighborhood is a twenty-minute trip with stoplights and traffic. It was the fancy neighborhood when I lived here, and I'm guessing from the way Frankie is dressed that it still is. One- and two-story houses and low-rise apartment buildings give way to high-rises with plate-glass windows that reflect the light of old-fashioned wrought-iron streetlamps. The wide avenues here are clean and lined with trees. At night, this could be a fancy part of Chicago, except for the palm trees and the occasional older Spanish-style building. I orient myself using the huge illuminated statue of the Virgin Mary on top of the Cerro San Cristóbal. To get to the restaurant, we pass the hill.

Frankie pulls into a parking space on the narrow street just past the restaurant and tosses a coin to an old watchman with bloodshot eyes and a rotten odor. I don't think he'll be much use if anyone tries to mess with Frankie's *moto*. When he opens his mouth to thank us, I see that he has no teeth. Frankie grimaces and turns away.

I had expected Frankie to take me to a McDonald's, which they have here, too, or a local fast-food place—like where I'd hang out with my friends at home. But this is a real restaurant, specializing in *asados*, different types of meat cooked over an open fire, which the waiter serves straight off the spit. I savor the aroma of all kinds of grilled meats mixed together. Most of the people eating here are in their early twenties. I see lots of couples.

This is a real-live date. On the way to our table I redo my ponytail and straighten my sweater, conscious that I wore jeans instead of the clingy, knee-length 1950s-style skirts that seem to be popular here. On the other hand, I rode here on a motorcycle. They probably came in cars.

The table for two has a sheet of thick white paper covering the tablecloth. I've never seen paper over cloth, but Frankie says a lot of restaurants do this. I guess it saves on laundry, but he says it has to do with the customs of immigrants from the Basque region who settled in Chile.

Frankie scans the handwritten menu and recommends the pork. Then he asks me to translate the entire menu into English and listen to him repeat the words I say. He slides an empty wine glass out of the way, pulls a small notepad from his back pocket, and writes down words that he has trouble remembering. Some I can't translate for him because we don't have those dishes at home.

"How long have you studied English?" I raise my voice above the din around me.

"Five years in school. But school . . . not good."

"How is it not good?"

"Classes very big." He holds his arms outstretched. His shirt pulls tight against the muscles of his chest. He has great muscles, but if these are his best clothes, he's outgrown them.

"How many students were in a class?" I ask.

"Forty. Maybe more. But many no come."

My classes have twelve to fifteen students. Lucky me, but it doesn't seem fair. "I hope you can come to the United States. You'll learn English fast. Just like I did."

"I have to take test in English to come. And I need money." He frowns.

"There are scholarships," I say, in as cheerful a tone as I can manage. "My brother got a full scholarship to Georgia Tech."

Frankie perks up, which makes me smile, too. "How?"

"They have a special program for Hispanic students to study engineering. He had good grades. And we didn't have any money, either."

"No?"

I shake my head. "My parents split up three years ago. And my mother went back to school in the United States. All of us were students at the same time." Even though we were poor, I liked that Mamá was in school along with Daniel and me.

"But you have a big house here."

"Papá's only lived in the house four months. He saved the money from his job with the radio station."

"What station?"

"Radio Colectiva."

"I don't listen to that one. Too much talk." He makes a talking gesture with his hand. I laugh.

"Yeah, you're right." I figure Frankie doesn't pay much attention to politics, since he doesn't like that kind of radio. Maybe something happened to his father to scare him away.

The waiter brings us a platter of pork still on the spit. Using a two-pronged fork, he slides the pieces onto our plates. The aroma of barbecue makes my mouth water. The meat is crisp on the outside and soft in the center, spiced with salt, pepper, and garlic. I've been to barbecues at my friends' houses, but I've never eaten a piece of pork so tender and juicy.

"How did you know about this place?" I ask.

"My uncle. Me, I'm a McDonald's guy." He winks, and I laugh.

"Yeah, me, too."

"You don't mind that I brought you here?"

"Of course not, Frankie." I slide my hand toward him, and he covers it with his larger, rougher hand. "It makes me feel special."

He gives my hand a light squeeze.

I know it's none of my business, but I want to know more about Frankie's father and what Frankie said at the ice-cream shop about the rats that drink and don't work. As soon as we finish our meal, I ask him, "Do you have any brothers or sisters?"

"Three younger sisters. No brothers." He pats his chest. "I'm the hope of the family."

I stare at him, open-mouthed. "What?"

Grinning, he switches to Spanish, "I'm the only son. King of the house."

Another *machista* like my father and brother. I can ignore his king of the house comment and write him off. Or I can try to change his mind. I switch to Spanish to make sure he understands. "You want to live in the United States, right?"

"Of course." He squints at me. "Is my English that bad?"

"No, you were perfectly clear. I just wanted to be extra sure because things are different there." Deciding to make my points with silverware, I pick up the fork. "First of all, women work at the same jobs as men, and even if it doesn't always happen, they're supposed to get the same pay." I point my fork at him. "Does your mother work?"

Frankie shakes his head. "She takes care of all of us. Even my father who doesn't deserve it."

"Second." I pick up the spoon. "Girls and boys go to school for the same amount of time. My mother went all the way to get her PhD and is now starting a job as a university professor. Girls don't have to drop out to get married and make babies. And they can go back to school even when they have kids like Mamá did."

I think I've silenced Frankie this time. I set the spoon down and hold the knife up. "When a girl is born, it's not like some huge tragedy for the family. It's not the end of"—Frankie's words come to me—"the family's hope." I tap the knife on the table. "Girls have value for themselves and not just for catching a husband. We're awesome, and we can do anything that you can do." I set down the knife, fold my hands across my chest, and bare my teeth in triumph. I make a mental note to give Papá this speech one day.

"Okay, okay. I'm sorry," Frankie says in English. He reaches for my hand, and I let him take it. All is forgiven by the warmth of his fingers.

"My father's the same way. And because he's old, he's probably never going to change his mind." I stroke the smooth skin of Frankie's wrist and smile at him, trying for what my counselor at school would call a win-win situation. I want this win.

"At least your father got a real house," Frankie says. "Mine, he doesn't do anything. That's the other reason it's all up to me."

"Is he unemployed?"

Frankie snorts. "He hasn't worked a steady job in years. All he does is drink." He lets go of my hand and waves it toward the door of the restaurant, where groups of people wait for tables. "That bum across the street where I parked my bike? That's him."

"That was your father?" Frankie wouldn't even talk to the guy.

"No, not really him. But my father is always passing out in the street, and people don't bother bringing him home anymore. Last weekend he was arrested for public intoxication, and my uncle had to pay his fine." He glances at his empty plate. "That's why I was late to pick you up. And sort of pissed off."

"I'm sorry."

Frankie holds his head in his hands. "Tina, I'm embarrassed to have his name."

I want to cheer Frankie up since it's our first big date. Besides, this is something we share—something nobody else in the world but he and I understand.

I scoot my chair toward him. "You want to hear a secret?"

Frankie nods, so I continue. "My father didn't work for the longest time, either. Remember when I said he was disabled? He drinks, too. A lot."

"Did he ever pass out in the middle of the road like a dead pig?"

"No, but he used to hit me."

Frankie leans across the table and points to the bridge of his nose. I saw a bump there before, but now I notice the way his nose bends to the right. "He broke it. Twice. When I was eight and when I was thirteen."

Papá never hit me hard or with his fist, not even when I talked back to him after he got out of prison. But I bet Frankie never had to take his father outside like a dog. I suck in my breath. "My father would pee on the bathroom floor because he couldn't find the toilet."

"At least he made it home. Mine was arrested for urinating in public." He pauses. "In public. In the middle of the day. With the whole neighborhood watching."

That must have been so embarrassing for Frankie's family. But there are worse things. "My father threatened to kill himself," I say.

Frankie jerks up straight. "You're kidding."

"I'm not. He tried to get a gun."

"My father hasn't done that." He stares at his empty plate again. "Sometimes I wish he would."

"You don't mean it?" I wouldn't want Papá to shoot himself, no matter how awful he's acted or how messed up he is. But maybe it's because he survived so much, and I can't believe after all that he really wants to die.

"Haven't you felt that way about your father? When he was hitting you, or drinking up all the money for food and rent?" There's a strange brightness in Frankie's voice, as if he's discovered a solution for a bad situation.

"No." I want to tell Frankie about Papá's time in prison, and what he was like before, but I can't. Even if his father is on our side, that doesn't mean Frankie agrees with him.

"You probably think I'm a horrible person," Frankie says.

I shake my head. "It sounds like you had it worse than I did. I haven't seen my father for three years. You see yours all the time."

He seems to accept my explanation. He changes the subject, to English words for fun things to do. Music. Movies. Soccer. Basketball.

When the check comes, I reach for my wallet, for the allowance money Papá gave me yesterday. "No," Frankie says. "That's not how we do it here."

He counts out a stack of bills, more than a delivery boy with an unemployed alcoholic father should be spending. Maybe we should have gone to McDonald's.

When he gets to the corner half a block from my house, he cuts the engine. I climb off. "Are you free on Thursday?" he asks.

"Yes!" I have to restrain myself from jumping up and down in the street.

"How's a movie and dinner?" He tells me he can get off work early and be at the house by six. Then he puts one arm around me and plays with the strands of hair that fell out of my ponytail. I smile. He stops and looks into my eyes. I see the streetlamp's reflection in his eyes, framed by his long lashes. Then he kisses me.

Frankie's lips are full and soft. The smoky taste of the *asado* fills my mouth. This isn't my first kiss, but it's easily the most delicious. I want us to stay like this all night, but he pulls away. My lips tingle. My whole body tingles. He straddles the bike. I give him a weak, stupid wave as he rides off.

I talk my way past Tía Ileana. My room hasn't been touched. I slide the letter to my mother from under the stack of books. Without reading it again, I tear it in half, then in quarters, and finally in little pieces that I slowly sprinkle into the wastebasket.

CHAPTER 9

Thursday, June 22: 60 days until I go home

"¡*Chuta!*"

Frankie's eyes are huge. He stares open-mouthed at our living room furniture and up the stairs to the second floor. Papá's house isn't *that* big. Sure, it's bigger than the various apartments where I've lived. But many of my friends' houses are the same size or larger, and Petra lives in a real-live mansion. Even the house my mother and Evan are fixing up without me has a separate living and dining room and bedrooms that can fit more than one piece of furniture besides the bed.

Maybe Frankie's home is one of those one-room cardboard shacks in the *poblaciones*. I don't know how anyone can live there. What do they do when it rains? And he said there are six people in his family. How do they all fit in? Do they all sleep together in one room, boys and girls? Where do they go to the bathroom?

He reads the titles of the books on the floor-to-ceiling bookcase. "I've never seen so many books," he says.

"Don't you have a public library?"

"Not where I live." He takes a book from the shelf. *I sommersi e i salvati.* "What's this?"

"I don't know. It's not in Spanish or English." I open the cover to the title page. The publisher's address is in Torino. My aunt said she was in Italy last year, so it must be her book. "Italian," I say.

Frankie scrunches his face. "Who knows Italian?"

"My grandmother was from Italy, so both my aunt and my father do."

He returns the book to the shelf and scratches the back of his head. "That's like my family. My uncle speaks German, but I don't think he reads it. Anyway"—he runs his fingers along the spines—"we don't have any books at home. Except ones for school."

"We always had lots of books. When I was little, my father used to read to me at night." I rub my cheek where his beard would tickle when I'd sit on his lap. "I learned how to read before I started school, but he'd still want to read to me. Except he'd make stuff up to see if I could catch him."

"I bet you did," Frankie says. "Because you're really smart."

I smile. That's what my old *papá* used to say: *I always knew I had a smart girl.*

Graciela eyes us suspiciously from the kitchen. Not only is she part of Papá's "security detail," so is the older couple next door, who she works for as well. Papá and Tía Ileana have made sure that Graciela is around when I'm home alone. They won't be back from work for at least another hour.

"Do you want to see the birds?" I ask. "Papá rescues injured parrots."

"Sure," he says dully, but then he puts his arm around my shoulders. "Show me the house first."

In the kitchen I introduce Frankie to Graciela. Avoiding eye contact, he shakes her hand. Graciela doesn't take her eyes off him. "I'm teaching him English," I explain before she decides to report Frankie's rudeness to my father and aunt.

Then Frankie says, "I want to learn the words for things in an office. For a job."

I lead Frankie down the few steps into Papá's office. I point out "desk," "chair," "books," "bookshelves," "pen," "pencil," "paper," and "typewriter." He repeats each word several times while lifting things on the desk and setting them down again. At first Graciela stands in the doorway, but then she leaves—bored, I guess. Or reassured that he won't take anything, including my sort-of-already-taken virginity. Frankie taps a piece of paper that Papá left in the typewriter. I peer at a title, a couple of sentences underneath, and a note in my father's handwriting.

"What does it say in English?" Frankie asks.

In both languages, I read the title aloud, "*Policías y para militares*. Police and . . . for military people?" It doesn't make much sense. I read the next lines to myself because Frankie would never understand them in English. *Despite the promise of democracy and civilian rule, suspicious acts of violence continue. As usual, they are classified as street crimes.*

I guess the article has something to do with the musician that was beaten up, but when I asked her after their phone conversation, Mamá said Papá had no proof. His note in the margin reads, *Guerra 1989 + Larranaga 1979,* which leaves me even more confused. *Guerra* means "war." Larranaga sounds like someone's name.

Frankie turns to a stack of newspapers and magazines on the daybed. The top magazine is open to an article with the headline, FOR MOTHERS OF THE DISAPPEARED, LIFE DOESN'T GO ON.

Frankie reads aloud the author biography, next to a postage stamp–size color picture of Papá at the bottom of the page, "'Marcelo Aguilar G. is the host of the weekday radio show *Oye, Nino.*' That's your father's article, right?"

"If it says so."

"What's it like to have a famous father?"

It doesn't make him happy. Or nice. I'd imagined him showing up with an entourage to meet me at the airport, but he didn't show up at all. "I've hardly seen him since I got here," I answer.

"Have you read any of his stuff?"

I shake my head. I haven't read his articles, just those two sentences about street crimes that make me think I shouldn't be walking around Santiago alone, day or night.

He picks up the newspaper underneath and flips through it. On the next to last page is another picture of Papá, another article, this one called, YOU BROKE THEM. NOW FIX THEM. He reads slowly, running his finger along the column until he gets to the end. I watch his face for a reaction. There's a tiny curl of the lip, then a grunt, and finally, two quick nods. After setting down the newspaper with the page faceup, he lifts a pencil from the desk and opens the right-hand desk drawer. I see blank paper and some stray paperclips. He takes a piece of paper and writes down the title of the article in neat block handwriting as if working on a school assignment. A smile crosses his face. I wonder if he didn't like what Papá said at first, but got into it later, as if Papá's words changed his mind.

I stand between Frankie and the door, in case Graciela reappears. When he's done, I refold the newspaper and put everything the way we found it. I also make a mental note to read some of Papá's articles myself because it's embarrassing that Frankie has read them and his own daughter hasn't.

"Come on. Let's go outside." I step toward the sliding door.

Still at the desk, Frankie writes something else. I squint to see the words: *Place item in right-hand drawer.* Suddenly, he glances back at me and claps his hand over the note. He folds it three times, presses the edges, and slides it into the inside pocket of his jacket. "Gotta show you something, Tina." He flashes his gap-toothed smile.

"What?" I ask, not smiling back. I thought he was finished with Papá's writing. And what's the item in the right-hand drawer? Before I can ask him, Frankie opens the drawer again, reaches way inside, and pulls out a half-full bottle of whiskey.

"Put it back!" I say, trying to keep my voice low and Graciela away.

"Want to see the other places they hide it?"

"No!" I snatch the bottle from Frankie's hand and shove it back into the drawer. "I already told you he has a problem." My voice breaks. Right now, I want to kick Frankie out and never see him again.

But then he touches me under the chin, and our eyes meet. His fingers are warm, and his eyes mournful. "I'm sorry," he says. "I do this at home all the time."

"Raid your father's desk drawer?"

Frankie drops his hand to his side. "He prefers the inside of the toilet tank. Mamá makes me do it."

"Why is it *your* job?"

Frankie stares at his feet. "If he catches her, he beats her. He can't beat me now. I'm too strong." He looks up and slaps his chest. It makes a hard, hollow sound.

I imagine him standing between his parents, defending his mother. I clasp his wrist. My fingers barely go halfway around it. I focus on his eyes and move down to the crooked bridge of his nose. "You are so brave, Frankie. Especially after he hit you."

Frankie shrugs. "Doesn't matter, though. He goes out, begs for money, and buys more."

"It's not your fault. You can't make him quit. They have to decide themselves." I have the Madison Metropolitan School District's Drug and Alcohol Awareness Program to thank for the advice. I grab Frankie by his jacket sleeve and tug him outside. I don't want to talk about it anymore; he looks so unhappy. And I don't want to think about finding another of Papá's bottles in the tank of the downstairs toilet.

"So where are these birds?" he asks when I flip on the porch light.

"Here." The wire roof glows in the light, and the bare branches cast jagged shadows onto the ground. Pablo perches on the top rung of a ladder. Víctor flies to the opposite end of the cage. I point to him. "He doesn't trust people yet." Then I slip inside the cage. The heels of my shoes sink into mud. "Papá thinks he was abused. And"—I hold my hand toward Pablo—"the previous owner broke this one's wing so he wouldn't fly away."

"That sucks," Frankie says.

Pablo hops onto my hand, and I stroke his back. His claws tighten around my index finger. "How can people be so cruel?"

"Welcome to my country."

I want to put my arms around Frankie, let him kiss me like he did the night before last, since the birds haven't cheered him up, either. But he doesn't even look at me. "How did your father get the parrots?" he asks.

"This one used to live next door." I nod toward the house behind us, on the other side of the high fence. All I can see is its terra-cotta roof in the shadows. "He made too much noise, but Papá got him to quiet down."

"And the other?"

"Graciela's husband brought him. He'd bitten off his foot."

Frankie steps into the cage and stands next to me. He and the birds are so quiet that I can hear him breathe. Pablo shakes his tail feathers.

I take a deep breath. "My father has a thing for crippled birds. I think he sees himself in them."

I expect Frankie to ask how my father became crippled, but he doesn't—just like he didn't ask me about Papá's seizure on Tuesday.

"This parrot can talk," I say.

Frankie jerks his head toward me. "What does he say?"

"All kinds of things. He knows lots of swear words."

"In my neighborhood everybody teaches their parrots swear words. They get together and have swearing contests with the birds." Frankie steps close to me and leans over so his face is level with Pablo's. "Say something," he orders.

"*Pégame un tiro ya*," Pablo squawks.

"That's all?"

It occurs to me that Pablo didn't think up "just shoot me" on his own. My vision blurs, and in my mind is the image of a pistol in Papá's hand. I change the subject. "I was trying to teach him English, but it didn't work."

Frankie kisses my forehead. "So that makes me smarter than a parrot."

He holds out his finger, and Pablo hops to him. "Say, 'I like Metallica,'" he says slowly. When Pablo doesn't respond, he tries again. And again. Víctor circles us and settles on a branch right above Frankie's head. Frankie twists around and smiles. "You! Say, 'I like Metallica.'" Greeted with silence, Frankie turns back to me. "Maybe we need to bribe them."

I've seen Papá give his birds grapes, so I go inside for a handful. When I return, Frankie stands nose to beak with Víctor, now on a closer branch. I poke a grape through the wire.

"I like Metallica," Frankie says, holding up the prize.

"I like Metallica," Víctor squawks.

I'm about to cheer when Frankie shushes me. I push the rest of the grapes through the wire, one by one. Frankie feeds a grape to Víctor and eats another one himself. Pablo, now back on the ladder, screams, "*¡Alfonso, conch'e tu madre!*"

Frankie laughs. "Okay, one for you, Mr. Jealous." He balances a grape on the ladder, and Pablo snaps it up.

////////////////////

"I think Víctor likes me," Frankie says while we wait in line at the theater to buy tickets for *Duro de matar*. Bits of paper tumble down the street, blown by the chilly southern breeze.

"Maybe you can come over this weekend and show Papá how you got him to go near you. And talk, too."

Frankie pops a grape into his mouth and shakes his head. "Forget it. Your old man's going to be as jealous as that other bird."

"Pablo." Realizing I should have borrowed Tía Ileana's old-lady wool gloves, I shove my numb hands into my pockets. "You think?"

Frankie munches another one of the grapes I snatched from the refrigerator on our way out. "Víctor wants to fly. He doesn't want to hear all the nasty stuff your father fed crazy Pablo." He snorts. *"Pégame un tiro ya."*

I clamp my mouth shut, but my lip trembles. Pablo's words and the liquor bottle Frankie found in Papá's desk drawer tumble through my mind.

"Sorry, Tina. I shouldn't have said that. But with everything at home, I don't want to meet your father right now." Frankie draws me into his body, blocking out the wind. "Okay?"

"Yeah. No problem."

"Really?"

"Yeah, really. It's not like you don't want to see me," I answer. Frankie squeezes me tight.

///////////////////////

Unlike *Gorillas in the Mist*, *Die Hard* doesn't leave me crying. We get dessert again at the *heladería*, where I try the *manjar* and discover that I like it even better than chocolate.

When we get to Papá's street, Frankie parks his bike at the corner. We walk hand in hand the half block to the house. All the lights are off.

"Good, they're in bed," I whisper.

Frankie kisses me. I put my arms around his neck and hold him to me, to feel his soft lips against mine. They taste salty. I press my swirling stomach against his. His mouth, his body, keep me warm in the cold night air.

The light clicks on in the living room, and Frankie lets go. I glance inside at my aunt, standing next to the curtains. My father leans against her, his arm draped over her shoulders.

I grab Frankie's forearm. "There they are. Look."

He turns away from the window. "When can I see you again?"

Last night, Papá said he wasn't working Saturday or Sunday, and he wanted to show me Valparaíso. Tía Ileana is driving us, and we're staying overnight with some of his friends.

"I have to go out of town this weekend," I tell him. Three days is way too long not to see Frankie. "How about Monday?"

"No good. But I'm free Tuesday again."

I sigh. Four days. "I'm going to miss you."

Frankie plays with the end of my ponytail. After a while, he asks, "So what did you do back home when your friends went away?"

"You really want to know?"

Frankie nods. After stepping in front of him so that he blocks me from the window, I squeeze my thumb and index finger together, hold them to my lips, and inhale.

"*Cuete*," he says.

Max, who's Mexican, calls it *mota*, but it's probably the same thing.

"Do you smoke?" I ask him.

Frankie pulls me closer, like he's going to kiss me again. Instead he whispers, "No, but I might be able to get you some on Tuesday. So you'll think of me when we can't see each other."

"Cool!" I whisper back.

He touches his finger to my lips. "Don't say anything, *¿cachai?* You can get ten years in jail if they catch you."

"I'll hide it in my room. Nobody will ever know," I say. He gives me a final long kiss. When we let go, it feels like I'm still in his arms, spinning through the dark universe. I unlock the gate, but before going inside, I watch him ride away from the corner and into the night.

CHAPTER 10

Saturday, June 24: 58 days until I go home

Two police cars with flashing green-and-white lights
block the intersection. The one-way street is a steep
uphill climb, with buildings right next to the street. No
way to go around the cops. When I peer through the
windshield of Tía Ileana's little car, I imagine the police
cars crushing us from above.

"Can we back out of here?"

My aunt presses her lips together. In the weak light
of the streetlamps, her lips appear dark against her pale
face before everything flashes green. "It's just a roadblock,
amorcita. They do this all the time." She slides three cards
from her purse and sets them on the dashboard.

For the first time tonight I'm glad Papá stayed back
with the other reporters at the building for the new
National Congress rather than coming to see the rest
of Valparaíso with Tía Ileana and me. He said he had
the weekend off, but once again, he lied. My aunt told
him the new elected government would still be in charge

next year whether or not he took two hours to show his daughter the city. He didn't change his mind.

My aunt rolls down her window and keeps her hands, fingers outstretched, on the steering wheel. "What are you doing here?" a *carabinero* barks.

"I'm taking my niece around Valparaíso. She's visiting from the United States."

The cop holds out his hand, palm up. "Documents."

Tía Ileana hands him the three cards on the dashboard. He shuffles through them. I wonder if he's going to ask me for my documents, too. I don't have a national ID because I've been living in the United States too long, but Tía Ileana made me bring a photocopy of my passport.

After a long minute the *carabinero* returns the documents, slaps the top of Tía Ileana's car, and waves us on. My aunt puts the car in gear and without another word climbs the winding street to the top of the hill.

She stops in a parking area next to an overlook. When I get out of the car and stand next to her in the darkness, I gape at a view that made our encounter with the scary cops worth it. Below us, the lights of the city dot the steep hill all the way down to the harbor. All around us are other hills with lit-up houses and streetlamps along their slopes.

"During the day, you can see the houses painted in a rainbow of colors," Tía Ileana says. "But the city at night has its own beauty."

A gust of wind chills me inside my down vest. Ghostly fingers of fog make the lights blurry and cast a white shadow over the black water of the harbor. When the fog recedes, small fishing boats and huge cargo ships appear. From the top of the *cerro*, the piled-up cargo containers that we saw on our way into the city earlier today are as tiny as matchsticks.

I wish I could have seen all the colors of the houses and ridden the cable car to the top of the *cerro* in daylight. But during the day I had to carry Papá's backpack and equipment while he interviewed people for the radio station. Because Valparaíso is built on dozens of hills, everything is steep slopes and staircases, none of which my father can manage easily. And nothing is handicap-accessible.

"I wish Papá could see this," I tell my aunt. There's someone else who I wish could be here, too. But even though Tía Ileana has met Frankie, I want to pretend that we've created a secret world—just him and me— far away from our families and their troubles. So far, neither my aunt nor my father has said anything about seeing us kiss last week. Maybe it was too dark, or we were too far away from them.

"He had his chance," Tía Ileana says. "Our grandparents Gaetani lived here when they came over from Italy. Our mother grew up here." She points toward the black seam in the hill where the cable car runs on hundred-year-old wooden tracks. "Neither Cecilia nor your father had the patience to wait for the lift. They used to chase each other up the stairs and paths, at least until she started wearing high-heeled shoes to impress the boys."

"How old was she then?" Perhaps this aunt I never knew was the one most like me.

Tía Ileana touches her cheek. "Younger than you. Around fourteen. But Marcelo never quit. He would meet us at the top, like this." She crosses her arms across her chest and sticks out her lower lip in an arrogant pout. "Our grandfather said he looked like a little Mussolini."

"They must have not liked my father very much."

"He did it to annoy them. Because they were always so serious." Tía Ileana pats my back, and when I glance at her, she smiles. "I think you inherited your outspokenness from him."

"Like when I told him off about being prejudiced against lesbians." I don't want to remind my aunt of his hate, but if you don't talk about it, you can't end it. Besides, I got him good that night. Then I describe how I made Papá pee outside like a dog.

I expect Tía Ileana to laugh but instead she says, "I'm sure it breaks his heart that he will never run up these hills again."

My old *papá* never took Daniel and me to Valparaíso— my great-grandparents had already died by then—but he used to take us to the big park in Santiago, the Forestal, every Sunday unless it rained. In the morning, before people arrived from church, we ran among the trees in games of hide-and-seek. Then we ate the empanadas Mamá packed for us, and in the afternoon, the three of us cheered Papá on as he played pick-up *fútbol*. Over the years we got to know most of the other guys, and they all wanted Papá for their teams. He could run almost as fast while dribbling the ball as he could without it, but mainly he could *run*. His team would take the ball all the way to the other team's goal and lose it there, and Papá would show up right away on defense to steal it back. He said he was so good because he had the loudest cheering section, but Mamá once told us he was invited to try out for the national team. *He liked fútbol, but he liked writing about it even more,* she said.

I was good, but not that good, he responded. *You focus on what you do best. And where you're going to help the most.*

Tía Ileana continues. "I'm reading this book, *amorcita*, so I can understand him better. I got it in Italian because he doesn't read Italian that well and doesn't have time to try."

The book Frankie took from the shelf? I sound out the title. *"I sommersi . . ."*

"Los hundidos y los salvados. What would that be in English?"

"The Drowned and the Saved," I answer.

"Maybe you should read it when you get back to Wisconsin. It's by Primo Levi, an Italian Jew who ended up in Auschwitz during the Holocaust. He writes about why some people survived the death camps and others didn't." Her voice breaks. "Two years ago, he committed suicide." She pauses for a moment. "Do you know who Elie Wiesel is?"

"Yes. We read *Night* in eighth grade." I remember the part where Eliezer watches his father die from the upper bunk of their concentration camp barracks.

"He said Primo Levi died forty years earlier, at Auschwitz."

"And you think that's what happened to Papá?"

"He's my baby brother. I want to help him. He needs to accept that he's a different person because of what they did to him in prison, and love the person that he is now."

"Love?" I don't get it. Love is what Mamá and Evan have for each other. What I want Papá to have for me. And Frankie? I don't know if it's love, but whenever I'm away from him, I can't stop thinking of him and the world of just us.

Anyway, I suppose it would be hard to love yourself if you were drunk all the time, like Papá and Frankie's father.

"Yes, *amorcita*." My aunt squeezes my hand. "Right now, he hates everything about what happened to him. And he hates his own body, which is probably why he won't take care of himself."

"Even though he was a hero? And his side won?"

She nods. "He's suffered a lot more than most."

I wish I knew where my aunt was going with this and what the answers were, because it sounds like Papá is on the drowning side of the book. "So what can I do?" I ask.

"You and Daniel are very important to him."

"*Daniel* is very important to him. I'm just a girl."

"And you're a fighter. Keep fighting, keep trying to love him. That's the only way he'll learn."

"To love himself, right? And love me the way he used to?" Tía Ileana squeezes my hand again, and I smile back at her. Could my love really be strong enough to change everything—not just for Papá but for Frankie, too?

CHAPTER 11

Is that my *abuela* in front of the jewelry store? *¡Carajo!* Even if she and my grandfather refused to come to Mamá and Evan's wedding, I should have visited them already. But I haven't even called. And what would she say if she saw me with a guy in a motorcycle jacket?

I back into a corner of the brand-new mall, near the fancy neighborhood where my mother's parents live, and pull Frankie toward me. Maybe I can hide behind him. Mamá and Evan are getting back to Wisconsin tomorrow, and when Frankie picked me up at the house I told him I still hadn't gotten them anything for their wedding. So he brought me here. I should have asked him to bring me somewhere else. So far, everything's way too expensive anyway.

The wrinkled lady in high-heeled shoes struts in our direction. She carries three different shopping bags—navy, brown, and pink-and-white. But she's not my grandmother.

121

I exhale. After she's safely past, I ask Frankie if he got the *cuete*.

"No, sorry, couldn't find any." Frankie puts his arm around my back and gives me a tug. "Don't you know drugs are bad for you?"

I shake my head and force a laugh. I guess that he forgot. Or he couldn't find anybody who had it. Or he didn't want to risk going to jail for ten years because of me. "You're too late anyway," I tell him. "I needed it last weekend."

"The trip was that boring?"

"Worse. I had to carry Papá's stuff. It was so heavy."

"What was he doing?" Frankie twirls a strand of my hair.

"Interviewing people. Getting treated like a celebrity. Acting like one." I pretend to take Frankie's picture, the way the photographers from the newspapers Papá writes for took his. If Papá hadn't treated me like a pack mule while he played Princess Diana, I might have been happier to see him so happy at work. Instead, all I could think about was kissing a certain hot guy with a motorcycle while sitting on a cliff overlooking the ocean at night.

"Did you see the city? Or take the lift to the top of the hill?" Frankie asks.

"I saw the inside of a building. I heard about the lift." I sweep the hair from my face. "My aunt drove me to the top of one of the hills to see the city at night. That was kind of cool."

"You probably won't believe this, but I've never been to Valpo. I've never been outside Santiago."

"Really?"

He nods. "My uncle says he'll take me before I go into the army."

"Why wait?" I clasp my hands behind Frankie's neck. "Let's sneak off together. Do what *we* want to do." I don't think my father would notice, but my aunt might.

"You mean it? You'd run away with me?"

"Like *Romeo and Juliet*." My favorite Shakespeare play, though so far I only have *Julius Caesar* to compare it to. I wonder if Frankie studied it in school. "Except things didn't go so well for them."

Frankie frowns. "What happened? Did they get killed?"

I guess he didn't study it. "I can't tell you. But I promise I'll get you a copy of the play if you work hard on your English."

"Deal." He holds out his hand for me to shake. So old-fashioned, given that we're already tongue-kissing. "And then we'll run away."

I can't tell if he's joking or not, so I watch his face. The beginning of a smile. A little nod. After we kiss and let go of each other, he pulls a folded piece of paper from an inside pocket of his jacket.

"Look what I found."

I take the paper and unfold it. It's some sort of flyer with the headline, OUR DUTY TO PROTEST. Underneath is the date and time of a demonstration two weeks from now. And a list of speakers that includes, right at the top, Marcelo Aguilar. "That's Papá's! Where did you get it?"

Frankie answers in robot-like English. "The office. The desk."

"And you swiped it when you picked me up?"

"There were a bunch of them. He'll never miss it."

I lean toward him. "Are you going?"

He winks. "Maybe. My uncle . . . someone told me it's an illegal demonstration."

"Your uncle told you?" His uncle must be a *momio*—a supporter of the dictator. Especially if he's the same one who likes fancy restaurants.

"It wasn't my uncle. It was someone else, from work. Besides, no one cares about illegal demonstrations unless a speaker incites a riot." Frankie slides the flyer from my fingers. "Your father would never do that, right?"

My insides sparkle like the flecks of light on the floor tiles. I haven't given him any reason to believe I'm so into politics, but he must really care about me to go to Papá's demonstration because of me. Ever since my aunt told me about his father's affiliation, I've figured Frankie's father must have been imprisoned and tortured for his views just as mine was.

Frankie leads me to a record store. The albums and cassettes are brand-new and in their original wrapping, not like the used and bootleg tapes at the store near Papá's place. I also see a few compact discs that are really expensive. Frankie buys re-releases of *Kill 'Em All*, *Master of Puppets*, and *Ride the Lightning* on CD, and I wonder where he got the money for them and the equipment to play them on. Maybe delivery boys make more than I think. I pick up a cassette of dance music from Brazil for Mamá and Evan but put it back. My old *papá* liked to dance. Evan jogs. And Evan doesn't listen to music when he jogs.

While we eat at the local version of McDonald's in the food court, Frankie asks me to translate his favorite songs. He likes "The Call of Ktulu," which doesn't have any words, so I don't have to translate that one, and "For Whom the Bell Tolls," which is one of my favorites, too. It was inspired by a scene in Ernest Hemingway's novel about the Spanish Civil War.

"I didn't know that," he says. "I mean the novel. We learned about the war in school. How Franco stopped the Communists."

I drop my french fry. That's probably what they learned in school under their own dictatorship like the one in Spain, but wouldn't his father know the real history? Maybe his father never went to school. And I'm sure Frankie couldn't read the novel *For Whom the Bell Tolls* because it takes the side against Franco and would have been banned.

Picking up my half-eaten burger, I change the subject back to Metallica. "What other songs do you like?"

He doesn't hesitate. "'Master of Puppets.' I got a concert version from the bootleg place where they played it in a medley with 'Welcome Home (Sanitarium).'"

"Oh, yeah! I heard it live. They call it the 'Mastertarium.' But I like 'Sanitarium' better."

Frankie sings the opening verses of "Sanitarium" in English. He sings in tune and hardly has any accent at all. I translate the words into Spanish, verse by verse, and then I translate the words of "Master of Puppets," after he sings those.

Everyone at the tables around us is staring at us by now. I'm sure they weren't expecting musical entertainment, even from someone with as fine a voice as Frankie has, but we don't care. He reaches for my hand under the table. His hand is warm and a little greasy from the french fries. Or maybe it's my fingers that are greasy. Heat spreads through my body.

"So what do you like about 'Sanitarium'?" he asks me.

"The opening. The melody. And it's the story of a lot of my friends." I tell him about Leslie, my first real friend in the United States, whose mother had her committed to a psychiatric hospital after she tried to run away near the end of our eighth grade year. "I see why you like 'Master of Puppets,'" I add.

Frankie folds his arms and leans across the table. "A lot of people around here think it's a political song. But it's really about drugs and booze. How they make you their slave."

My smile evaporates. Maybe this is Frankie's way of telling me he doesn't want to bring the weed. "Is Metallica popular here?"

"Guys like them. I've never met a girl who did. Except you." He touches the ends of my hair. "Girls here are different."

"More girlie-girl?" I think of my aunt Cecilia, running up the hills as a kid and then wearing high heels at fourteen.

He takes a sip of his soda. "They know their place. There are things that boys do, and things that girls do."

I'm not shocked. Daniel has said the same thing. Problem is, the boys get to do all the good stuff.

"But I'm not like that, you know," I say. And he better be okay with it, because that's the way it is where he wants to live.

He shakes his head slowly. "Me, I want to see the world. This country is just an itty-bitty corner." He holds his thumb and index finger a centimeter apart. "But whenever I'm with you"—he extends his arms— "it's like the whole world opening up for me. Like when you told me about how boys and girls aren't so different in your country."

I give him a huge smile. "Maybe you can visit me in Wisconsin. I'll talk to my mother as soon as I get back." I say before popping the last bite of hamburger into my mouth.

"You promise?" His eyes meet mine. "Really?"

"Promise." I rest my arm on the table. Frankie strokes my pinkie, then each of my other fingers in turn. His touch is electric; the sensation moves up my arm and through my body.

"How will I get there?"

"She got a new job and my stepfather's an architect. We'll send you a plane ticket."

He gives me a doubtful look.

"They can afford it. Honest."

"You say you have a stepfather?"

I nod. "His name's Evan."

"Do you like him?"

"Yeah, he's really nice. You'd like him, too." I tell Frankie about the *mitzvah* house, as coherently as I can with his fingers caressing my hand and wrist.

"He sounds cool," Frankie says. "I wouldn't have thought to fix a busted-up house if I had the money. I would have torn it down and built something new."

"My aunt said the same thing. But she works for a company that builds high-rises."

For a few seconds Frankie stares at me without saying a word. Then he asks, "So who would you rather have for your father? This Evan guy or . . . you know?"

What kind of question is that? "I have both."

But he presses me. "Who? If you were forced to choose one."

"Evan's easier to live with. He lets me get away with

more, because I guess that's the way the gringos are. And because he's not my real father."

"Does he drink?"

"No. Maybe a glass of wine at dinner." I've never had to choose between Evan and Papá before—not even Papá has asked me to do it. "But there are things I like about my father, too."

"No way." Frankie blinks rapidly.

"I'm proud of the things he does. And that with all his problems, he still gets up and goes to work every day."

"Yeah, that's a concept." Frankie slurps down his soda and lifts his hand from mine. "Ready to go? Maybe tonight we can see the stars."

My eyes don't sting when I step outside. Yesterday's rain and wind have cleared most of the smog. Fifteen minutes until closing time on a weeknight, the mall's parking lot is nearly empty. And the stars are out, the brilliant southern constellations I had forgotten in my years away. To the east, I can see the snow on the mountains and the lights of the Farellones ski resort. I imagine the skiers from all over the world coming to this itty-bitty corner that Frankie has never left.

Frankie lays his arm across my shoulders and turns his head toward me. His mouth closes on mine. I taste french fries and secret sauce. I explore the gap between his two front teeth. He pulls me tight against his body. I was standing on tiptoes, but it seems as though my feet have left the ground completely. I can no longer tell where I end and Frankie begins. *Is this what love is like?*

When the long kiss is over and I feel my feet on the pavement again, I bury my face in his leather jacket. It's smooth against my cheek and makes a soft crackle when I move. I inhale a thick, slightly oily smell.

Mastertarium. The word, the thoughts, echo in my head like the opening bars of "Sanitarium" and the glistening lights of Farellones. *You like "Master of Puppets." I like "Sanitarium." The two fit together.*

CHAPTER 12

Wednesday, June 28: 54 days until I go home

When Mamá gets back from her honeymoon in Spain, she calls. A frowning Tía Ileana hands me the phone. "She thought you would have sent a card at least. She's not happy."

"I did write," I tell Mamá. "I just didn't mail it."

"Oh?" My mother's tone demands an explanation.

"It was really boring here at first, and then I met a boy." I tell her about how I met Frankie and the movies we saw together.

She asks me how old he is, what neighborhood he comes from, and how we get around. Typical mother questions.

So I lie. For her, he's sixteen, he lives in Papá's neighborhood, and we walk or take the *micro*—the bus.

"May I speak with your father?"

"He's outside with his birds."

"Get him, please."

I was hoping it wouldn't come to this. Not because I thought he'd expose the stuff I made up—he's still completely out of it—but because I remember her crying every time she talked to him. I don't want to hear whatever he tells her that upsets her like that.

He comes to the phone right away, like he's actually eager to talk to her.

First he asks her about Spain. He listens for a while. Then he tells her about the election campaign and the candidates who've stayed at the house. In the nearly two weeks since I met Frankie, two more have crashed on the sofa.

Finally, they get to me. "She's fine. Having a good time," Papá tells her.

There's about thirty seconds of silence.

"Ileana has met him a couple of times. She says he's very polite. Volunteered for us in the election. And he hasn't brought her back past her curfew."

Why didn't Frankie—or Tía Ileana—tell me he actually volunteered?

Papá talks again. "No. I guess I should meet him. I didn't expect to be this busy at work."

Sitting across the coffee table from him, I can now hear my mother shouting all the way from the other side of the planet. From what I can make out, she's accusing him of being a bad father for not having met Frankie yet and letting me go out with him anyway. Doing so takes her eighty-five seconds.

"Look, Vicky, you weren't going to take her on your honeymoon. And she would have been underfoot when you were working on the house." *No, I wouldn't have.* Clueless Papá holds the phone to his ear with his shoulder while reaching for his cigarettes on the end table. "Of course, she's safe. I give her a lot more rules than you do."

I can tell the conversation is degenerating quickly. I have three choices. One. Do nothing and hear the whole ugly mess between them. Two. Leave the room and let them fight in private. Or three. Try to stop them before someone gets hurt.

I can be a good daughter when I set my mind to it. And besides, Papá will cut me more slack if he thinks I'm taking his side.

I cross the living room, rest my hand on my father's shoulder, and reach for the phone.

"Mamá," I say as soon as he hands it over. "Papá's doing a great job watching me. And he's a good father. He's helping me learn about my country."

"That boy," she sputters in English.

I switch back to Spanish so Papá can understand. "I'm teaching him English so he can come to the United States to study. We're not doing anything."

Cigarette in his mouth, Papá mumbles, "She thinks you'll go home pregnant."

"I heard that. Tell your father it's not something to joke about," Mamá says.

"I'm not stupid, Mamá. Nothing is going to happen. You should be happy I'm having a good time and not begging to come home." I think of the letter I almost sent her, now sitting in pieces in a garbage dump somewhere in the Andean foothills.

After about a dozen warnings to stay out of trouble, she hangs up. Meanwhile, Papá's swigging whiskey straight from the bottle, and he hasn't eaten supper yet. Ninety minutes of lucidity are going down to about forty tonight.

I sit him down and boil water for poached eggs so he has something in his stomach besides toast and avocado to soak up the alcohol. His hair hangs over his glasses and he makes no move to push it away, even while smoking. I'm afraid he's going to set his hair on fire, but I also know he doesn't like people touching his head. Before I call my aunt to supper, I ask him what's going on between him and my mother that she ends up crying when she talks to him.

He perks up. "She does?"

I nod.

"Good." He stabs out his cigarette.

You're a jerk. I dash up the stairs and knock on Tía Ileana's bedroom door to tell her we're off the phone and ready to eat. At the table, she asks me how the call went.

"She's worried. Because I'm friends with a boy," I answer. *Like I don't have friends who are boys at home.*

"She's just being a mother," Tía Ileana says.

Papá glares at her as if to say, *How would you know?* He pierces the poached egg with his fork. Yolk streams from multiple holes and pools on his plate.

Tía Ileana covers his hand with hers. "I think you're the boy she's worried about."

Papá shrugs one shoulder. "Vicky's moved on. She has a gringo now."

And that's all he says about it for the rest of the night.

///////////////////

I'm wide awake and buzzing with anticipation when Frankie comes for me at eight thirty the next morning. It's Thursday, the sun is poking through the haze, and he's going to take me on his deliveries with him so I can see Santiago in the daytime. We weave in and out of rush hour traffic on our way downtown. While gripping Frankie's jacket, I stare at the giant snow-covered mountains to my right, the peaks so high I can't see them through the blanket of smog. No more than an hour from where we are, we could be up there skiing.

At the edge of downtown farthest from the mountains is a shabby row of warehouses and small offices. An orange and yellow metal sign above one of the offices reads SPEEDY COURIERS, the name in English. The tail of the S ends in the shape of a sneaker. I wait outside while Frankie punches in and picks up his first delivery. He returns with a plastic envelope, hands me his leather jacket, and puts on an orange rain jacket with the sneaker logo.

135

I touch the rubbery sleeve. "You were the one who splashed me!"

"I did?" His eyes are wide. Innocent. Or faking innocence.

"The day after I got here. It was raining, and you sped through a puddle. Got my jeans all wet."

He flips my ponytail. "I didn't notice. But if I was rushing to a delivery and did, I'm sorry." He kisses me, then says, "Check your pocket. There's a surprise."

I pat both pockets of his jacket. In the left one is something hard with sharp edges. I pull out a book. *Romeo y Julieta.*

"My uncle loaned it to me. I'm up to the part where he goes to the party where he's not invited, looking for some other girl."

I laugh. "You just started!"

"I'll finish it. I promise," he says. I examine the slender paperback. The papers' rough edges are yellowed with age but the unbroken spine tells me no one has read the book, ever. Frankie drops the envelope into the milk crate. "Job number one. Pick up documents from a law office in Bellavista, deliver to a law office in Macul. I'll show you the river right away."

He guns the engine. We take a wide avenue along the Río Mapocho, which runs from the mountains east to west through the city. The current is fast and the water gray and smelly, as if the river is the city's main sewer. We stop in front of a three-story building in the shadow of the Cerro San Cristóbal. Frankie runs up the outdoor staircase to the top story, taking the steps two at a time. Minutes later, he's back with a manila folder.

We cross a bridge over the river, pass by the downtown skyscrapers, and end up in an area of one-, two-, and three-story buildings not far from Papá's house. Frankie drops off the documents.

After another errand we stop for hot chocolate while he calls his boss from a pay phone. He gets assigned a doctor's office in the La Florida neighborhood, with files needing to go to a specialist in Providencia.

"Get ready for a long ride," he tells me. "It's about twenty kilometers."

La Florida is a newly built suburb in the shadow of the Andes. When I lived here before, it was nothing but fields and shantytowns. Seeing the almost identical brick houses with shingle roofs makes me think of the new suburbs just outside of Madison, like Middleton and Fitchburg, where people have moved to get away from the big city.

On the way back to downtown along a flat highway, Frankie shouts, "My family lives one *comuna* over." He points to the opposite side of the highway, where there's a field and beyond it, a row of squat plywood homes that look like barracks. A pack of stray dogs—nearly two dozen of them—roams the field next to the highway.

"Can we stop off there?" I shout back. I think I'd like his mother and sisters, from what he's told me about them, and I'm guessing that his drunken father, far less functional than mine, won't be up this early.

"No," he snaps. I can tell that this has nothing to do with the tightness of his schedule.

I don't have a city map with me, but I've drawn a mental picture of all his delivery routes. With the exception of one run to the airport, we've stayed in the eastern half of the city, from La Florida in the south to the hilly, rural La Dehesa in the north, where Pinochet has one of his homes. Frankie points this out matter-of-factly. I would have expected him to say something critical of the dictator, but he doesn't say anything, and I don't want to say the wrong thing. As Papá explained, there are many different parties in the opposition known as the Concertación, from the Christian Democrats who once supported the military government to the Communists and Socialists who were enemies number one and two from the start. And just because Frankie's father is with the Socialists doesn't mean Frankie is, especially since Frankie hates his father.

Things get quiet in the early afternoon, so we stop to eat at McDonald's in the Plaza de Armas, in the center of the city. The plaza is between a bunch of government buildings and the Metropolitan Cathedral, near where Papá worked as a human rights investigator after he sneaked back into the country. I see soldiers all over the place, which makes me realize how good a cover Papá must have had when he was underground. Daniel said he disguised himself as a beggar. I believe it. There are plenty of those, and enough of them look the way Papá used to before he cleaned himself up.

In the late afternoon, Frankie picks up bank documents to deliver to an office in one of the glass skyscrapers downtown. He squeezes his motorcycle into a small triangle of striped pavement. "Watch my bike, okay?" he says. "This space is very illegal."

"What if a cop comes?"

"Tell them I'll be back. They don't care as long as someone's standing by." He lifts off my helmet and kisses me. I wrap my arms around his neck and inhale the mixture of rubber and sweat from his Speedy Couriers jacket. His leather jacket that I'm wearing smells so much nicer, and I can't wait until we finish the deliveries. Tonight he's taking me to a different mall with what he says is the best pinball arcade in the city. I plan to kill him at *Ms. Pac-Man* there.

Fifteen minutes pass while I babysit Frankie's motorcycle. Fumes from the cars and buses make me dizzy. Well-dressed men and women push past me, knocking me into the bike. I wonder if there's been a mix-up that Frankie's had to sort out upstairs. My head swirling, most likely from lack of oxygen, I wander into the lobby. I know waiting inside rather than on the street won't make him return faster and will probably get him a ticket. But it wouldn't help if I passed out from the pollution, either.

Then I see him, next to a bank of elevators. Standing with him is a short brown-skinned girl with long straight hair and a big butt. They appear to be talking. He has his arm around her shoulders. She snuggles against him and rubs his back, just above his waist.

The dizziness returns. Frankie and the other girl turn into one big blur.

Hey, maybe you should change the name on the jacket from Speedy Couriers to Cheaty Couriers. I can't think of the words in Spanish, I'm so mad.

Frankie turns his head toward me. Quickly, he pulls away from the girl and calls my name.

But it's too late. I stomp over, ready to make a scene. "I'm waiting outside and you're—"

"Tina, this is Sofia Méndez. Sofi, meet Tina Aguilar." Frankie clasps my elbow. I shake his hand away.

Frankie continues, apparently oblivious. "Sofi is a friend from *colegio.* She's a secretary." He pauses. "Tenth floor, right?"

Sofia names a company, but I don't listen. How could Frankie do this to me? But two days ago he asked me to choose between Papá and Evan. Maybe that was his way of saying he wanted to choose, too.

The girl holds out her right hand, but I stick mine behind my back. She shrugs and looks at Frankie, as if to say, *Let's get rid of this little twit and do our thing together.* I notice her bright red lipstick and eyelashes three times thicker than any normal eyelashes. None of my friends at home wear makeup like that, unless they're going for total Goth. This Sofia looks at least twenty years old, and going for total skank.

Frankie glances at his watch and frowns at me. "I hope I don't have a ticket."

"Good luck, Pepe," Sofia says.

Pepe? What the hell is that? Some pet name?

She stands on her tiptoes and hugs him. He kisses her on the cheek.

Frankie runs back to the *moto*, leaving me to follow. There's a ticket attached to the handlebars. "*Mier . . . colés!*" he shouts, shoving the paper into his pocket.

"I didn't come to be your ticket insurance while you go off with your girlfriend," I yell at him.

"She's not my girlfriend. Just an old school friend," Frankie says.

"Old is right. She's, like, twenty."

"She's eighteen. Same as me."

"Right. And what's this 'Pepe'? What your sweetheart calls you?"

Frankie stammers. I can't make out what he's saying. He shakes his head.

My voice breaks. "I thought you cared about me. We were going out."

But he never said, *I love you.* Neither did I, though I couldn't stop thinking of him. Maybe I should have said the words. Maybe it would have made the difference.

"I'm sorry, Tina. You and I are . . . going out."

"You like her more." That's the way it always is. Papá likes Daniel more than me. Max dumped me for a freshman at the beginning of our sophomore year. Their romance lasted six weeks, but it killed ours forever.

Frankie reaches for my arm. I yank it away.

"You go back to her. I'm leaving!" Pedestrians stop to watch us, but I don't care.

"It's nothing. I mean it. She's just a friend," Frankie says.

"How can I believe you? You spend two days a week with me. What are you doing Mondays? Because we never get together Mondays." I do the math in my head. Two days, me. Five days, *her*.

Frankie squeezes the handlebar of his motorcycle. But he's looking at his hands. He won't look me in the eye because he's lying. I know it. "I can't. It's a family thing."

"Yeah, right. And how about the other days? The weekends?"

"You're the one who went out of town last weekend. Remember?" He stares up at the hazy purple sky. "You don't know how good you got it, you selfish little brat."

I rip Frankie's precious leather jacket off and hurl it into the milk crate. "Jerk!"

Sofia's tits and butt are bigger. She isn't a brat.

She calls him by another name. *Pepe.* Pepe is normally a nickname for José, but who knows what they have going?

142

"I'm sorry." Frankie steps toward me, and I back away. "I'm just dealing with a lot, Tina."

"That's right. A lot of girlfriends." I turn from him and fast-walk to the end of the block, where I let the crowd push me around the corner. He doesn't follow me.

CHAPTER 13

Thursday, June 29: 53 days until I go home

The afternoon's purple-gray haze has darkened to charcoal. Streetlamps flicker on. Shivering without Frankie's jacket, I hunt for a bus stop. The sign lists at least a dozen lines—which one goes to my house? People surround me, sharks circling a drowning person. I pat my pocket to make sure my money is still there. Did any pickpockets see me? See that my money's in the right front pocket of my jeans?

Next to the bus stop is a pay phone. I drop the coins into the slot and dial Tía Ileana's office number. *Please be there.*

A receptionist puts me through. "Is everything all right?" Tía Ileana asks. On hearing her voice, I let out my breath.

"Frankie and I had a fight and broke up. I'm stuck downtown." I read off the nearest street signs.

"I'll be right there."

Ten minutes later, she pulls up to the corner. As soon as I

get in, she hugs me. Tears run down my face and soak into her blazer. She waits until I stop crying before letting go.

"I'm sorry." She pats my leg. "It was nice to have a friend your age."

"He wanted to choose between me and someone else. Someone in his class at school." I snuff back a wad of snot. "Her name is Sofia Méndez."

"Is that what he told you?"

"He didn't have to tell me anything. I saw them hugging and kissing. And a couple of days ago, he asked me who I'd pick if I had to choose between Papá and Evan."

"That's not right," Tía Ileana says. "First of all, your father and Evan are family."

"Mamá chose." Maybe that's how half of me is Papá. People love others more than they love us. Papá doesn't even love himself, so he's already lost.

And me? I'm sick of always coming in second.

Tía Ileana steers with one hand and squeezes my hand with her other. "Your parents loved each other. That they cared about each other and were faithful to each other despite everything that happened is a beautiful testimony to their love." We stop at a light, and my aunt's hazel eyes connect with mine. *Beautiful* isn't a word that I'd use to describe what happened between Mamá and Papá, but I want to hear more—such as why Tía Ileana doesn't totally hate my mother.

"But they still got divorced. So Mamá could marry Evan." Which is why I'm here, getting my heart broken. The light changes. Tía Ileana breaks her gaze to watch the road. Several months after coming back from prison, Papá got into a huge argument with Mamá and accused her of having a boyfriend, which she didn't—at least not then. That night she threw him out of the bedroom and he slept on the living room sofa until he went back to Chile.

"That prison changed your father so much." Tía Ileana reaches for a tissue from the box in the center console. I grab one, too, and wipe my dripping nose. "And your mother also changed, going back to school and raising you and Daniel on her own. They weren't the same people anymore."

She's right. My old *papá* is dead, drowned in flashbacks and anger and alcohol and his obsession with his work like in the title of that book. It's as if my mother became a widow.

"But I didn't change. Frankie doesn't have that excuse. He just doesn't love me." I blow my nose. "He may have acted sweet, and we had a lot in common, but he only pretended to care about me. And he certainly wasn't faithful."

My aunt laughs. "Two weeks is a bit early to be talking about love."

"What about love at first sight? Mamá said it happened to her when she met Papá." I fold my arms across my chest.

147

"Well, it's over now. I have nothing to look forward to."

My aunt's expression goes from amused to stricken. I wait for her to yell at me for being ungrateful. She comes home every day to eat with me. She drove me around Valparaíso last weekend. She just left work early to pick me up, and she talked about my parents' divorce even though it made her sad.

She slows the car. Maybe she's going to kick me out and make me walk home, like Mamá sometimes did when I was in middle school and pissed her off.

"You know what I look forward to?" Tía Ileana says at the next light.

I shake my head.

"You being here." She sighs. "Getting to know you after all these years." She squeezes into a parking space in front of a pizza shop with a funky hand-lettered sign that reads LA PIZZA PELLEGRINO. "We can do some things together, too."

"Like what?" I say.

"Don't you like movies?"

I nod to be polite. And because there might be take-out pizza in my future.

I slouch into the store behind her, hood over my head. The menu board has the same hand lettering, lines alternating red, black, and green. *What flavor for a girl who's had her heart broken?* Tía Ileana says Papá likes mushroom, so I pick sausage.

But when we get home, the lukewarm pizza tastes like dirt. I ask to be excused.

Papá glances at Tía Ileana. "What's wrong with her?"

"Boyfriend trouble," my aunt answers. I don't want my father into my business but at least she told him so I don't have to talk to him.

Papá shrugs one shoulder. If I had any hope of getting insight from him on the male species, I'd better forget it.

"You encouraged her, Chelo. I warned you that she'd get hurt."

"So says the queen of 'I told you so.'" My father picks a piece of sausage from his slice and throws it on the table. It stains the tablecloth next to his quarter-full glass, and I suddenly feel guilty for not enjoying the flavor he won't eat. Frankie's words, *selfish little brat*, gnaw at me.

"Go on upstairs, Tina," my aunt says, nodding at me. Papá's face twists ugly. "She's had a hard day, so if she doesn't want to sit for dessert, we shouldn't make her."

I jump in to reassure Papá. "It's not going to happen again, I promise." *No more boys for me.*

And a gazillion weeks more of two crabby old people who fight with each other and know nothing at all about me.

I give them both a good-night hug and apologize for leaving early. Tía Ileana pats the top of my head. Papá grunts, but at least he's not scowling at me.

Upstairs, I shut the door and turn up the volume on the TV. Yesterday, Papá and Mamá talked on the phone.

He drank himself unconscious in record time afterward, and she probably cried again. I don't know why those two keep picking at old wounds until they bleed and throb. When it's over, it needs to be over.

On top of my desk is the Metallica cassette that I bought the day I met Frankie. I rip out the tape, twist it up, and leave it in tangles on the floor.

CHAPTER 14

Wednesday, July 5: 47 days until I go home

The phone rings while I'm cleaning up from supper. I expect my mother again. As I dry my hands, I debate whether to beg her for a plane ticket home, or if going shopping and seeing movies with my aunt is enough to keep me here. Tía Ileana is trying hard—maybe too hard. I can't imagine she really likes *The Naked Gun*, which has the stupid and meaningless title *¿Y dónde está la policía?* because the censors don't like anything having to do with sex.

Papá, on the other hand, hasn't tried at all. He spent much of the weekend at meetings to plan the demonstration next Tuesday. Until it's over, I know I'm not going to see him.

"Hi, Mamá," I begin.

"It's Frankie," an out-of-breath voice responds.

"How did you get my number?" I don't recall ever giving it to him, and it's not in the Santiago phone book. And why is the Cheaty Courier calling? I squeeze the receiver so it won't slide out of my sweaty palm.

"I wrote it down one time when I came over. The number's on the rotary."

"Oh." I try to sound unimpressed. But at least it shows that he liked me once and wanted to hang out with me. Even if he likes someone else more.

"Tina, don't hang up. Listen."

I let a few seconds of silence pass between us, while I scan the living room for Tía Ileana. Papá's already in bed, but I'm sure she's hiding somewhere, eavesdropping. "Okay," I finally say. I know I'm acting just like my parents by staying on the phone, but it's going to be a long six weeks in upside-down-land if I don't listen to him.

"I've been trying to call you all weekend."

"I was out with my aunt." I twirl a strand of hair around my finger, wondering how he's going to explain himself out of this one.

"I'm sorry for what I said to you on Thursday."

"When you called me a . . ." I can't say the words: *selfish little brat.*

"I was mad about getting the parking ticket. And you were right to be jealous. I left you standing in the street while I talked to some other girl."

"Your girlfriend."

"We were friends in high school. Honest. I haven't seen her since graduation."

"How can I believe you?" I pull my finger away, making the corkscrew strand unwind to my natural wave.

I can't think of anything he can say that will make me believe him.

There's silence, then a series of clicks on the line. A bad connection, or maybe Papá's phone is tapped. Frankie speaks up again. "My grandmother just went out of town, and I'm taking care of the apartment for her. I'm free every night. Weekends, too."

"There's no one else?" I replay the scene in the office building, wondering if I jumped to conclusions without listening to his side—like Papá jumped to conclusions about Mamá. After all, Frankie seemed not to know the office where Sofia worked. I switch the hand holding the phone and wipe my damp palm on my jeans.

"No one." He pauses. "I mean, I went out with other people in high school. Didn't you?"

"Yes. But it's all over." Frankie's right. They could have broken up and stayed "just friends."

"And my uncle gave me his videos and a Nintendo. Have you played *Super Mario Brothers?*"

He can't see my big grin. "I'm the *capo* of *Super Mario Brothers.*"

"Are not."

"Are, too."

"I challenge you. Tomorrow at six," Frankie says.

"It's a deal."

I hang up and turn around to face my aunt. "Who was that?" she asks.

Hot blood rushes to my face. "Frankie. The boy you met."

She raises an eyebrow. "The boy you broke up with last week?"

I nod slowly. "We're going to try again. We're getting together to play video games." I don't mention an empty apartment. "He said Sofia Méndez wasn't his girlfriend. Just a friend from school he hadn't seen in a long time."

"And you believe him?"

"I guess."

My aunt frowns, and I wonder if it's because I'm getting back together with him, or bailing on her.

"Boys don't always tell the truth." She squeezes my shoulder. "Don't let him hurt you."

///////////////

The apartment is on the fourth floor of a six-story concrete building with no balconies. The elevator is slow, and Frankie and I stand in opposite corners, avoiding each other's eyes. He lights a cigarette, and between us, the elevator fills with smoke. I don't know what to say to him, and I guess he doesn't know what to say to me, either. *Promise you won't go off with someone else* is what I want to say. When the elevator gets to our floor, he drops his cigarette, grinds it out with his foot, and kicks it through the gap into the shaft. He leads me down a dingy hallway with a worn parquet floor.

"Here it is," he says, unlocking the gray metal door. His key ring has a yellow smiley face.

I step into the living room. When he said the apartment belonged to his grandmother, I expected something old-fashioned with overstuffed sofas and Oriental rugs and a mothball smell—kind of like the house in Las Condes where my *abuelos* live. I'm surprised to see a modern-looking white sofa and love seat—like the living room at Papá and Tía Ileana's house except for no books, a way bigger TV, and a combo cassette and CD player. Fancy electronics, even by my *abuelos'* standards. A beige oval rug covers the middle of the parquet floor. Our living room has a plank floor and no rug—nothing that Papá can trip over.

"So are you going to show me around?" I say.

"Oh, yeah. Sorry."

He takes me to the kitchen and points out the bathroom. There's another door, closed. "What's that?"

"My grandmother's bedroom. She doesn't want anyone going in there." He jiggles the locked doorknob. "Paranoid about her jewelry."

Why would she think her own grandson would steal her jewelry?

We stare at each other. He shoves his hands into the pockets of his leather jacket. I hook my thumbs in the belt loops of my jeans and twist. One of the loops has a loose thread.

A week ago we would have hugged. And kissed.

"*Super Mario Brothers?*" I suggest.

Frankie nods, then smiles. Finally.

"Prepare to lose," he says.

I massacre Frankie at *Super Mario Bros.* We gringos get so much more practice. He blows me away at *Duck Hunt*, though. And by the end of the first match, we're talking and laughing again like we used to. After we get tired of playing, Frankie leads me into the kitchen. He takes two glasses from a cabinet above the sink and two cans of Coke from the refrigerator. Then he sticks his head into the cabinet under the sink, setting dish detergent, floor polish, and powdered bleach on the tile floor next to his feet. "Here it is. Eyes closed. Both hands out."

I obey him. He sets what feels like a small plastic bag in my hands. Whatever is inside is lightweight and crunchy.

"Open your eyes."

I look at the dried, rolled leaves and savor the familiar woody smell. Then I stand on my tiptoes and hug him tight. First hug since *that day.* "Shall we try it?"

He shrugs. *Is that a yes or a no?*

"Do you have any papers?" I ask. "I can roll us a . . ." I hesitate, not knowing the word in Spanish. I say it in English. "A *blunt.*"

"Blunt?" he repeats.

I make a rolling gesture, then say, "*Gordo*"—fat— and hold my thumb and index finger to my lips.

"That's what *cuete* is." He points to the weed in the bag. "This is *macoña*."

"Oh."

I'd figured *cuete* was the herb, not the cigarette. But Frankie knew, and he still didn't get it. "Sorry. No papers," he says. Either he's totally clueless, or he really doesn't want to do this.

"And you probably don't have a bong."

"Bong?"

Once again I explain.

"I have this." He ducks under the sink again and comes out with a small packet of white powder. "Cocaine. You put it up your nose with a straw."

My heart races at the sight of the powder. I've never done coke. Ever. And I can't believe he has. I remember what he said about "Master of Puppets" two weeks ago, how drugs could take over your life, and it made me think how innocent and old-fashioned he is. Has he been lying to me? "How do you know? Have you used?" is all I can say.

"I've watched *Scarface*, like, a dozen times."

My heart slows to near normal. My thoughts rearrange themselves in straight lines. "And what are you doing with cocaine—in your grandmother's apartment?"

"I thought you wanted it." He stares at his feet.

"I wanted weed. And some way to smoke it. I don't do hard drugs."

"You don't? My uncle says . . ." Frankie sets the bag on the counter.

How could he think that someone who smokes weed from time to time would automatically be a cokehead? Talk about jumping to conclusions.

And what does his uncle have to do with this? Could the uncle—the one who likes fancy restaurants—be a drug dealer?

"Can you take it back? Get your money back?" I ask Frankie, my voice hushed even though we're alone in the apartment. If his uncle is the one who got the stuff, I'm sure he'll understand.

"Maybe."

"Well, try." I raise the bag of weed to his eye level. "Because this is better than drinking. It doesn't make you puke and it's not addicting. That"—I point to the white powder—"is really dangerous."

Frankie takes a step backward. "I don't know. Drugs are drugs. Drinking isn't illegal, and look at our fathers."

I grab his forearm and tug. "*Tranquílate.* You sound like my *abuelito.*"

"I'm not your little old grandfather." He crushes me in a hug. "But you already said we have no way to smoke it."

I pat his shoulder. "Brownies, Frankie. Marijuana brownies."

He has nothing to make brownies with, either. In fact, there is no food in the kitchen at all. His grandmother must have cleaned out the place before leaving town. It doesn't seem fair—Frankie being a growing boy without much money doing her a favor by watching her place. I check my purse for the allowance my father sets on my desk every Monday morning.

"Is there a supermarket around here?" I check my watch. "And we'd better hurry, because they close soon."

Frankie hesitates before answering, "Yes, but—"

"You don't want me running into any more ex-girlfriends."

Frankie grabs his jacket and keys. "Okay, let's go."

"I'm not an insanely jealous person. Honest," I say. Well, maybe a little. It comes from being the younger sister of the boy everyone considers the perfect child.

At the supermarket a block and a half from his building we buy a package of brownie mix, the kind where you have to add butter. I add a few other things to the cart before my money runs out—milk, cereal, oranges, ramen noodles, and as a treat, a tube of frozen cookie dough.

On the way back he carries both bags on his shoulders as though trying to hide his face with them—easy enough to do in the pitch-black evening. We get back without anyone he knows seeing him, and I successfully reproduce Petra's brownies. Frankie tastes one, and when nothing happens, he eats another. And another. By the time we finish the batch, we're high for real.

"Your uncle got us some good stuff," I say, suppressing a giggle. "Thank him for me, okay?"

"It, uh, wasn't him." From the silly grin on Frankie's face, I know he's lying. I suppose I shouldn't be hanging out with a guy who's related to a drug dealer, but I brush away my worries.

"And I bet he didn't get you that copy of *Romeo y Julieta*, either," I say.

"Actually, he did. But I gave it back."

"Why? Did you not like it?"

He puts his arm around my waist. "Because I want you to teach me enough English so I can read the original."

He kisses me. The room spins. We slow-dance in the kitchen, bumping against the table and chairs and walls. He reaches for my belt.

"No. Not now," I whisper as I push his hand away. He steps backward and mumbles an apology. I guess being high makes him super horny. And I'm tingling all over, too, but we've never gone this far before and stoned isn't how I want to do it with him. Besides, Papá's words, *she thinks you'll go home pregnant*, run through my mind even though we're supposed to be in our own secret world, like the laws of nature chasing us down no matter where we go.

CHAPTER 15

Saturday, July 8: 44 days until I go home

Frankie and I were supposed to spend Saturday afternoon and evening together since he gets off work at noon, but Mamá has arranged for me to go to my grandparents in Las Condes. "One day with them, and that's all you have to do," she tells me over the phone on Friday morning.

I don't protest because I have forty-four more days with Frankie—and a mother who will owe me big time when I want to see him after that.

On Saturday morning Tía Ileana drives me to the house where Mamá grew up and where she, Daniel, and I lived for the months between Papá's arrest and our move to Wisconsin. Mamá's two brothers, my *tíos* Alberto and Claudio, join us for *la comida* along with her sister, my *tía* Francisca, their spouses, and a bunch of their kids who I've never met before.

Tío Claudio brings his guitar and plays children's songs for my cousins. During the week he's a music teacher, so he knows how to get kids to join in, and before long, I'm singing, too.

"How's your father doing?" he asks afterward as he sets his guitar in its case—leaving early because his four-year-old twins have a play date.

"Okay. Always working."

Tío Claudio laughs. When we stayed here, he was always super nice to us and told us how much he admired Papá and wanted to help get him released from prison. I don't think my *abuelos* know how cool he is, or they would have acted as stone-cold to him as they do to Mamá.

"Tell Nino I'm looking for him. We just moved out to La Florida, and the place has a clubhouse and a pool." He snaps the case shut and lifts it. "We'll have to wait on the pool until summer, but there's a park with hiking trails and a zip line."

I think of my long ride with Frankie to La Florida, the identical squat brick houses with shingle roofs and newly seeded grass. I can't imagine Papá traveling all the way out there or hiking and riding a zip line, though my old *papá* would have done it for sure. "I'll tell him you said hello," I answer.

Tío Claudio's dark brown eyes turn serious. "Tina, we have to get him moving. He'll feel a hundred percent better." I nod slowly. He's right, but the only thing I've gotten Papá to do so far is let me go out with Frankie.

After Tío Claudio leaves, I find the Lego box in the closet where my *abuelos* kept them for Daniel and me, and play with Tía Francisca's kids until it's nine o'clock and time for me to go. On the way out, my grandparents comment on what a nice older cousin I've turned out to be.

"I was the coolest," I tell Tía Ileana in the car. "Just call me the family hero. Mamá should send me a present." In my mind I run through the possibilities: Metallica cassettes. Videos. Nintendo games. All stuff Frankie and I can do together, since he told me he has to stay in the apartment and can't take me out to the movies or the arcade until his *abuela* returns. He said she's worried about break-ins at night.

Back at the house Papá sits at the dining table, squeezing his rubber ball with his bad hand. In front of him is an open box of take-out pizza with one slice of mushroom left, an ashtray with three crushed cigarette butts, and an empty glass.

"Tío Claudio says hi," I say. "He wants you to go out to La Florida and hike some trails."

"Good for him. Maybe he should teach gym rather than music." Papá pushes the rest of the pizza toward my aunt. At least he ate something. After a few more squeezes of the ball, he speaks up again. "I thought Tina should know what I found out from Sofia's father."

My insides clench. "You mean the other woman?" I ask, wondering if Papá has taken to spying on me now.

He lets the ball slide from his fingers and wiggles the glass at Tía Ileana, the fingers of his bad hand surprisingly nimble.

"You've had enough, Chelo. I don't want you to get sick," she says, as if he's a little kid stuffing his mouth with candy. She brings a bottle of mineral water from the kitchen and fills his glass.

Papá gulps the water and frowns. His speech is slurred but understandable. "Your aunt asked if I knew Sofia Méndez or her family from the 'NO' campaign. She's afraid this Frankie is a big-time womanizer."

I don't know whether to thank Tía Ileana for her concern or kick myself for giving her way too much information.

"In fact, I do know her father quite well," Papá continues, sending another jolt through my insides. "We were detained together in a concentration camp right after the coup. He got tuberculosis there and has been in and out of hospitals ever since."

Mamá told me my father had been imprisoned once before, for six months after the 1973 coup, and then blacklisted from working as a journalist, even though he only covered sports in those days. I was only a baby then.

"What did her father say?" My knees weaken, and I drop into a chair across from Papá.

"Sofia never dated anyone named Frankie, or Francisco, Zamora. So if the boy tells you he and Sofia were 'just friends,' he's probably right." Tía Ileana's lips are pressed together, so I try not to make my sigh of relief too audible.

Papá shoves another cigarette between his lips and fumbles with the lighter. "On the other hand"—he glances at Tía Ileana—"he didn't know anyone from the *colegio* with that name who volunteered for the 'NO' campaign. He said Sofia went to visit friends in Concepción, but he promised to check with her when she gets back. She was one of the captains for the school."

Papá takes a puff and blows out a stream of smoke. "It could be that he goes to another school, or was in a different level. Or he wanted to make it seem like he did more than he did. Everyone wants to be on the winning side." Another puff, another stream of smoke. "Or he may not be who he says he is."

My throat closes, and I can barely swallow. Sofia called him Pepe, not Frankie. I bite my lower lip to keep from telling Tía Ileana and Papá that nugget.

Papá bats the ball with his weak hand. It hits the pizza box and bounces back. He stops it with his splint. "My guess is that he was in a different level. That *colegio* is quite large and in a very mobilized working-class neighborhood. It had one of the largest contingents for the 'NO' in the city."

"I don't want Tina to get hurt," Tía Ileana says.

Papá leans forward in his chair. "And because you nagged me to check the boy out, this guy thinks I can't control my daughter."

165

And does the guy have any idea what his daughter looks like when she leaves the house for work? I can't control my giggles.

Papá turns toward me so quickly he nearly falls out of his seat. "And what do *you* think is so funny?"

I lower my gaze. "Nothing."

"Fine." Papá slaps the table. "I'm going to feed my birds, which I couldn't do before because of this little investigation." He stands, knocks his chair over, and stumbles into the door to the kitchen.

Tía Ileana rushes to him. "Let Tina do it. I'll take you upstairs."

He waves her off. "My responsibilities, okay?"

He lurches through his office on the way to the backyard. My aunt takes off her jacket and hangs it in the entryway. She turns her face away from me.

"I'm sorry, Tina," she finally says. "I only wanted to protect you."

"I know." But it's okay. Frankie isn't going out with Sofia, and no one's going to keep me from seeing him. Still, I feel bad for Tía Ileana because Papá acted so mean to her. And I remember what she asked me to do when she showed me around Valparaíso—stand up to Papá so he'd change. "I'm going to check on the birds. And Papá."

"Be careful, *amorcita*."

Outside, the light mist sparkles in the floodlight. Papá throws birdseed around the cage. I never took my coat off inside, so I'm still warm despite the damp cold. Papá's face is flushed even though he wears no coat, only a wool sweater. When I slip through the wire door and squeeze past him, I smell the whiskey on his breath. He sets down the bag of seed, leans against a scrawny tree, and takes a bottle from his back pocket. It looks like the one Frankie found in the drawer, and it's nearly empty. He gulps the rest and tosses the bottle toward a corner of the cage. It pings when it hits the wire.

If he gets sick because I didn't stop him, I don't want to see it. I step toward the cage door. Víctor flutters to the branch above my head, startling me. I have nothing in my hands, but I pretend to pass him a grape.

"I like Metallica!" he screeches.

"I . . . like . . . Metallica," Papá repeats in heavily accented and slurred English. "Where'd he learn that shit?"

"Frankie," I answer. "That's how we met. He showed me this record store, and it turned out we both liked the same music." I don't tell Papá what else we have in common.

I wish Papá would talk about how he and Mamá met and fell in love. I already know the story because Mamá told me. They were students at the university—he in his first year, she in her second. One day, he gave her his seat on a crowded bus, and when the bus broke down, they had a lot of time to get to know each other. If he told me the story, though, it would show me that he still knows how to love.

167

I swallow. "Papá?"

"What is it?" Papá's eyes are half-closed, and leaning against the tree in the rain, he appears relaxed, comfortable. Fine droplets of water cling to his hair and glow silver in the light.

"Do you think a person has to love himself before he can love someone else?"

"No," he says sharply. "Why?"

"Tía Ileana said—"

"Tía Ileana said," he mocks. He bends forward and spits onto the dirt floor of the cage. "Hasn't she caused enough trouble for one day?"

"She's only trying to help. Anyway, I'm the one you guys were spying on. If anyone should be mad, it's me."

Papá stares up into the fog. "Just shoot me." He turns his back to me and stumbles from the cage into the house, leaving me alone with the birds and the cage door open.

CHAPTER 16

Sunday, July 9: 43 days until I go home

rankie picks me up after he's done with church on
Sunday. Although Papá has already left for a meeting
about Tuesday's demonstration, Tía Ileana demands
specific details for our day—plus, she wants me home
by eight for supper. Frankie tells her we're going to
McDonald's and a double feature at the cinema.

On our way to the motorcycle parked at the corner, I
ask Frankie, "Did you really go to church this morning?"
He's wearing jeans and a threadbare sweater—but then
I notice a white button-down shirt and dark red tie under his sweater. They're the kind of shirt and tie I see
on the kids—both boys and girls—coming home from
school in the afternoon.

"Yes. With Mamá and my sisters. My uncle, too." He
looks away. "Got to pray for my father."

"Because he won't go?" Papá doesn't, either, even
though he used to work for the Catholic human rights
organization and the radio station broadcasts the

Cardinal's sermons. He says he doesn't believe in God and people should work for justice on earth rather than wait for it in heaven. In my family, the only ones who attend church are my *abuelos* in Las Condes. And Evan goes to temple, the Jewish version of church that happens on Friday night or Saturday morning.

We arrive at the corner, and Frankie hands me a helmet. "He doesn't go much, but now he's really sick. Spitting up blood."

"Does he have tuberculosis?" Like Sofia's father?

"No, cirrhosis. Do you know what that is?"

I shake my head. Frankie adjusts the chin strap of my helmet. My insides go from zero kilometers to a hundred when his fingers brush my skin.

"It's what happens after you drink for years. The liver turns to scar tissue, and blood can't get through. So it comes out everywhere else."

"I'm sorry. That must really hurt." I envision Papá's liver turning to a wad of useless collagen.

Frankie shrugs. "His choice, his consequences."

"But you're still praying for him." I climb onto the seat and wait for Frankie.

"What else we can do?"

I expect Frankie to take me to McDonald's like he told Tía Ileana, but we go straight to the apartment. He parks in a motorcycle space and helps me to the ground.

"What about lunch? And the movies?" And why is he

spending the day with me if his father is dying?

"I have to be where my family can reach me," he says. "But I have some surprises."

Upstairs in the apartment, he takes a package of rolling papers from his back pocket. Then he shows me a well-stocked refrigerator and pantry. Good, because I'm broke.

"I brought the double feature, too. My uncle loaned me *El Padrino* and *El Padrino II*."

I switch to English because it's been two days since we practiced. "I love *The Godfather*."

"Yeah. Lots of bang-bang." He makes a gun with his thumb and index finger. Then he lifts me up and kisses me.

"Are you sure this is okay?" I ask as soon as my feet return to the floor.

"What? I kiss you all day."

"No. Your family. Don't they need you to be there?" I hope they don't, but if it were Papá in that situation, I think Tía Ileana would make me stay home rather than go out and have fun all day.

Frankie shakes his head. "He sleeps all the time." He pretends to raise a bottle to his lips. "Drinks and sleeps. And pukes."

With Frankie and his little sisters watching? Frankie pulls me to him, and I hug him tight. My friends and I had wanted to give Boomer in *St. Elsewhere* a hug when his wife died. Now Frankie's father is dying, and I'm hugging Frankie for real.

And could my father be that far behind his? I have to find out.

I lead Frankie to the sofa, sit, and pat the place next to me for him to join me. When he does, I press my body against his and rest my head on his shoulders. He brushes a strand of hair from my face.

"I'm worried about my father, too," I say. "He says he drinks to get to sleep. But now he's drinking more and more and it doesn't seem to make much difference."

"You mean it doesn't affect him?" Frankie fumbles with the top button of my shirt. I grab his wrist and move his hand to my shoulder. My body is revved up, but I know where this is going. The word *inoportuno* sticks in my mind. Inappropriate. The wrong time.

"No, Frankie." His hand stays where I put it, even though he could have thought my "no" meant his question rather than his roaming fingers.

"I'm sorry," he says. "It's hard to put them out of your mind when they get like that."

"It's so scary."

"Not anything a kid should see. They ought to think about that before they do it."

The one time I watched Papá puke from drinking totally freaked me out. It happened in Madison on a Saturday in early spring, after the snow had melted and it was still light outside at five in the afternoon. Yet another news-paper had rejected one of his articles that morning, and his friends had taken him to their favorite Mexican restaurant to console him. They brought him back while I was sitting in our tiny living room doing my homework, and he let loose like a burst sewage pipe right after they came through the door. I screamed, and Mamá shoved the guys out of the apartment. I remember her screaming, too, and beating their muddy feet with a mop. They weren't even supposed to be there; she had banned them from the apartment for bringing Papá home messed up once before, when I was asleep but my brother wasn't.

"Your poor sisters," I say.

Frankie takes a deep breath. "I'd do anything to save you from the same thing."

I stroke his hand, which still rests on my shoulder. At least I can go back to Mamá and Evan and forget about Papá. But not if I want a father who takes care of himself and loves me.

"About your father." Frankie's voice is gentle. Patient. "You said he drinks more and more and nothing happens."

"Yes." I pull on the loose thread of my belt loop.

"Mine went through that stage, too. For years." He touches his crooked nose. "That's when I really wanted to kill him." His jaw trembles, as if he's trying to swallow but can't. "Now it looks like he's gone and done it to himself."

I stare at the little bits of hair on Frankie's upper lip and chin. Some of the skin along his lower jawbone is still smooth like a boy's. I let go of my belt loop and touch his baby skin with my index finger. "Last night Papá said, 'Just shoot me.' Like he wanted to kill himself, too."

"We can work that out."

I jerk up straight, away from Frankie. "No!"

But Frankie is laughing. "I'm just playing with you, Tina. Sometimes you've just got to laugh." He holds his palms out. "Or you're going to be crying and miserable and have no life." I realize that Frankie's right—and the reason he decided to spend the day with me rather than stay home with his family. "Anyway, your father has developed a tolerance, which means his liver is about twice the size of normal and three times as efficient."

"How do you know this?"

"Looked it up at school last year. On account of my old man." He stands, drops the rolling papers on the table, and heads toward the kitchen and the cabinet with our stash. "If he gets body slammed, his liver explodes. Otherwise, it's his last chance of having his show, chasing street crimes, and all that other stuff he does instead of paying attention to you."

///////////////////

The rest of our weed, a pile of ham-and-cheese sandwiches, two bags of microwave popcorn, and a *Godfather* double feature help put Papá and his problems out of my mind.

"Can you get more *macoña* for tomorrow?" I ask Frankie as the credits roll on *The Godfather: Part II.*

"We, uh, can't get together tomorrow." He avoids my eyes.

"But you promised."

"I know. I . . . have to watch my sisters Monday nights. My mother works late."

"You didn't tell me she works." In fact, he told me that she didn't work—that taking care of a falling-apart family was her work.

"She's . . . a maid. Up in Las Condes. It's her *señora*'s canasta night."

What must he have thought, when I introduced him to Graciela? And what about his grandmother, with jewelry and a nice apartment? Then I think of my *abuelos* on Mamá's side, and the way we used to live when Papá drove his taxi before his arrest. We lived in an apartment—not a tin roof and plywood shack like where Frankie probably lives—but it had a leak in the ceiling, cold cement floors, and bedrooms even smaller than the ones in Papá's new house.

"I'm sorry," I say as I caress the smooth part of his cheek again. The video clicks, then whirrs as it rewinds. "How about Tuesday?"

"Okay." But then Frankie leans forward and covers his face with his hands, leaving my fingers in mid-air. After a few seconds, he sits up straight, facing me.

Making eye contact. "I have the day off. I'll pick you up in the morning."

"And go to Papá's demonstration afterward?" I hug Frankie without waiting for the answer. "That would be so cool!"

"We'll see." He nuzzles my neck. "You don't want to show up reeking of weed."

"Good point." I rub the short, wiry hair at the back of his head with the palm of my hand. The tape stops rewinding, leaving the apartment completely silent except for our breathing. "Anyway, I'd rather spend all day with you."

"Enjoy the time while we have it," Frankie whispers. He presses his lips to mine. The earthy taste of the *cuete* fills my nose and mouth. His warmth spreads through the middle of my body as if I'm melting into him.

I love you, Frankie. I would say it out loud, except that our lips are attached to each other, our tongues touching. And when we stop kissing to catch our breath, I hear the words I've most wanted to hear.

"I love you, Tina. You're everything that's good in my life."

///////////////////

Can you love someone without loving yourself? I ask myself that question on Monday, which seems forty-eight hours long rather than twenty-four. I can't believe I used to go days without seeing Frankie—now I can't stand even one day without him. And I decide that he really does love himself. After all, he said once that he was the hope of his family.

After supper, I lie on my back in bed, staring at the ceiling. I used to imagine us riding off on his motor-cycle, into our own secret world, but now I imagine him at home in my world.

How can I convince Mamá and Evan to bring Frankie to the United States so he can finally have the life he deserves?

Chapter 17

"¡CHELO!" A scream awakens me at dawn. I was half-asleep, imagining Frankie's body pressed against mine, and it takes me a while to recognize my aunt's voice.

She keeps shouting my father's nickname, but I get downstairs before Papá does. Tía Ileana stands in the middle of the front yard in her bathrobe, holding the newspaper. At her feet is a bloody bird—a parrot—its head twisted at an acute angle.

Sour liquid fills my mouth. I turn away from the carcass and swallow hard.

My father limps outside, wearing his pajamas and leaning on his cane. His hair sticks up, and his glasses are askew. He takes one look at the dead bird, mutters, "*Mierda*," and lurches into the house. Tía Ileana and I follow him to the backyard. In the pale sunlight, Víctor flutters from branch to branch. Pablo walks upside down along the wire roof of the giant cage. Usually, I love watching Pablo do that trick—I imagine him clowning around just for me—but this morning I ignore him. Papá pounds the side of his fist against the stucco wall.

"Fascist sons of whores," he spits.

I don't understand. His birds are fine. "What's going on?" I ask.

Tía Ileana shakes her head. "Maybe you shouldn't speak at that demonstration today, Chelo. Let someone else—"

"They can't stop me," Papá snaps. In the kitchen, he hunts under the sink for a plastic bag. Then he goes outside again, scoops up the dead parrot, and dumps it into the large trash bag in the garage. "There. It's gone. Now you can stop worrying."

Maybe Papá thinks we can forget about the dead bird and what it means, but I can't. By the time Frankie picks me up at ten, I've already had three hours to think about it.

As soon as we get to the apartment, I tell Frankie.

"A hawk probably got it." Frankie lights a cigarette. Tobacco, and I wonder if he managed to get the other stuff.

"Its throat was sliced, almost all the way through. It was disgusting."

"It could have been a super hungry hawk. Or a falcon." His other hand slips my top button from its hole.

"But wouldn't a hawk carry it away? To eat it?" I scoot away from him. "My aunt said it was some kind of death threat."

He inches closer to me again. His warm fingers slide from my collarbone toward my breast. My heart speeds up. "Tina, love, if every dead bird in front of a house was a death threat, there wouldn't be any people left in this country." He sets the cigarette in the small copper ashtray and leans into me for a smoky kiss. Afterward, he says, "Let's say a hawk grabs the parrot and is taking it to his nest. To feed his family, you know? Another lazy-ass hawk wants what he has and attacks him. Well, he's going to fight for what's his. Even if it means dropping the parrot and picking it up later."

"I suppose." I snuggle against Frankie.

He kisses me again, and then says quietly, "I hope I didn't make a mistake." My insides squeeze tight. He seems nervous—like he's planned something huge but isn't telling me.

I guess at what it might be. "Did you find more weed?"

He shakes his head. "I took back the other stuff. The cocaine. He gave me some pills, but I don't want to try them. Maybe you?" Frankie digs into his back pocket and takes out a small black cardboard box, the kind that holds those velvet jewelry boxes. He opens the top. Inside are eight white tablets. I have no idea what they are.

"Why would I take something if I don't know what it is?" I've heard about guys slipping tablets into girls' drinks in bars so the girl falls asleep and the guy can do anything he wants with her. But Frankie isn't that kind of guy.

Frankie picks up his cigarette and takes a long drag. "My uncle says that's what the gringos do."

His uncle? The drug dealer? Who also goes to church to pray for Frankie's father?

"I don't think your uncle knows much about the United States."

"Probably not. He's never been there." Frankie flicks ashes into the tray.

I grab the open box from the coffee table and march into the bathroom, where I shake the pills into the toilet. I don't bother flushing. "So what *is* this uncle like?" I ask upon returning to the living room. I want the truth, even if the guy deals drugs. After all, Frankie's not into drugs, and if he likes that his uncle has money, there are other ways of getting money where I can help. "Is he the one that got you the pills?"

"No," Frankie answers quickly. Maybe too quickly. "That was a guy from the neighborhood. My uncle hates drugs. Alcohol, too, because of what it's done to my father. They used to be close when I was really little, like two or three, and then something happened."

"Like what?"

"I don't know. It had to do with my father's drinking." Frankie stabs out his cigarette and nestles his head against my shoulder. When he speaks again, his warm breath tickles my skin where he's unbuttoned my shirt. "How would you feel if your father died?"

I gasp. "I'd be sad. Even though he's a jerk a lot of the time, I don't want him to die."

"But you hardly know your father. It's not like you grew up with him. Or he spends any time with you now," Frankie says.

I run my fingers along the bridge of Frankie's nose, try to understand the hatred he feels for the man who shares his name, wonder if he really does want his father dead. I clear my throat. "Do you remember yours ever being different from what he is now?"

Frankie shakes his head and lights another cigarette. When he moves away from me, my neck and shoulder go cold.

"Were there any good times with him?"

"We used to rebuild stuff together," Frankie says. "Bikes, cars. He had this motor scooter he used to take me out on until one night he rode it drunk into someone's home." He blows out a stream of smoke and sets the cigarette down. "Every good thing with him eventually went rotten."

"And if he dies, he'll never be able to make it right?"

Frankie clasps my hand and doesn't let me go. "I love you, Tina."

I throw my arms around him. "I love you, too, Frankie."

He returns to snuggling against me. His short hair scrubs my neck and chest. I run my fingers through the hair on the other side of his head, pushing it backward and feeling the sharp ends. After a while, he says, "Remember when you talked about Romeo and Juliet, chucking it all and running away?"

"Yeah, but you didn't read it." He doesn't know how badly it ends for them.

"I want to do it for real."

"How?" I squeeze his shoulders. "You don't mean it?"

The weird thing is—I think he does. And I don't, at least not since Mamá and Evan got back from their honeymoon. Now I dream of convincing them to send Frankie a ticket to the United States. I've already worked it out in my mind. He goes into the army for two years. I finish high school in two years. We go to university together.

Frankie kisses my breastbone. "I told your aunt I'd bring you back at eight thirty tonight. And tomorrow I have to go away to help my uncle. But sit by the phone after that, and I'll have a surprise for you."

"No way!" I pull away from him and rub my skin where he kissed me. This is more than talk about running away. Frankie has a plan.

I start to shake my head, but Frankie says, "We can have an adventure. Like a camping trip."

My old *papá* loved camping. For a week every summer we used to drive to a place five hours south of Santiago, where we slept in a tent, caught and cooked our own fish, and drank lake water that we boiled. Papá taught me how to skip stones on the water and gave me books as prizes when my stones skipped more times than Daniel's.

Could I convince him and Tía Ileana to let me go with Frankie? Maybe they'd want to come with us. Tío Claudio told me Papá needed to get moving, that it would be good for him.

"Camping. What a great idea!" I imagine that once Papá gets out in the woods, he won't need to drink. He'll be my old *papá* who loved me.

Frankie grins and says, "Perfect." He scoots upright and kisses me for real. His hand slips under my bra strap, to my breast, and this time I don't stop him.

"So what do you want to do now?" His voice is breathless.

"You want to see the Minus World?" I ask him.

"The Minus World?"

I turn on the television and Nintendo. "It's a secret level of *Super Mario Brothers*, underneath the regular world."

"Like here." Frankie points to the floor. "Underneath the regular world."

He puts on his new CD of *Ride the Lightning* and hits the MUTE button for the TV. At the end of World 1-2, I break the blocks at the pipe that leads to the flag, jump backward, and go through the wall. "Okay, I'm in the Minus World. It's not supposed to be part of the game but it got left in by mistake." I scroll through the hidden underwater level to the rhythm of Metallica until a school of evil jellyfish ices me. Then I hand him the controller.

"That's it?" he asks as soon as his unscathed Mario scrambles into a green pipe at the edge of the screen—and right back into the same world. "Just a bunch of stupid fish? And how do you get out of this thing?"

"You don't. Either you get killed or time runs out."

"That's stupid." He tosses the controller to the end of the sofa and turns off the machine.

My stomach growls. I'd skipped breakfast because of the disgusting dead parrot, but now I'm famished. I check my watch. One fifteen already. "Maybe we should go out somewhere, like McDonald's." I fan myself with my hand. Our warm bodies and an overenthusiastic heating system have made the apartment stuffy.

"I can't," Frankie says. "In case something happens with my father, again."

"Then why don't we go close by?" I ask, thinking, *camping trip—the way I'll save Papá from the same end.*

CHAPTER 18

We end up at a food stand half a block from the apartment, on a traffic circle with three different bank branches. The stand sells hot dogs called *italianos* because the avocado, mayo, and ketchup covering the meat look like the Italian flag. Tía Ileana once told me people in Italy don't eat hot dogs that way—it's only a Chilean thing. Frankie buys two cans of Coke from the stand as well. The cans are so cold that chips of ice cling to them and don't melt until we get to his building.

Back in the apartment, he pops in the CD of *Kill 'Em All* and sets our *italianos* on a large plate. Steam rises from the still-warm hot dogs. He takes a half-full bottle of pisco from under the sink. My breath rushes past my throat.

"I thought you didn't drink."

"I don't drink much," Frankie says. "But today's special. Because you're here."

He puts on a show of mixing our drinks. "Two *pis-colas*," he announces, handing one to me. He's made mine strong. I can definitely taste the pisco over the Coke. After a few sips, I pour in more Coke.

"You'd make a lousy bartender," I say. "You're supposed to water down the drinks. That way the owner makes more money."

"You're not my owner." He carries the plate of *italianos* and his drink to the coffee table, sits, and pulls me onto his lap. I pick up an *italiano*, wrapped in thick foil, and take a bite from the avocado end.

"Mmm, good," I say, mouth stuffed.

He twists around and bites off half of the mayonnaise section of mine.

"Frankie, you little thief!" In retaliation, I grab his untouched *italiano* and chomp the ketchup end.

"Sorry," Frankie says. "I just love mayonnaise."

"Then why don't you go back to the supermarket and pick up a loaf of bread and a jar of mayonnaise?" I really wanted the entire *italiano* experience. In Valparaíso with my aunt, I was too timid and chose the chili dogs.

By the time I finish my hot dog and drink, my head feels fuzzy. I lean into Frankie for a pisco-flavored kiss. My stomach does a dive loop when his tongue touches mine. My limbs relax.

"Frankie," I say when our mouths separate. "I think you got me drunk." With a used napkin I fan my face and smell ketchup mixed with *piscola*. "I guess you can take advantage of me now."

"I don't want to take advantage of you," he says. "I

want to make you feel good." He massages my shoulders. "How's this?"

"Super." I exhale. My arms and legs tingle. My heart beats to the rhythm of Metallica. The digital clock on the stereo reads 2:45. Fifteen minutes before Papá's demonstration, and I want to stay like this forever.

I remember my father in the birds' cage on Saturday night, the moments when he seemed completely relaxed and free of pain before I annoyed him.

Frankie rubs my stomach under my shirt, and I realize that I've pushed his turtleneck sweater and undershirt up to his armpits and am running my fingers up and down his bare back.

I've gone this far before, and a lot more, with Max. We were stoned and awkward and silly. Frankie moves his body and hands like someone older, someone who knows how to make a girl feel good. Whatever didn't happen with Sofia Méndez must have happened with someone.

The CD ends and goes back to the beginning. Frankie kisses me again. The pisco has faded, but he still tastes sweet like fizzy soda.

He stands, takes off his sweater, and goes to switch the CD. I suddenly have a craving for chocolate chip cookies. I suggest we make the package we bought last week.

When I hop up from the sofa, I wobble. "Easy, love," Frankie says, rushing over from his CD collection to steady me.

"Am I that wasted?" I wonder how much pisco he poured into my glass. I thought I watched him carefully, but maybe he's one of those magicians who can somehow distract a crowd to make it look like they're pulling coins out of their ears and rabbits from their hats.

"Low blood sugar," Frankie says. "You're not used to drinking."

I drop back on the sofa, surprised at how hungry I am. When Papá drinks, he usually doesn't like to eat at all, and after he knocked back nearly a dozen *piscolas* the night of my first date with Frankie, he was off his food for days.

Frankie, though, takes care of the cookies—and me. From the living room I watch him cut the frozen dough into neat quarters and set them on the oiled baking sheet in a perfect grid. Evan would be totally impressed. The smell of baking cookies makes me dizzy.

I think I fall asleep because the next thing I know, Frankie is kissing my forehead and holding the cookies in front of my nose, the way a paramedic would hold smelling salts under the nose of someone who's passed out. Behind me, the TV flickers, and I make out English dialogue and the screeching of brakes. I bite into a warm, soft cookie and let the chocolate chips melt on my tongue.

"What the doctor ordered?" Frankie says.

"I think you like taking care of me."

"Better than you know who." His experience shows, but I don't want to tell him that because it would keep reminding him of his dying father. And I can't let myself get this way again. I don't want to end up like his father—or mine.

Turning slowly toward the TV to keep my insides where they belong, I recognize *Back to the Future.* I take a deep breath and zoom in on Frankie's eyes. "I want you to know I'm sorry. About not trusting you when you said there was nothing between you and Sofia. Papá—"

"What did he do this time?" Frankie's voice suddenly turns hard.

"He called Sofia's father. My aunt made him do it. But the guy didn't know who you were."

Frankie groans. "I need to get out. Go somewhere else and start all over."

"I'm going to have my mother and stepfather bring you to Wisconsin."

"Please. The sooner the better."

Two years. When he's done with the army and I finish high school. And we'll visit each other before then. But can he wait that long? Can I?

I push up Frankie's undershirt, press my face against his smooth chest, and stroke the fine hairs on his stomach. If Papá and Tía Ileana join us on the camping trip, we won't have any privacy. And Frankie is so much more experienced than Max. He could make me feel so good. He's already made me feel good.

At the end of last summer, Max and I tried. We smoked a lot of weed and made a lot of stupid condom jokes to stall for time. Petra told me it hurt the first time she did it, and I expected the same. The first stab of pain made me cry out, and it either scared Max or he'd smoked way too much because he couldn't go on. And that made me sort of no longer a virgin and him sort of no longer interested in me. He said I made him feel like a failure, even though I never told anyone what happened—or didn't happen.

"I love you, Frankie," I whisper into his warm skin. With cookies joining the *italianos* in my stomach, the too-strong *piscola* is starting to wear off. But my limbs still feel anesthetized, and my body is telling me to let him make me fly.

"I love you, too. I'm so happy I met you." He holds me tighter and rocks me back and forth. We've hit a quiet part of the movie, where Marty and Doc are having a heart-to-heart. I've seen the movie so many times I've practically memorized it.

I peer over Frankie's shoulder at the VCR clock. It's already four thirty. Less than four hours until I have to go home. Ninety minutes after the demonstration started. "You think they'll have the demonstration on TV?"

"Nah. They never do. It's like it doesn't exist."

"That's terrible. All that work for nothing."

Frankie strokes my hair. "They know the rules. You wonder why they bother."

And if they didn't bother, Papá would have more

time for me. More time to take care of himself.

"Forget about the demonstration, Tina." Frankie's lips caress my neck, then inch lower, lower. I stretch his undershirt over my head and nuzzle his stomach. "We're going to get away from all this. Soon."

I want to get away now. And I think sex with Frankie will be ten times better than weed and pisco. I reach up and tickle his ear. "Let's do it."

"Not all the way. Just part of the way," he says. "You've had too much to drink. And so have I."

I giggle. "And you don't want me telling my aunt you got me drunk and took advantage of me."

"Something like that."

With Max it never felt the way it does with Frankie. First comes the little jolts of electricity, the swirling in my stomach, the weightlessness of my arms and legs. The roller-coaster dizziness returns, even more thrilling than before, as if I don't have a care in the world and will never hurt again. I was wrong. This isn't ten times better than weed and pisco. It's a hundred times better.

"You like it?" Frankie asks as I'm toweling off my sweat in the bathroom. The door is open, and he smokes a cigarette.

"It was awesome." But I'm greedy. I want more. "Let's go all the way."

"I can't."

"Why not?" He's not a little boy like Max. It occurs to me that he didn't plan this. He doesn't have protection.

And if I go home pregnant, it will screw up everything for both of us. "Don't they sell condoms here?"

Maybe not. Tía Ileana said it's a very conservative country—and not just politically.

"Yes, but I have to stay here."

I take the cigarette from his mouth and drop it into the sink. "It will only take a few minutes, right?" He nods. I stand on my tiptoes and kiss him, pressing myself to him, skin to skin.

I glance at the clock. Just six. The TV plays white noise, *Back to the Future* done and auto-rewound.

"I don't have to be home until after eight," I remind him.

He steps into the living room and gathers his jeans, undershirt, and sweater. "Okay, be back soon." He smiles. I think he's drooling.

When he leaves, I wrap myself in a towel and peer outside through a crack in the curtain. It's already dark, and the streetlamps cast a yellowish glow on the sidewalk. The street is jammed with cars, trucks, and buses, their tail lights growing brighter as they hit their brakes, then fading back to dark red when they sit, stuck in rush hour traffic. I try to spot Frankie's motorcycle, but at least six of them weave among the cars, and three of the riders wear helmets like Frankie.

The phone rings. Could it be news about his father? Expecting that Frankie would want to know if his father is dying for sure, I hurry to the kitchen to answer it.

Even though it would ruin our plans.

"A . . . *Aló*," I say.

I hear silence.

I say hello again.

There's a *click* and a dial tone. Probably a wrong number. I blow out my breath.

Minutes later, Frankie returns. He tosses a small box on the table, drapes his motorcycle jacket over the back of the sofa, and strips off his sweater and undershirt. "Showtime. You choose the music," he says.

"'Mastertarium.'" I swing the towel, as if I'm a bullfighter waving it in front of the bull.

He sorts through the cassettes, finds the bootleg with the concert medley, and holds it out to me. "This one?"

The phone rings again.

CHAPTER 19

Frankie drops the cassette and runs to the phone. The clear plastic case shatters.

"*Aló.*"

My watch is in the pocket of my jeans, lying on the floor, but I estimate thirty seconds.

"Yes, sir, I'll be right there."

I count off another twenty seconds.

"What call?" he says into the phone. "You must have dialed the wrong number."

"Oh, yeah, Frankie," I shout. "Someone called while you were gone, but they hung up."

Frankie says, "No, sir, I'm alone. It was just the TV."

I clamp my mouth shut. Am I not supposed to be here?

It seems like forever before Frankie speaks again. "You said between ten and eleven. It's not even seven. What happened?"

Another long pause.

"What about Rambo? Our meeting?"

A shorter pause. "Yes, it was her."

My heart speeds up. I hold my breath, listening.

"Her, too? Why don't I take her home?"

Rambo? A meeting? This doesn't sound like a sick father.

I blink and hug myself tight. No more fooling around. He *has* to take me home.

"That's, uh, going to be hard to handle. Especially if I have to wait for Rambo." More silence, then Frankie says, "Yes, sir. I'll take care of it."

In the next instant, he appears beside me, clutching his T-shirt. "Can you be any more stupid, Tina?" His face reddens.

"What do you mean?" Acid burns my throat.

"Get dressed. Now." He yanks his undershirt over his head but doesn't tuck it in.

The phone call—I should have never picked it up. "Wait! I'm sorry!" I reach for his shoulder, but he jerks away. "Are you taking me home?"

He bends down and flings my bra in my face. It makes me ashamed of my nakedness. "Dress warm," he says. He throws the rest of my clothes at me on his way to the stereo, where he slams *Ride the Lightning* into the CD player and turns up the volume on "For Whom the Bell Tolls."

While he puts on his turtleneck and leather jacket, he jerks his body to the song's rhythm as if performing some kind of bizarre ritual—as if he went out for condoms and joined a cult instead. I expect the people in the next apartment to bang on the wall or call the police.

As soon as I'm dressed, he shuts off the music and pulls a dark gray wool blanket from a closet. "Come on," he says. When I don't move right away, he clamps his hand around my upper arm and drags me out of the apartment.

"Stop! You're hurting me!" But he doesn't let go. His jaw is clenched. "What's going on?" I ask over and over.

No answer. He snaps his fingers while we wait for the elevator. My heart pounds so hard my whole chest aches.

Outside, the night is damp but not cold. I don't know why he told me to dress so warmly. He hands me a rope, several bungee cords, and the blanket, then hurls the plastic crate from his *moto* and one of the helmets into the bushes next to his grandmother's building. My arm still aches from where he grabbed it. He puts on the other helmet, leaving nothing to protect my head except the hood of my sweatshirt. I fumble with the things he handed me. I really have to hold on to him now. He guns the engine.

I expect him to take me to Papá's house, but we speed north. "You're going the wrong way!" I shout over the engine. He acts as if he doesn't hear. We still have time before my curfew, but if he's taking me on a surprise trip, it's not a nice surprise.

We race past the lights of downtown into a rundown neighborhood, through dark *poblaciones* lit up only by the *cantinas'* neon signs, passing gangs of kids and stray dogs. My head feels strangely light without the helmet.

My scalp and ears go numb in the raw wind. Frankie pulls up to a one-story cinderblock police station.

We've been busted. I should have known better than to ask him to get weed for me—a boy I barely knew at the time, in a foreign country with tough drug laws. I feel like I'm going to throw up, right on his leather jacket. How will I tell Papá and Tía Ileana?

Frankie jumps off and clutches my arm. "Leave that crap here," he says, pointing to the rope, cords, and blanket. I drop the stuff to the ground. His helmet makes a hollow *thunk* on top of the pile.

A uniformed man stands in the doorway under a floodlight. They shake hands.

Shake hands, like they know each other?

The man is stocky, with olive skin and short black hair under his cap. His pants have several dark spots on one leg.

"We've been waiting for you. Where have you been?"

They do know each other! My breath catches.

"Slightly delayed, sir."

"Is this a setup, Frankie? Are you friends with these cops?" He doesn't look at me. I pat all my pockets, to make sure I don't have any illegal drugs, not even a stray seed.

"And who's she?" The *carabinero* looks me up and down. I'm sure he sees that I can't stop shaking.

"You'll find out soon enough," Frankie says. My legs

wobble as I follow Frankie and the *carabinero* inside and down a narrow hallway.

The man unlocks a heavy metal door and flicks a switch. A single overhead bulb lights a low-ceilinged room with bare cement walls and floor. A table has been pushed to the side. A chair lies broken beside it. Rags are piled near the back wall.

A moan rises from the pile of rags.

I know that voice.

I scream.

CHAPTER 20

I kneel beside Papá, who lies curled up on the pile. His eyes are closed. A line of blood-tinged saliva runs from the corner of his mouth onto a thin towel. I inhale and recoil from his rancid odor, as if they'd picked him from a Dumpster behind a bar.

The *carabinero* hoists my father upright against the wall. "Here's your guy," the cop tells Frankie.

"Ex-excuse me? I'm his daughter."

But no one turns my way. Papá's head drops to his chest. His light gray sweater has a whitish stain in the shape of a jellyfish. He doesn't have his glasses. I don't think he knows I'm here.

Frankie pulls a folded-up newspaper clipping from the inside pocket of his jacket. He unfolds it, holds it up to the light, and nods.

From the reverse side, I recognize one of Papá's articles, with his photo in the bottom corner. But why is he in the police station, so beat up? And why did they call Frankie and not me to get him?

"Papá, wake up!" I place my hand on his back to feel

his breathing. He raises his head and opens his eyes.

His stare is empty, unfocused, lifeless.

"Who did this to you?" I ask him.

"Him." He turns his head toward the *carabinero*. I can barely understand his words. "And another one. Rifle butt . . . my ribs."

Papá's lips and the ends of his mustache redden with blood. Crouched next to him, I look for something clean to wipe his mouth. I pat his lips and mustache with the cuff of my sweatshirt.

Behind me, Frankie and the *carabinero* are talking.

". . . bit his tongue . . . seizure . . . We thought he was going to die on us," the cop says.

"We'll take care of him, sir," Frankie answers.

"Get him to a hospital—now! Please!"

"Who is this?" Papá mumbles.

"It's me. Tina. Don't you recognize me?" I take a panicked breath and try not to cry. "No. Don't talk." Turning to Frankie, I shout, "Call an ambulance!"

"Not so fast, girlie," the *carabinero* says. He stands over me, one hand on his holster. His fingers drum the leather. "Your father was arrested for public intoxication and inciting a riot this afternoon."

I pat my pockets again. Papá forgot my allowance this week, not that it would have been nearly enough. "I don't have money for bail. Let me call my aunt."

The officer lays his other hand on my shoulder. I twist away.

"We've decided to release him without charges, as long as he signs a statement admitting that he was drunk and resisted arrest."

Papá clears his throat and spits a pink gob that lands on the officer's boot. "How can I sign? You broke my fucking arm," he rasps.

I look to his side. His right arm—the only arm he can really use—hangs limp. His hand is red and starting to swell.

"Use your teeth, cockroach," the man says.

Papá bares his teeth. They're covered in blood but all the ones he had before today—the crooked and broken survivors of his years in prison—are still there. From his expression, I can tell that he'd more likely spit on the statement than sign it.

The *carabinero* whistles to someone else in the hall. A taller man strides into the room, sniffling and rubbing his nose. *The other one?* His nose is flared and red, as if he has a cold. The cops whisper for a minute or two. The red-nosed *carabinero* leaves and a few minutes later returns with a different sheet of paper.

"You win this one, Aguilar," he says. "I'll have the kid sign a release form."

He slams the paper onto the table. Handwritten, in jagged, sloppy handwriting, is my father's name, the name of the police station, and the date and time of release. Nothing more. My hand shaking, I sign. I wonder if the dictator's newspapers can use this against him anyway, report him as drunk and disorderly the way they reported the beaten-up musician as a druggie.

The two officers lift Papá to his feet. There's blood on the crotch of his jeans. He seems to have passed out again, so they drag him outside, his feet scraping the ground, and help Frankie sit him on the motorcycle in the space where I usually sit. Papá screams when he straddles the bike. My legs are weak, my feet numb. We have to find a hospital. Fast.

"Hold him up," Frankie tells me, his tone matter-of-fact, no longer angry like he was at the apartment. I sit on the motorcycle behind Papá and lock my arms under his armpits to keep him upright without touching his ribs. I adjust my grip when Frankie wraps the blanket around my father's body and pulls at the top of it to create a makeshift hood. The blanket fails to stifle the stench—blood, vomit, and more than a hint of hard liquor—that clings to Papá.

Frankie avoids my eyes while he works on the blanket. I shake Papá's shoulder. "Papá? Can you hear me?"

The only thing I hear is Frankie humming "For Whom the Bell Tolls." And dogs barking in the distance.

"Come on, Frankie," I beg. "We gotta get to the hospital."

"I'm almost ready," he says. "You don't want him falling off."

The tall, red-nosed *carabinero* hands me a plastic bag with Papá's wallet, watch, belt, cigarettes, lighter, glasses, and pill bottle. I pull my hand back quickly after taking the bag. I don't want to touch those creeps who hurt Papá. After shoving the bag into the kangaroo pocket of my sweatshirt, I lift Papá to my lap to give Frankie room.

Frankie squirms, trying to make more space for himself. I push Papá toward him so I can get a grip on Frankie's jacket. Frankie hands the short, dark-haired *carabinero* the rope and bungee cord.

"Secure him to me, sir."

"Good idea, Romeo."

Romeo? As in *Romeo y Julieta?* If this is another high school nickname like Pepe, these guys are way too old to be Frankie's high school friends.

And I'm trapped here, holding Papá up. I suck in air through my mouth to avoid the smell. "You're taking him to the hospital. Right, Frankie?"

Silence.

"You are Frankie, aren't you? Frankie Zamora?"

When the man touches him, my father shivers under the blanket. I feel the rope pulled around my back, the three of us bound together. My skin crawls. I whimper with each breath but make myself stop because I don't want Papá or Frankie to hear me.

Then Frankie shakes hands with both *carabineros.* "You're in with these guys!" My throat is parched. I can't swallow.

Frankie steps to the motorcycle and shushes me. "I have a plan, okay?" he whispers.

I tug on his jacket. "The hospital. Now!"

"Hold on, we're going," he says without looking back. He puts on his helmet and kicks the motorcycle to life.

Frankie steers carefully, avoiding the heavily traveled avenues. I hold tightly to his jacket so Papá won't slide off the bike. My father's body is limp and still. I press my face against his back from time to time to make sure he's breathing. The wool blanket scratches my cheek. I cough out fibers and grime.

"Where's the hospital?" I yell over the wind and engine noise.

"Not far," Frankie answers, staring straight ahead. But I don't recognize where we are and it seems to be taking a long time to get there. There are no streetlights in this part of the city. And no traffic at all, even though we're at the tail end of rush hour. The cold fills my lungs and penetrates my body. An icy wind slaps my face. There are hills where we're going. I can feel the up and down in my stomach and ears. Papá twists and groans.

"Wait a minute! You're lying!" I don't know where Frankie has taken me, but it's not the hospital. It's nowhere near the hospital. I run through the events, one by one: the phone call, his sudden change from hot boyfriend to total lunatic, telling me to dress warm, throwing my helmet in the bushes as if he didn't care about me anymore, the name Romeo, the small talk, the handshake with the two cops.

He said he had a plan? How can this be the same person who made me feel so good a few hours ago . . . who said he loved me?

A cry escapes my throat. Sweat runs down my body inside my layers of clothes. I shout, "Stop! Go back!" but Frankie doesn't hear me in the roar of the wind and engine. I can't see a thing.

I beat my fists on Frankie's jacket. Still no response. And the trembling I feel is not mine but Papá's. I'm afraid he's having another seizure. I push him harder against Frankie.

We leave the paved blacktop and climb a hill. Gravel crunches under the tires.

Finally, Frankie screams, a long, agonized wail.

"Where are we?" I pound his shoulder.

He slows the bike and cuts the engine. I look down and see snow. Packed snow with bits of gravel on the narrow road. Fresh snow—I can't tell how deep—on each side. And beyond that on our right side, the rock face of a cliff.

"What are we doing in the mountains?" It's the kind of place where you can kill someone and no one will find them for months.

Frankie dangles his helmet by its chin strap on the handlebar, unhooks one of the two bungee cords around himself and Papá, and takes something from the inside pocket of his jacket.

It's a switchblade. Its sharp edge reflects the motorcycle's headlight. Frankie cuts the rope with a single motion of his wrist.

"Frankie, don't!" I plead.

He unhooks the other cord. He's breathing hard, his shoulders rising and falling. My father stirs.

"And who's Romeo? Is this some secret name? Like Pepe?"

"Shut up!" Frankie shouts. "I can't think with you screaming!"

"You said you loved me!"

Papá's back stiffens against my chest. He coughs into Frankie's jacket, a muffled sound like squashed innards spilling out. "Tina, was this right-wing thug your boyfriend?" he says.

Frankie slides off the bike and raises the knife to Papá's face. Frankie's cheeks glisten. Has he been crying? "You drunken subversive, you have no idea what your daughter's doing," Frankie says, his voice breaking.

Papá teeters, and I hold him steady around his shoulders and chest. He tries to raise his weak arm as if to point or grab Frankie. "You. You're the one who beat up Rodolfo Guerra."

"Was that the musician, Papá?" My teeth chatter.

Papá turns his head slightly in my direction. "A paramilitary gang. As I suspected. One that recruits boys, too."

Paramilitares? Not "for the military" but "paramilitaries." Gangs that support the military dictatorship but aren't part of the military. I realize that's what Papá's article was about, the one Frankie read in his office. Frankie took notes, and I believed he was on our side. Tía Ileana said he was on our side, that he worked for the "NO" vote.

How could we have been so stupid?

And yet . . . ? Over my father's sagging shoulder, Frankie's eyes connect with mine. With his free hand, he pulls out the folded article and slowly hands it to me. Still holding my father, I shake it open. In the dim light I can read only the title: "GUERRA: VÍCTIMA DE LAS DROGAS? O DEL FASCISMO?"

"Go ahead. Kill me," my father says. "But take her home. I'm sure she can keep her mouth shut. She's obviously been doing it with me for the past month."

"Have you ever asked her? Or are you too busy poking your nose into places you don't belong?" Frankie takes a single step toward us. "I love her. We're running away together."

"Excuse me? You never told me this plan, Frankie." I hold one arm in front of Papá's face. This was supposed to be a camping trip. With all of us. And fun. Not some *Romeo and Juliet* remake, where everyone's family hates each other and they all die in the end.

Frankie points the tip of the knife at Papá. "You, communist, you don't even want to live. You tried to get a gun to kill yourself."

My tears start out warm but freeze in the blast of

wind. "Sorry, Papá," I whisper. "I shouldn't have said anything."

"That's it," Papá says. "The people have voted. Leave me here for the vultures."

"No! I'll stay with you. I didn't mean to betray you." I raise my voice so he's sure to hear me. "I love you, Papá." I press his body to mine to keep both of us warm, to let him know that I do love him and want him to live. I measure his breaths, to see if there's any fight left in him, or if there's no more hope.

Frankie stands in the ankle-deep snow, half his body glowing in the headlight, the other half in total darkness. The hand holding the knife shakes. My chest throbs. I hear each of my heartbeats. I wonder if Frankie's going to run away by himself now, leaving Papá and me to freeze to death. Or if someone else is coming to kill us, like that Rambo guy I overheard him mention on the phone in the apartment.

"Frankie," I say, tightening my throat muscles to keep my voice from wavering, "do you really love me?"

Frankie steps back into the darkness. I can't see him anymore.

I try again. "I thought we were the 'Mastertarium,' you know, meant to be together. And I was everything that's good in your life." The chords play in my head. "How could you say you love me and then do this?"

Frankie's voice is almost a whisper coming from

nowhere. "I need you, Tina. I do love—"

I don't wait for him to finish. "If you really love me, Frankie," I call back into the night, "put the knife away and take my father to the hospital."

After a minute that seems like an hour Frankie appears in front of the headlight, folds the knife, and slips it into his jacket pocket. His face is now dry but a whitish film covers both cheeks. "Hold tight to the old man," he says as he puts his helmet back on and slides onto the seat. He starts the engine, circles, and turns the bike down the mountain road. The rope and bungee cords lay lifeless in the snow.

CHAPTER 21

Inside the city, a section of blanket over Papá's head on his left side falls away across my arm. With his clumsy hand, he reaches for Frankie's belt.

I put my mouth to his ear. "Hang on, Papá."

"Got it," he says. There's a flash of light in his hand, a streetlamp's reflection. Afterward, he goes limp in my arms, as if the light has left his body.

It takes less than an hour for us to get from the mountains to the hospital in our neighborhood, the same hospital where Frankie dropped off some X-rays two weeks—an eternity—ago. Everything that happens next is a blur—the hospital staff taking Papá away on a gurney, me calling Tía Ileana, her arriving pale and shaken and holding me for what seems like forever.

While we wait to hear whether Papá's going to be all right, I walk outside, back to where Frankie dropped us off. He's still there, sitting at the curb under a streetlamp, his motorcycle parked next to him. He has a roll of paper towels and a plastic basin, and he's trying to wash the back of his leather jacket.

"Who the hell is Romeo?" I ask, though my hands keep shaking.

Frankie glances up. "No one."

"You're lying." I shove my hands into my sweatshirt so he won't see them. "Someone ordered you to kill us. That uncle you talk about all the time?"

Frankie grimaces. "Just your father. And I was only supposed to kidnap him. The others wanted to get information from him first."

"And me?"

"You weren't supposed to come along. You weren't even supposed to be at the apartment today." He dips a paper towel into the basin. "I thought I'd have you home before everything went down."

My fingers curl, as if on their own mission to strangle Frankie. "And then what? You'd show up at the house in a few days, like, 'Sorry your father died, let's go camping this weekend'?"

"Something like that." He sets the basin aside, a paper towel hanging from it. "We can still run away together."

"Forget it." I step away from Frankie.

He turns his head toward me, eyes pleading. "Look at the way he treats you, Tina."

"Yeah?" I glare back at him. "He may suck as a father, but he's *my* father. I thought I made it clear that I didn't want him dead."

"Sooner or later, he's going to drink himself to death.

Do you want to go through that?"

"I'll take that chance." Maybe now that Papá knows how much I love him, it will be enough to save him.

"Look, Tina . . ." Frankie stands, facing me.

"What do you want? And why are you here? Instead of out there, you know"—I sweep my hand away from him—"killing people."

"I never killed anyone."

"You beat up that musician."

"He was a druggie. And a subversive."

I clench and unclench my fists. "I thought you weren't into politics." I can't believe I fell in love with this guy, that I wanted to have sex with him. Without his jacket, he's not even hot—just a small-time gang banger worshipping his *momio* uncle and their beloved dictator.

He holds out his hands, palms up. "I'm not. Honest. It was a family thing. You know, like *Romeo and Juliet.*"

"Sounds more like *The Godfather.*" I look from his hands to his eyes. Under the dim streetlamp, they're wide open. Scared. "Papá was on your trail for what you did. So you had to go after him next." I jab my chest with my thumb. "Through me."

"It's a little more complicated, but yes."

"Why didn't you just kill him before I showed up?" It would have simplified Mamá's marriage to Evan. And saved my summer.

"Because we don't go around having shootouts in the street here. At least not anymore. And your father has a ton of security."

Mostly to protect him against himself. But I don't tell Frankie. I've told him way too much already.

"We were looking for a way inside. To get at whatever weak points we could find." Frankie scoops up his leather jacket, stained with Papá's blood and the remains of whatever he drank before speaking at an illegal demonstration. One Frankie found out about from a flyer at my house.

"You needed me to spill his secrets," I say.

"But then I fell in love with you." Suddenly, he grabs my hand. "Please run away with me, Tina."

I yank my hand away and stick it behind my back. "No. This isn't some play from four hundred years ago. This is real life, and I'm staying with Papá."

"Okay." Frankie takes a few raspy breaths. "I lost the key to the apartment."

"Don't you have a home? With some made-up drunken father?"

He doesn't look at me. Did I catch him in yet another lie, or is his home really as bad as he said?

"I need that key. Do you know where it is?"

I replay the moments before we left for the police station, when he dragged me by my arm and wouldn't answer my questions. At no point do I remember him holding a key. "You probably locked yourself out."

He sits again and hides his face in his hands.

"Don't you have someplace else to go tonight? So I don't have to look at you?" My chest aches, as if I've been crying for hours.

"I can go home. I should . . . get right with the old man while there's still time." He runs his hands along the top of his head.

"Your father, you mean? He exists?"

"Yeah, and he's as messed up as I told you he is." For a second, I want to touch Frankie, to hold him, to comfort him, but I know that it's all over. Forever. Even if he couldn't bring himself to do it, he was supposed to kill Papá, and me as well. His real name isn't Frankie Zamora, and I don't know who he is.

How can you love someone when you don't even know his name?

"Frankie?" I say after a long silence.

"Yes?" He raises his head.

"What's your name?"

"Francisco Zamora, but I like Frankie."

"No, it's not. And that's why you made me stay in the apartment after I caught you with Sofia." I step forward, slide my toe under the lip of the basin, and tip it over. "She called you *Pepe*."

"*Frankie es el nombre de mis sueños.*" And then he switches to English. I feel like I haven't heard him speak English in a long, long time even though it's only been a few hours. "The name of my dreams."

"And when you don't dream?" I ask as the last of the water soaks into the dirt.

He switches back to Spanish. "When I wake up and realize that I'll either be killed or my crappy life will just run out, like in the Minus World?" He sighs. "José Francisco Heider Villalobos."

"For real?"

He nods. "You can report me to the police if you want."

"Yeah, and they'll probably arrest *me*." I turn away and walk back into the hospital.

CHAPTER 22

Wednesday, July 12: 40 days until I go home

The hospital waiting room has chipped paint on the walls and layers of grime on the linoleum floor. The TV set in the corner emits white noise because programming ended at midnight. A pregnant woman moans and clutches her belly while an older woman—I guess her mother— squeezes her hand. At the other side of the narrow room, a young man stinking of beer slumps in his chair while holding an ice pack against his swollen jaw.

Clipboard in hand, the doctor reads Tía Ileana and me the damage: a lacerated right kidney, which means Papá will be peeing blood for the next week. Bruised genitals. Stitches in his tongue. Three broken ribs on the right side. Stage-two trauma to his liver, which might have escaped injury if it hadn't been so enlarged because of his drinking. These thugs knew his weak spots, thanks to Frankie and my big mouth. On the positive side, his right arm isn't broken, only bruised from him using it to protect his head.

"Keep him away from alcohol until his liver heals," the doctor says.

Tía Ileana sighs. "One more thing to do." Louder, she asks, "How long?"

"Six months. Maybe nine."

My aunt shakes her head slowly.

The doctor hands her a pamphlet with the title ENFRENTE UD. EL ALCOHOLISMO. "Face Alcoholism." And another: EL ALCOHOLISMO: UNA GUÍA PARA LA FAMILIA. "Alcoholism: A Guide for the Family."

"We'll keep him through Monday for observation and to ease his withdrawal symptoms," the doctor continues. That's a long time for Papá to stay in this dingy place. But I'm also relieved that I won't have to see him, he won't be drinking, and people who know what they're doing will take care of him.

I suppose that's what Tía Ileana also means when she pats my shoulder and says, "He's in good hands, amorcita."

At three in the morning, she and I leave without seeing Papá again. I don't tell her about our detour into the mountains. Maybe they'll drug Papá so much that he won't be able to talk, and no one will find out how I almost got him and me killed.

I hear Tía Ileana getting ready and leaving early in the morning, but when I finally crawl out of bed at noon, she's home. Graciela is there, too, and there's a strange man in our living room. He's stocky, with thick charcoal hair.

Tía Ileana introduces us. The man is Rafael Jaramillo, Graciela's husband, and he's going to be staying at the house with us for a while. For our protection.

So they already know what happened. I wait for the accusations.

Rafael moves to the chair next to the sofa where I sit. In his hand is a yellow enamel smiley-face key ring with two keys. I recognize it immediately.

"Your father took this from the boy's back pocket last night." Rafael waves the keys in front of my face. "Seen 'em before, *chica?*"

"Frankie was looking for them. I thought he left them in the apartment," I blurt out. That must have been what I saw flash in Papá's hand last night, when we got back to the city and he wriggled out from under the blanket.

"Where's this apartment?" Rafael asks. His voice sounds like car tires crunching gravel.

I shake my head. It feels heavy, unbalanced, and I realize I haven't brushed my hair from when I put it up in a bun to take a shower.

Tía Ileana stands behind me and squeezes my shoulder. "Give her time. She's just been through a traumatic experience," she says.

"Nino wants the place raided before they can remove or destroy evidence." Rafael glances toward the front door, then at Tía Ileana and me. "If he wasn't drugged to the gills with four different tubes stuck in him, he'd do it himself."

Drugged? Tubes? Like the dying patients surrounded by beeping machines in *St. Elsewhere*. I swallow and almost choke.

"That's enough, Rafa," my aunt says.

"Doesn't she have somewhere else to go? Some grandparents?"

I shrink back against the sofa. "No way I'm going there." With my grandmother's rules, it would be like spending the next six weeks in jail. And everybody, Mamá included, would find out and blame me for what happened.

"You're not safe in this house. The boy is out there, along with the people who set him up. They're going to come after you and your father again," Rafael says.

"Does Papá want me to go away?"

Rafael and Tía Ileana look at each other.

Rafael scoots to the edge of the chair. "As head of your father's security detail, I advised him this morning to send you to a safe place. He wanted you to stick around, to help him locate the gang your boy is working with."

"He wants me to rat out Frankie?" I yank out the rubber band and shake my hair loose. My scalp stings from where the band pinched and pulled.

Rafael stands and slips the key ring into his pocket. "Your so-called Frankie," he says, "brought you and Nino into the mountains to slit your throats and leave you in the snow for the vultures."

I spring to my feet. Tía Ileana and Rafael are a blur in front of me. "But he didn't! He took us to the hospital. He saved Papá's life!" I back toward the stairs. "Send me to Madison, okay? Where it *is* safe and the people aren't crazy!"

I run upstairs to my room and, slam the door. How can I call my mother without everyone seeing me? How am I going to explain everything that's happened? And how quickly can she get me a plane ticket?

One just for me. No Frankie—because the Frankie I thought I knew doesn't exist.

I hear a soft tapping at the door. When I open it, Tía Ileana holds an armful of sheets and the blanket from Papá's bed. The dark circles under her eyes stand out against her pale skin.

"I'm leaving for the hospital," she says.

I point to the sheets and blanket. "What are those for?"

"You have to bring your own change of sheets."

"That's awful." I picture the grimy floors and walls of the hospital, then Rafael and Graciela downstairs. "I bet everyone hates me now."

"No one hates you. They just don't trust you." My aunt sets her bundle on the desk. "There's a lot more to it than what Rafa said."

"Like what?" I stare at the white sheets, at the quarter-size light brown stain near one edge.

"For one, I met the boy. Multiple times. I believed his story, too. Besides, you didn't make your father speak

225

at that demonstration. You're not the only one who did something foolish and dangerous."

"I'm the one they blame." I sit in the chair and fold my arms across the bedclothes, fingering the stain.

"Maybe." She rubs my back. "Because of what Marcelo stands for and what he did to end the dictatorship, a lot of people act as though he can do no wrong."

"Except for the ones who want to kill him."

"True, *amorcita*." My muscles start to relax under Tía Ileana's hands. "I'm more worried about the harm he does to himself."

I stare at my fingernails, all of them picked ragged since last night. "When he spoke at the demonstration, he may have been, uh, drunk." I sniff. "I could smell it on him at the police station five hours later."

"I'm not surprised." I catch a whiff of her perfume.

"And the police wanted to charge him for public intoxication and starting a riot, but then they changed their minds."

Tía Ileana's sigh tickles my neck. "I'm surprised none of this has made the TV or newspapers. Maybe it's because they dropped the charges."

Or maybe because the cops thought they'd killed him, when it was supposed to be the job of Frankie and his gang.

"Daniel said he didn't use to drink when he was working," I say. But I can't say what else I'm thinking—that it's only a matter of time before he'll be unable to work. Like one José Francisco Heider if Frankie is telling the truth.

"You're right. It's getting worse. And I wish you didn't have to be here to see it." My aunt stops rubbing my back and slides the bundle from under my arms. "I have no idea how we're going to do this. I need your help."

"Remember the book you told me about? The one in Italian about the guy drowning?" I also envision it on the shelf downstairs, in Frankie's hands, then in mine—neither of us able to read it. "Did it give you any good advice?"

"I wish it did. But it wasn't that kind of book." She kisses the top of my head.

I want to spend more time with her, to figure out what we can do and how I can make up for my mistakes, but she says she has to get to the hospital soon to relieve one of Papá's coworkers. She sighs a lot, so I know she's not happy about it. I wouldn't want to see that hospital again. Or Papá, in the condition in which Frankie and I brought him there. I promise her I'll take care of the birds while she's gone. At least that's one problem she won't have to deal with.

After she leaves, I put on my headphones and slap my cassette of Pink Floyd's *The Wall*—my number-one favorite album—into my Walkman. No more Metallica for me. I flop down on the bed, listen to "Hey You," rewind the tape, and listen to it again. I sing the words, committing them to memory, hoping maybe they will tell me what to do.

CHAPTER 23

My last hope is my mother.

After the cassette ends, I tiptoe down the stairs, hoping to get to the telephone in the kitchen without Rafael or Graciela seeing me. The living room is empty, and there's no one in the kitchen, either. But men's voices float in from the open door to Papá's office. I carry the phone into the living room and dial the fourteen digits of my home number. The rotary dial clicks, and holding it next to my body fails to muffle the sound. Why does my home number have so many zeroes and nines? Finally, I dial the last digit.

Strong hands grip both my shoulders and spin me around. I glimpse Rafael's dark eyes. "What do you think you're doing?" He lifts the phone out of my hands, but I can still hear ringing.

I gaze at the gaps between the floorboards, as if I could squeeze through and escape. "Calling my mother," I say.

"She's calling her *mami*," Rafael shouts, followed by laughter from two rooms away. He holds the receiver toward me. Ring after ring tells me no one's home.

A skinny man totters in. He's no taller than I am, with dark hair and a thick black mustache. He grips the neck of a whiskey bottle—the whiskey Papá usually drinks.

"Well, well," the small man slurs. "If it ain't the little girl who started everything." He takes a swig and nods at me. "Look on the bright side, *pendejita*. We get to drink up Nino's stash."

I break into a sweat at the word *pendejita*—little fool. "Where's Graciela?"

"Next door. Where she normally works when she's not looking after you." Rafael spits out the words. "You spoiled gringa brat." I back away from him into the kitchen. He follows me and sets the phone on the counter.

I scoot toward the sink. "Leave me alone!" The words come out an octave too high for anyone to take me seriously.

"Typical gringa. Thinks the whole world revolves around her." The smaller man appears next to Rafael and laughs. I try to look him in the face, the way the counselors told me to do when kids pushed me around in middle school. But I can't make myself do it, and my gaze falls to his body, where a pistol sticks out of the waistband of his jeans.

"And I hear you're a real *puta*." He staggers toward me. His hand grazes my hair. "We ought to teach you a lesson."

My stomach lurches. My gasp sounds like a cry.

"Watch it, Héctor," Rafael says. "That's Nino's daughter."

"I was only kidding, man." The man named Héctor taps the grip of his pistol and shakes his head. "Damn, if I had a kid like her, I'd want to blow my brains out, too."

Rafael claps him on the back. I slide along the kitchen counter toward the door to Papá's office and backward down the three steps. A large man with red hair and freckles sits in Papá's desk chair. On the desk are a can of Coke and a bottle of pisco. The man belches. I push open the sliding door.

Outside, I suck in the damp, smoggy air and gag. I look for an escape, but high walls, the house, and the birds' cage trap me.

In the silence I hear the flutter of wings. Víctor darts to the other end of the cage. He hovers over a branch before perching with his single intact foot. On the tree branch nearest the cage's door, Pablo stares at me, his beak quivering. I unhook the latch and squeeze through the wire door. My eyes sting and then I'm crying for real. I don't even bother to muffle the noise or wipe the tears that stream down my face.

Pablo hops onto my trembling finger. "Help me, buddy," I say.

No answer. I repeat the words in Spanish, somehow expecting advice from the bird my father trained to make suicide threats.

"*Te quiero, flaco*," Pablo squawks. A moment later, he adds, "*No te me mueras.*"

I love you, skinny. Don't die on me.

My throat burns. "I love you, too."

A ruffling of feathers overhead startles me. Víctor lands on the branch next to Pablo. He's as close to me as he used to get to Frankie. I wipe my face with my sleeve. What did Víctor see in Frankie, that he went to him when he wouldn't go to anyone else?

"Hey, Víctor," I say, forcing a smile. The stump of his leg twitches. Papá said that Graciela's husband brought him here. Was Rafael the one who abused him?

I've got to get away from this house.

There's a tree next to the back wall, but the lowest branch is too high to reach unless I stand on my tiptoes. If I had a rope, I could get up there, but if they won't let Papá have a gun or knives, what are the chances of a rope lying around the house?

Near my bedroom window is a drainpipe. If it's close enough, I can use it to swing to the top of the wall, and maybe there's a gate on the other side.

I decide to set Víctor free, so he won't be left alone with Rafael. I open the cage door wide. "Go, Víctor." I wave my hand. But the bird just sits there. I fetch a handful of birdseed from the bag under the eaves and scatter some of the seed outside the cage. He still doesn't leave.

With a shrug, I say, "Good-bye, birds," toss the rest of the seed inside, and close the cage door. I sneak back into the house and upstairs without the goons noticing me. I switch from my boots to my pink high-top Chucks with rubber soles to grip the metal pipe. After throwing a change of clothes into my backpack along with my hairbrush and toothbrush, I slide the window open.

A blast of cold air greets me. I reach for the drainpipe, test its sturdiness. I jump up to the pipe and hang on.

I have to close the window, or someone will notice I've gone. I thrust out my backpack, hook the handle of the window with the shoulder strap, and pull the window shut. Then I slide down a few feet and plant my left foot on the top of the wall.

In a crouch I sidestep along the wall, looking for a way out through the neighbors' yard. There's a shed in the middle next to the wall and a gate at the far end. I lie flat on the shed's corrugated metal roof and peer below to make sure Graciela isn't there. Then I climb down, dash across the narrow yard, and push the wrought-iron gate open.

I'm stunned to find myself in the street. Then I realize I have no money and no place to go. The only place within walking distance is the apartment where Frankie and I used to get together. Where his grandmother lives. Where his motorcycle may still be.

She won't be back anytime soon, Frankie said last week. He said last night that he planned to go back home. He also said he planned to run away, with or without me. But can I believe anything he said? And Rafael has the keys in his pocket. How would Frankie have gotten in?

My chances of finding a safe place to go are zero, but still I trot up the street and around the block to avoid passing Papá's house. Before long, I'm pushing through crowds at the shopping plaza, trying to remember which street leads to the apartment. It's already getting dark. Landmarks, I tell myself. The traffic circle. The three banks. The hot dog stand with the *italianos.*

I count the blocks. A fine mist drifts down from the purple sky. At eight blocks I see the traffic circle. The building is in the distance, lights on in most of the apartments. The raindrops get heavier. I break into a run. Icy water pelts my face and soaks into my clothes.

Frankie's motorcycle is not on the street in front, where he usually parks it. Stupid idea—I knew he wouldn't be here. I turn around to go home but alongside the building spot the silver and black Suzuki behind the bushes.

Someone has propped the lobby door open, as if expecting me. Inside the elevator I shiver in my wet clothing. *Why am I doing this?* Frankie was supposed to kill Papá. But he couldn't bring himself to do it. Because he loved me? Because I loved him—even if I can't anymore?

I knock on the door. The voice that answers is unmistakably Frankie's. "Just a minute."

The door opens. Frankie has wrapped a towel around his waist, as if he stepped out of the shower. His hair glistens. He sucks in his breath. "Why are you here?"

I don't know the answer.

CHAPTER 24

Frankie pulls me into the apartment, shuts the door, and holds me in his arms, his soft cheek resting on the top of my head. He smells fresh—of aftershave and soap. I press my face against the warm skin of his chest.

Can we still be friends after all this, the way I am with Max?

"You're soaked," Frankie says after a moment.

"It's raining."

"I haven't been outside since this morning."

I wriggle out of my soggy sweatshirt. "How'd you get in without the key?"

"My . . . uncle let me in."

"Are you in trouble?" I ask.

He nods. "You?"

"Big time."

I follow him into the living room. He unwraps the towel and steps into a pair of white briefs. He picks his wrinkled and dirt-streaked jeans from the floor and puts them on, then bends over again and pulls a black T-shirt over his head. I sit next to him on the sofa. Hands trembling, he lights a cigarette and takes a few puffs. A blanket covers one of the armrests.

I fold my arms across my body, trying to warm myself. "Papá's still in the hospital. Three goons are guarding the house. One of them called me a whore and said he should teach me a lesson."

"Wait. Slow down," Frankie says. "What did they do?"

I don't want to repeat the bad things they called me. "They've got guns."

Frankie jerks up straight. "Did they follow you here?"

"I don't think so." But how would I know? It didn't even occur to me to look. "I'm scared to go back."

Frankie sighs. "You can't stay here." Before I can ask him why, he says, "I'm leaving the country next week."

"Where are you going?"

"Not allowed to say. But I'll try to get to Miami." He grabs my hand. "Can you meet me there?"

He told me that he's never been outside of Santiago. He has no idea how far away cities in the United States are from each other. It's more than three hours by plane from Madison to Miami.

But he has a phone. The one I shouldn't have answered yesterday. "Why don't I call my mother now? To send us both a ticket." I can't believe I've just said this.

Frankie shakes his head rapidly. "I'm not allowed to make international calls. They'll catch me for sure." He takes another puff of his cigarette and blows the smoke straight ahead.

"Who'll catch you?" When he doesn't answer, I ask, "The people who wanted you to kill Papá and me?"

Another puff. "I'm sorry I brought you into this. I wanted to spend the day with you, but I put you in danger." He grinds out his cigarette. "I had to tell them you were dead. Both of you."

"So they're going to come after me?" I can barely breathe.

"You? I doubt it."

"Really?" My hands shake. I want to believe him, but I can't. He could change his mind because I chose Papá over him. Or *they* could burst in at any moment and finish me off.

"They don't care about you. They're going to come after *me*"—he touches his chest—"as soon as they find out I lied to them."

I search for the truth in his eyes. He doesn't look away.

"I did it for you," he says.

"Why?" I hold his gaze, waiting for the words. For him to convince me I'm not going to die thousands of miles from home, never to see my mother and Evan and my friends again.

"Because I love you. I really do. But I have to get out of the country." He lights another cigarette.

"Everything you've told me about yourself is a lie."

"Only some things." The tip of his cigarette glows as he sucks in more smoke. "I really did fall in love with you. I wasn't supposed to, but I did. You were . . ."

I finish his sentence. "Everything good in your life."

Frankie nods. "And that's the other true thing. My life sucks. I'll do anything to escape it."

"Like beat up some musician who never did anything to you and kill my father because he was on your trail."

"More than that." Frankie takes another drag. "My uncle says someone assassinated one of his closest friends because of what your father wrote."

Daniel said something like that, too. Papá's underground newspaper named people in the military who tortured prisoners, and that's why he got beaten so badly in prison. But that was years ago. "You and I were little kids then. They shouldn't drag us into this." I raise my voice. "You shouldn't drag me into this, either."

"No, I shouldn't." Frankie scoots toward me and touches my arm. I twist away from him. "If you never forgive me, I would totally understand," he says. "But I need you to help me."

"And what about Papá?" Maybe I should tell Frankie that Papá has to quit drinking—maybe that will make Frankie care about my father, too.

"If they find out he's still alive before I leave, I don't know what they'll do. It could come down to him or me."

I pull my knees up to my chin and wrap my arms

around my legs, keeping a barrier between Frankie and me. "Nobody should have to die."

"Then I can't get caught."

"So what am I supposed to do?" Panic makes my voice shake.

"Go someplace where they can't see you. Don't you have those grandparents in Las Condes?"

"We don't get along that great. And my grandmother will want to know everything."

"*Metete*. Not good." He lets go of me and picks up the cigarette in the ashtray. "And the keys. I couldn't find them anywhere here." He takes a long drag. His eyes bore into me. "Do you know where they are?"

"The goons have them."

"How the hell did they get them?" Frankie clenches his right fist.

I take a deep breath of the smoke that he blows out. "Papá swiped the key ring from your pocket last night."

"He what?"

"When we got back to the city. Right before the hospital."

"*¡Puta cucaracha!*" He punches the armrest of the sofa.

I jump to my feet. "He's not a cockroach!"

"I saved his worthless life"—Frankie slams the armrest again—"and the drunken bastard ruined me!"

"Don't call him a drunk. He quit drinking."

In the next instant, I realize it makes no difference to tell Frankie that Papá won't be able to drink anymore.

Frankie can't take back his words. I understand now that he would kill Papá to save himself.

I grab my sweatshirt and back toward the door. "Tell your uncle or your grandmother or whoever that you lost the keys on the ground."

Frankie shakes his head. "I'm stuck here until I leave."

"Can't you ask your uncle to loan you his keys?"

"Are you kidding?" Frankie's face crumbles. "They're paranoid about crime. He'll want the locks changed, and I don't have the money to do it. Besides"—he reaches for the cigarette—"I screwed up in so many ways. One more, and all my lies come crashing down."

"I think they already have." My hand closes on the doorknob.

"No, Tina!" He doesn't try to get up. "Don't go! Listen!"

He presses his hands against the top of his head. I don't know which Frankie to believe—the one who tried to kill Papá and me, or the one who tried to save us.

He reaches one hand toward me. All the times he held me in his arms and all the times he said he loved me draw me back to the sofa. As I come closer, I make out words. "He won't be able to quit. They never do. It just gets worse."

This isn't about Papá. "What happened, Frankie?"

"After the hospital. I went back home like I told you I would."

"To check on your father."

"Four in the morning, the bars were closed. I heard him cursing outside. I went out to tell him to shut up—these little shacks, you can hear everything. He was two doors away, and all around him were cops." Frankie takes my hand. "I couldn't let them see me, so I couldn't stop them."

"Did they beat him?"

Frankie shakes his head. "No, but they were laughing and calling him names. Lush. Garbage. Cockroach. Then they started pushing him from one cop to the other, spinning him around until he fell down and couldn't get up." He closes his eyes. "And all I could do was hide and watch. After they left, I carried him inside and put him to bed." Frankie squeezes my fingers until they hurt. "You know what he said to me?"

The way Frankie asks the question, I know his father didn't thank him. "What?" I ask.

"'You're just like me, boy. A coward.'"

CHAPTER 25

I sprint through the darkness toward the traffic circle, my hood pulled low over my eyes to keep out the fine rain. After passing the last of the three banks, I slow to a walk. My side throbs, and the wind rips through my damp clothes. By the time I get to the shopping plaza, storekeepers are lowering their metal gates for the night. I might as well give up and beg Tía Ileana for mercy so I have a place to sleep tonight.

I check every one of my pockets for coins to call my aunt. There's nothing. Not even a lint ball.

Then I do what I saw so many kids my age doing when I lived here years ago.

I hold out my trembling hand, palm up. "Excuse me, sir?" I call out to a man who's already walked past me. He doesn't turn around.

I grasp my wrist to steady it. To keep from dropping any coins that someone might give me. "Excuse me, sir . . ."

Another man looks away as he passes me.

A woman approaches. She wears a calf-length wool coat with horizontal stripes and spiked heels that click on the pavement. "M-ma'am? Ch-ch-change so I can eat?"

She crosses the street.

My arms drop to my sides. A few people pass without looking at me.

I pull my hood lower, make my voice smaller, close my eyes. "Please? Just a peso?"

A coin drops into my outstretched hand. Gripping it tightly, I dash to a pay phone. I dial slowly to avoid a wrong number.

"Hello. Who's this?" Right away, I recognize Rafael's gravelly voice.

The coin clicks inside the pay phone. I hang up.

My money is gone, and the plaza is now deserted, except for a few storekeepers sweeping up. I ask one of them for directions to the hospital. If Tía Ileana isn't home, she must still be there, where she'd taken the sheets for Papá. The storekeeper points to a wide avenue and says, "But it's very far."

"How far?"

"Almost three kilometers."

I walk fast to get there with no one noticing me—a girl alone at night. Even so, cars honk and guys on motorcycles call out to me, asking my price. I consider giving them the finger but don't want to call more attention to myself. I dash the last block to the hospital.

Out of breath, I ask the receptionist. "I'm looking for my aunt. She's with my father. Marcelo Agui—"

All along the way, I hadn't thought about seeing him in the hospital, what he'll look like, what he'll say. He probably hates my guts for what I did to put him there.

"Your name?" The receptionist's curt tone startles me. When I tell her, she says, "You're not on the list."

"But I'm his daughter." Now I know. He does hate me.

She shows me a logbook. "He's only allowed one visitor at a time. And no one under eighteen."

I drop to my knees on the dirt-streaked floor in front of the reception desk and hide my face behind my hands. Someone touches my back. The receptionist kneels next to me.

"He's going to be fine, dear," she says, voice softening. "He's here to rest and get better."

I want to scream, but I let her keep talking, reassuring me that Papá isn't going to die.

"Have you seen my aunt?" I finally ask.

"The tall, red-haired woman?"

I nod, sniffling.

"She left about half an hour ago."

"May I call her to pick me up?"

The receptionist hands me the phone. This time Tía Ileana answers. She has no idea I'd run away, and she thinks I'm here because I'm worried about Papá. I wait until we get inside her car before I tell her what happened with Rafael and Héctor.

"So they were drinking his liquor rather than pouring it

out?" I nod. She turns toward me and holds my gaze with hers. "And they made advances toward you?"

"The guy named Héctor did. Rafael told him to stop, but they were saying horrible things. Like I'm the reason Papá wants to kill himself."

Tía Ileana's grip tightens on the steering wheel. I can hear her teeth grind before she turns the ignition. "I'm sorry you had to hear that, *amorcita*."

"Don't make me go back there," I plead. "If you don't want me, take me to my grandparents. Or put me on a plane home."

"No." Her voice has a hard edge. "I can't give up on you and your father."

///////////////////////

Tía Ileana drives to the neighborhood we passed when I first arrived, to the four-story apartment building where she said she used to live before she moved in with Papá. The cement balconies on each floor reflect the streetlamps. The sidewalk is wide and clean. About half the windows are lit, and when I look inside, I see the tops of bookshelves in a few living rooms or bedrooms and the flickering of televisions in most of the others. My aunt whips into a parking space in the median of a divided avenue.

She leads me to an apartment on the top floor and unlocks the door. The place smells of tomato sauce and garlic.

Berta steps into the living room and wipes her hands on her jeans. She glances at me, then at my aunt. "What's she doing here?" Berta asks, as if I'm not there.

"Some problems at home," Tía Ileana answers. "She's going to have to stay here for a few days."

My aunt takes me by the arm through a hallway to a small room with a desk, a tall file cabinet, and a twin bed pushed up against the wall. I drop my backpack on the bed.

Berta stands in the doorway. "I can't have her here."

"She has no place to go," Tía Ileana says.

"What about the house?"

My aunt looks at me, expecting me to tell Berta what happened, I guess. I take a deep breath. "It's full of these security guys. One of them threatened to hurt me."

Berta doesn't ask me why. Maybe she doesn't know what I did.

"You have to be at the hospital. And I can't watch her," Berta finally says to my aunt.

"I don't need watching," I say.

Tía Ileana glances at me, eyebrows raised. Then she nods at Berta and they leave the room. Afterward, I hear voices from the living room, getting louder and louder—Tía Ileana and Berta arguing because of me.

"She got into some trouble. It's not safe for her."

"I'm not taking time off work for her."

"It's important to me. Her father . . ."

"You should have never moved in with him, the ungrateful pig."

"This is my family, Berta."

"Family? He hates us."

"This isn't about my brother. It's about Tina."

"I don't care. It's not safe for us with her around. . . ."

"I'm not like him, okay?" I shout above them as I step into the living room. They stop talking and stare at me. "Please let me stay. I promise I won't run away again."

Berta and Tía Ileana look at each other. Berta nods. My aunt hugs me.

"Thank you, Berta," I say.

Then I remember Frankie, holed up in the apartment without his keys. And if he doesn't get out of the country before the gang leaders find out he didn't kill us, it will come down to his life—or Papá's.

Maybe if I return to the house and get the keys, I can help him run away. But I just promised that I wouldn't leave Berta's. I will save myself instead.

CHAPTER 26

When I wake up the next morning in Berta's guest room, I glance at my watch. Ten after twelve. Not even morning anymore.

The birds! Yesterday before she left for the hospital, I promised Tía Ileana that I would feed them and clean their cage for Papá. But how can I go back there now? And the keys—I don't even want to think about Frankie.

I hear rustling in the kitchen, and while I'm in the bathroom washing up Tía Ileana calls my name. I stick my head out, mouth full of toothpaste. "Aren't you going to the hospital?" I ask.

"I'm staying here today," she answers. I'm sure it's because I can get into a lot more trouble than Papá, who, according to what my aunt said last night, has only three tubes attached to him now.

After I shower and get dressed, she asks if I know how to cook. I wonder if she wants me to make *la comida*. Since I just woke up, it's like breakfast time for me.

251

"I do a little cooking," I answer. "Mostly cut stuff up for my mother."

"Sous chef." She drops a package of raw chicken onto the kitchen counter. "You've been promoted." Her earrings, dangling feathers, swing back and forth as she hands me more ingredients. Olive oil. Salt. Black pepper. A box of spaghetti. A can of tomato sauce.

Given that Tía Ileana hasn't done anything more than heat leftovers, it makes sense that she sticks me with the cooking. It makes even more sense because I showed up uninvited, caused a fight between her and Berta, and screwed up everyone's life. I find a black plastic cutting board labeled CARNE—the block printing doesn't look anything like my aunt's—and set to work chopping the chicken.

"Is this enough for Berta, too?" I ask.

"She's out for the day."

"Is she mad at me?"

Tía Ileana frowns for a moment. "She'll get over it."

While I heat the oil in a heavy iron skillet, Tía Ileana sets a pot of water to boil and opens the tomato sauce. She hums under her breath, like she's really happy to be here. With me. I drop the pieces of chicken into the skillet, one by one, trying to keep the oil from splattering all over. It pops and I jump back a step. "I actually like cooking," I say. "It's fun."

"That's what Berta says." My aunt smiles at me.

"When we get home, we should make something nice for supper. Not just leftovers."

Tía Ileana's smile vanishes. "Your father won't eat it."

"What's it to him? He hardly eats anything." I roll a chicken leg away from the skillet's edge with a fork. "We should do what we like."

My aunt puts her arm around my waist and pulls me to her. I snuggle against her, feel her head touch the top of my head, and sniff the lemon scent of Berta's shampoo. I chew my lower lip, thinking about how miserable it's been living with my father for the past few weeks, how she's had to do it for months and will probably be stuck with him until . . .

Until he ends up like Frankie's father?

Maybe Tía Ileana can read my mind, because she says, "I talked to him yesterday about what happened at the demonstration."

"Was he . . . ?"

"Yes, *amorcita*." Her arm drops from my shoulder to her side. "He said someone gave him a bottle to calm his nerves. He didn't know who."

I suck in air. "They could have poisoned him."

"It wasn't opened. But he shouldn't have opened it and given the cops the excuse to arrest him."

"So he knows it wasn't totally my fault, right?" But what unknown person got him drunk? Someone he worked with, or someone who wanted to destroy him?

Little bubbles rise from the pot of water, not quite a full boil. Tía Ileana slides spaghetti from the box into the pot anyway. The water hisses. I realize she hasn't answered my question.

Because she can't make him change his mind.

After a minute or so of staring at the water, I ask, "What about Papá's birds if I'm here? Will they be okay?" *And if so, will he change his mind about me?*

"I took care of them this morning. And I brought you fresh clothes."

"Thank you." I kiss her cheek.

"It's no trouble. When your father brought the first bird home, I thought I'd have to take care of it. I'm surprised how responsible he's been." She lays her hand over mine. "As a child he'd pick up stray creatures all the time and right away lose interest in them."

"Kind of like what he did with his family."

My aunt sighs. My mother would have gone on for at least half an hour about how he abandoned us.

Tía Ileana lets go of me so I can finish cooking. But I want to know more. "What was my father like as a kid?" I ask.

"Spoiled. As the youngest and the only son usually is." While I turn the chicken over to brown the other side, Tía Ileana continues. "Your grandfather Aguilar lost so much in the Spanish Civil War—his home, his cause, two of his brothers killed. He had to start over in a new country. I think he lived the rest of his life through Marcelo. Your father loved soccer and every match he played it was like your grandfather was fighting the war again."

"But he was so good. Daniel and I used to watch him." It seems kind of crazy for someone to think a soccer game was the same thing as the Spanish Civil War, but when we played soccer in Madison, plenty of parents went crazy and yelled at their kids or the other kids or the referees if their team lost. They must have had their reasons, too.

"Growing up, his whole life was sports, but I also think he understood what it meant for our father."

"Mamá said he gave *fútbol* up to write."

"He did." Tía Ileana reaches past me to stir the spaghetti. "When he was a teenager, he filled up a notebook with *fútbol* poems. Our father found it and made him burn it. He called it a waste of time, and Marcelo got the message. After that, even when he wrote about sports, he'd always bring politics into it."

"Which is how he got himself messed up." With a fork I stab a drumstick and bat the other browned pieces around the pan. I step closer to take in the aroma before tomato sauce buries it.

Tía Ileana dumps the sauce in. "At least your grandfather wasn't alive to see it."

"Was my grandfather any different?"

Her face scrunches up. "In what way?"

"I mean, is this something passed down from father to son?" I think of Daniel, who's not exactly a barrel of laughs, either. "You know, how Papá sucks all the happiness out of everyone else and instead of going to him, it goes into this hole. Like some sort of Minus World where stuff goes in and it can't ever get out." I make a loud sucking sound, then pop my lips.

Tía Ileana laughs at my sound effects. "You remind me of Cecilia," she says.

"Because I'm the wild one?" I pick up the impaled drumstick and twirl it in the air.

"And don't ever change." My aunt hugs me again. "Only be more careful."

///////////////////

They start to trust me. On Saturday afternoon, Tía Ileana leaves for the hospital, and Berta goes shopping. Left alone, I dial the number to the apartment where Frankie's holed up, which I wrote down the first day I went there. I want to make sure that he's still all right. And that no one's coming after me.

He isn't surprised when he hears me.

"Is it safe to talk?" I ask.

"Yeah, they just left." His voice sounds strange. Thick, but not like he's been drinking. More like he has food in his mouth that he can't swallow.

"Who left?" When he doesn't answer, I ask, "The people you work with?"

"Uh-huh." Another pause. "Did you find a place to go?"

"Yeah." I chew a hangnail on my index finger.

"Your grandmother's in Las Condes?"

I swallow and almost choke. "Can't say."

"But you're all right?" His voice breaks.

"Yeah. And you?"

"I didn't tell them about the keys," he says. The walls of the kitchen close in on me. I've had so much fun cooking and hanging out with Tía Ileana that I didn't think about the keys once.

"I'll get them tomorrow." I hold my voice steady so he thinks I mean it.

"They know."

"Know what? To change the locks?"

"That you and your father are still alive."

"Crap." I bite the nail itself.

"They don't care about you anymore."

My finger stings. I taste blood. "What about Papá?"

There's a moment before he says, "They haven't decided," and right away, I know he's lying. The room spins. *I can't give up on you and your father*, Tía Ileana told me.

"They've ordered you to kill Papá, haven't they?"

"Tina . . . there's something else."

"What?" I suck on my finger.

Frankie clears his throat. "My father's not on your side like I told your aunt. He was in the army. He supported the general. And he started drinking in the army. After the coup they made him interrogate people."

"You mean *torture* people? Papá wasn't interrogated—he was tortured. It ruined his life." All those memories I had of my old *papá* before I came here—I can't conjure a single one of them now.

"At one point, he couldn't do it anymore. So they demoted him. Humiliated him. And when he got drunk and crashed a jeep, they kicked him out."

"So what does that have to do with Papá? He doesn't even like the army." Once again, Frankie lied. His family made him follow their politics the same way my grandfather from Spain got Papá involved, but on the opposite side.

Frankie sighs. "I can't end up like my old man."

No, he can't. This has to stop.

"So what are you going to do?" I say out loud.

"Leave the country."

"And you need the keys. So they don't think you're an incompetent who let them fall into enemy hands."

"Yes."

"And you need to do what they tell you." My voice trembles. "Kill my father for real this time."

"Tina, I love you. I don't want to do anything to hurt you." I can tell he's breaking down. "Please help me."

Like you didn't help me when I had no place to go? Like you want to kill Papá to save your own ass? But I can't hang up on him, and I can't let him hurt Papá. My teeth grind my fingernail once more. If Frankie won't stand up to his gang, I'll have to rescue my father myself.

"How do I get the keys to you? And when?" I ask.

"Take the *micro*." He lists the bus lines that go to his apartment. I write them down on the notepad next to the phone. "Tomorrow morning, before nine."

"Why so early?"

"My grandmother gets back at ten thirty."

I roll my bloody finger on the notepad, like a fingerprint. "There's no grandmother."

There's silence on the line. I hear a key in the lock.

"I gotta go." I rip the page off and stuff it into my jeans pocket.

"I love you, Tina."

I hang up. In my mind, I repeat, *ten thirty—something's going to happen.*

Seconds later, Berta comes in with an armful of grocery bags. I jump to help her, but as I reach for the first bag, the words rush out, "Take me to the hospital!"

She looks at me, mouth gaping.

"Please! It's an emergency!"

CHAPTER 27

They won't let me go up to Papá's room. Instead, Tía Ileana meets me in the hospital lobby. "What happened?" she asks in a weary tone as if to say, *Can't I go away for more than a few hours without some crisis?*

"I found out something." I stand on tiptoe and whisper in her ear. "The people who hurt Papá. They know where he is and they're coming back for him. Frankie told me."

My aunt covers her mouth with her hand. Then she turns to Berta. "Take Tina back to the apartment. I'll call you later."

At the apartment, I try to help Berta with supper but cut my finger slicing tomatoes and burn my hand taking a sheet of empanadas from the oven. I'm in the bathroom putting ointment on my palm when I hear the door open and Berta exclaim, "Oh, no, not *him!*"

I rush into the living room in time to hear slurred words: "You think I want to be here?"

Tía Ileana and Ernesto hold Papá upright, his arms draped over their shoulders. Tía Ileana carries his cane

261

and leg brace. He has the beginning of a beard, and his face is pale with an orangeish hue, like the picture on a messed-up color TV. He wears an oversize shirt, plaid pajama pants, unlaced sneakers, and a pressure bandage on his right wrist in addition to the splint on his left. Slowly, they lower him to the sofa, stuff some pillows behind his back, and help him stretch out his legs. Behind his glasses, his eyes are nearly shut.

He waves me over. I kneel next to him. He smells of the hospital, of antiseptic and disease.

I touch his purple fingers. Though hardly swollen, they're soft, like rotten bananas. He closes his eyes the rest of the way.

Ernesto lifts Papá's other arm and squeezes his hand. "Good luck, Nino. And call if you need anything."

Papá's lips move but no sound comes out—that's how zonked he is on whatever they gave him.

I find my aunt and Berta in the kitchen, in the middle of another argument.

"This is my home. I though our safehouse days were over," Berta says.

"You don't have to take care of him. He said he wanted Tina to show some responsibility."

"He's in no condition to decide, Ilé. Look at him."

I step between them. "Hi, guys."

They shut up and stare at me.

"Hey, no big deal. He's asleep," I say.

My aunt frowns. "It's not as easy as you think, *amorcita*."

I leave the door to my room open, waiting for Papá to wake up so I can ask him about the keys he stole and gave to Rafael. Around eleven, after Tía Ileana and Berta have gone to bed, I hear a long moan.

I flip the light switch in the living room. Papá groans and shields his eyes with his bandaged arm. "You okay?" I ask.

"What do you think?" he snaps.

"Can I get you a painkiller?"

Sweat beads on his face. "Turn out the light, damn it." In the darkness, he says, voice low, "You can turn on a lamp if you want."

Dim light and shadows fill the room. "How's this?" I ask.

"Good." Under the blanket, he shivers. "I'm going off the painkillers."

"Why?"

He reaches under the blanket across his body, a motion that causes him to let out a strangled scream. He holds up the smiley-face key ring and two keys. "Where does he live?"

I try to grab them but Papá jerks them away. "Whose side are you on?" he says between gritted teeth.

I blow out my breath. What's left of my old *papá* after all these years lies on the sofa, broken and angry. Across town, the boy I was stupid enough to love will surely be killed because of my decision.

"He wasn't the one who beat you up," I answer.

"But he's in with them." He grimaces, as if slammed by a wave of pain. "My own daughter, running around with a fascist punk."

I was prepared for him to blame me, but steaming blood rushes to my face anyway. "You made me come here."

"To show you my life. Your country. Not to hang around with—"

I scrape my chair back, though I know he can't touch me. "What life? All you do is work all day and then get piss drunk. You treat Tía Ileana like crap. And here people murder each other because of stupid politics."

For a long time he says nothing. I listen to his breathing, try to gauge his reaction. With concentrated effort, he pushes himself to a sitting position. "Are you so blind to politics that you go out with an assassin because he rides a motorcycle and says he loves you?"

I leap to my feet and glare at him. "It's more than you ever said." It takes all my effort to keep from shouting.

He closes his eyes and mumbles, "Shit," like he forgot something. Like he is completely incapable of being a father—or of loving anyone—because of what they did to him.

I press on, in case he believes Frankie somehow converted me. "We never really discussed politics. Mamá and Daniel told me not to, and Frankie said he wasn't into it. He paid attention to me and was nice. That's all."

"That's all? That's all?" Papá's sarcasm stings me.

I flop down in the chair. "The only thing that matters to you is politics. Not us."

He gazes at me. "Of course you matter. I did this for you, too."

"That's crap. You did it for your country. For your"—I search for the word he used when they let him out of prison—"*compañeros*. Your family came after. When there was nothing left."

"I wanted to protect you." He clears his throat. "So you kids could grow up without having to live in fear. The life I led all those years when you were younger . . ."

"When you acted like a real father?" How could I have believed he'd still be that person?

"When I worked underground." His breath is shallow. "I didn't want it to become your life."

I think about all those years in Madison, getting teased by the other kids and not having my old *papá* to listen to me or help me. "I needed a father. A family that wasn't separated."

He nods. "I know."

"But you didn't do a thing about it. Except abandon your family."

"I arranged for you to come here. So we could be part of each other's lives again." He shakes his head slowly. "I didn't have to. It would have saved me a lot of pain."

He sinks into the sofa. I clench my teeth so hard my jaw aches. But there's so much more I have to say. I inhale, and the hospital smell almost makes me gag. "Frankie was with me on Wednesday. Not at the demonstration and not with those cops. And he wasn't drunk, either." *Well, only a little.* "So stop blaming me."

"You don't get it."

"Because you tried to *protect* me."

But then I think about what Tía Ileana told me, about his father dragging him into politics, and where that got him. Maybe Papá meant it when he said he didn't want his life to become my life. Maybe he wanted me to have a different life—one with safety and the freedom to make my own choices and say what I wanted to say. Like my life in Madison with Mamá and Evan.

But where did that leave him? And how long would he wait to see me again?

I let my face drop into my hands so Papá won't see it and think he was right all along.

I feel cloth against my wrist, then Papá's icy fingers. When he first got out of prison, he would jerk my hand away from my face when he thought I wasn't paying attention, but this time he just holds my wrist steady. And he doesn't say a thing, only stares at me.

There's so much more I can say about him not being there for me, and for blaming me when he was the one who spoke at an illegal demonstration while under the influence of a bellyful of hard liquor. But I can't keep hurting him and then expect him to help me.

"I'm sorry, Papá. I messed up. But now you're in trouble and Frankie's in trouble unless I do something."

Papá jingles the keys with his weak hand. "I got out of the hospital before he could kidnap me. What happens to your boy is his problem."

"No!" I shout, then lower my voice to just above a whisper. "The people he's with will keep coming after you. You'll never be safe."

"Is this what he told you?"

I nod. "I called him this afternoon. That's when he warned me."

There's a long silence. "Okay, bring me a glass of juice. Some aspirin. And one of those empanadas." His voice is calm. "I need to think this over."

When I return, I place the pills on his stitched-up tongue and hold the glass to his lips so he won't spill it because of his shaky hands. He finishes both the juice and the empanada before we speak again.

"Do you really love the boy?" he asks.

"I did. And we're kind of still friends." The line *divided we fall* runs through my mind, because this isn't the kind of friendship I have with Max. If Frankie and I act like people who hate each other, we all get killed.

"I suspect he loves you." Papá touches his mouth with the back of his bruised hand. "He saved my life because of you."

I think of what Frankie said to Papá in the mountains, cruel words that nag at me. I stare into my father's eyes. "Is that what you wanted? For him to save your life?" I want to push his hair away from his eyes, but don't.

"I wanted the pain to end." Papá takes a deep breath— the kind of painful breath he needs to take to avoid a lung infection—and coughs. "But, yes. I need you guys to keep me from doing things I won't have a chance to regret." He smiles weakly.

I smile, too. It doesn't quite count as loving himself, but it's a start. "I sort of said I'd help Frankie escape," I tell Papá.

"Escape to where?" Papá bats his hair from his face. His eyes are bright. Alert.

"I don't know. He wants to go to Miami."

"That may be hard. The gringos don't let just anyone in." He holds up the keys again. "But if you tell me where the apartment is, I'll get him out of the country. I know some people through work. People in other countries who've published my articles."

"You won't just raid the place?" How can I be sure he won't turn Frankie over to Rafael and Héctor—who'll surely do to Frankie what the cops did to Papá?

Papá's voice is steady. "I need the names of all the other gang members. Will he give them to me?"

I nod. "If I promise to sleep with him."

"Tell me that's a joke."

"Lots of people make promises they don't keep," I say.

Papá stashes the keys under the blanket and holds out his bruised hand, as if he wants me to shake it. Or slap him five, which I hesitate to do because he's already so beat up. "All right. We'll go together," he says, gripping my hand. He squeezes a lot harder than I expected. His fingers are dry, as if covered in powder.

I let everything spill out. The address, the streets and buildings nearby, the fake grandmother, the phone call ordering Frankie to go to the police station and to take me with him. I don't tell Papá what Frankie and I were doing in the apartment that day, only that I would visit to play video games. I don't expect Papá to believe me, but he doesn't say anything. I tell him, "Frankie said he'll be there alone until ten thirty in the morning. And there's a locked bedroom. He said it was his grandmother's bedroom, but it isn't and I don't know what's in there." I imagine guns, lots of guns. Ammunition. And more cocaine and weed. Maybe even dead bodies.

"Okay. Bring me the phone," Papá says when I'm done.

He dials a number. "Hey, Ernesto. It's Nino. Sorry to wake you. . . . I'm surviving. . . . I need you here at eight in the morning. Call Rafa at the house and tell him you're picking him up at seven forty-five. . . ." *Oh no, not him.* "Shit, yeah, you're picking him up at seven forty-five. Don't be late. We don't have much time for this action, and it's big. Real big . . . One more thing. Bring a pair of jeans, because I'm not doing this in pajama pants. Your jeans, *guatón,* not mine. I've swollen a few sizes. And a set of screwdrivers. Got all that? Repeat it. . . ."

He goes over the plan with Ernesto twice more before he hangs up.

Operation Minus World has begun.

CHAPTER 28

Sunday, July 16: 36 days until I go home

Papá and I spend a sleepless night plotting as he comes down from the painkillers and the sedatives they gave him for withdrawal, but at breakfast I wonder if he's still high. While eating his toast with jam, he jokes with me and with my equally surprised aunt. His euphoria is catching, and even she gets into the act, gossiping about people I don't know. I push my plate away, unable to swallow a single bite. I can't say anything anyway—Papá has the job of assuring Tía Ileana that the apartment's empty and Ernesto and I will be sitting in a café a block from the building while he and Rafael raid the place.

And guess what, Tía Ileana? There's no café within a block of the apartment building, either—just three bank branches and a hot dog stand.

"You know what makes your *papá* happy? Doing something really dangerous," Ernesto tells me while driving to Frankie's apartment.

"No, finding the truth," Papá says. "But for sixteen years, that's been dangerous."

Rafael laughs. I shrink into a corner of the backseat, as far away from Rafael and his sour breath as I can.

"So how are my birds doing?" Papá asks.

Rafael leans forward, toward Papá in the front seat. "Plucking out their feathers. Both of them." I turn from the stench. Does the guy brush his teeth when he wakes up?

"Víctor, too? I didn't think he cared about me."

Rafael nods. "He started a day after the other one. Guess it's contagious."

"He misses me." Everyone stares at me. But when no one says anything, I go on, "He started talking to Frankie first. And then to me."

"The bird's a *momio*. A traitor. And ungrateful," Rafael says. "He'll make a nice stew."

"No!" Papá and I shout together. Then Papá says, "He's my bird now, Rafa. You gave him up."

As we approach the building, I think of the good times I had there—the video games and movies, hanging out with Frankie. Ernesto parks on the side street, where Frankie's motorcycle is still chained to a light pole behind the bushes. The four of us get out of the car. Rafael pats his hip—I know he has a holster and gun there. Ernesto taps his calf, and I try to tell from the looseness of his pant leg if he's hidden a gun or a knife. I carry a walkie-talkie and the box of screwdrivers, Papá the keys. He leans on his cane.

At the door to the building, he hands me the keys. My hand trembles when I try both keys twice, finally get one into the lock, and turn the handle. Ernesto and Rafael stand guard downstairs while Papá and I take the elevator to the fourth floor. My knees bang against each other, and I press myself into one of the corners to keep them from buckling. Papá wedges himself into the other corner and taps his cane on the rubber floor to the rhythm of a popular chant, *Tap-tap. Tap-tap-tap,* over and over as the elevator makes its slow climb.

I drop the keys before I unlock the door to the apartment. Frankie calls out, "Tío Jorge? You're early."

His uncle? The leader of the gang?

We push through the door, me first and then Papá with his weak left hand clutching my shoulder. Frankie jumps up from the sofa and stumbles backward. He's barefoot and wearing only a white undershirt and jeans. Clothes are scattered all over the living room floor. Soda cans and crushed cigarette butts litter the coffee table. Next to the ashtray is his switchblade. I glimpse the Mass on TV, the Cardinal on the pulpit.

"Tina!" He blinks rapidly, then holds his arms outstretched. "Thank God, it's you." The left side of his face is purple, the color of a birthmark, with a thick black ring under his eye.

"What happened to you?"

"I . . . fell. In the bathroom."

I step forward, scoop up the knife, and drop it into the kangaroo pocket of my sweatshirt. Papá steps around me.

"Mr. Heider Villalobos, I believe we've met," he says.

Frankie pushes himself against the built-in cabinet. His body covers the TV. He turns his gaze to me, then to his unlaced sneakers, everywhere but to my father. "Please don't hurt me, sir."

I slide toward the entryway and lock the deadbolt. Frankie continues to beg for his life, even though Papá is unarmed except for his cane. Papá leans on the sofa and sets the cane on a cushion.

"Want to see what your comrades did?" Papá lifts his untucked shirt to reveal a thick, jagged purple line across his rib cage. A giant bruise darkens his lower back. His belly is swollen, with purple and black patches, and there's a square bandage above his navel. His entire midsection is battered even worse than Frankie's face.

Frankie's color drains, leaving only bruises. "I'm sorry, Mr. Aguilar."

Papá lowers his voice to a growl. "Okay, fucker, here's the deal." I suck in my breath. He was going to give Frankie *la dura*—the deal—but calling him a *culiao* was not in the script. "My daughter loves you. You love her. Right?"

Frankie nods.

"Look at me."

Frankie raises his head to look into Papá's yellowed eyes and winces. He could be seeing his dying father's eyes in Papá's.

"Your face, kid?" Papá's tone softens.

"I fell," Frankie says.

"No, you didn't." Papá picks up his cane and raises it toward Frankie's head. Frankie cringes. "Someone pistol-whipped you."

I gasp. "How do you know, Papá?"

My father ignores me. Still staring at Frankie, he asks. "Who did it?"

"I . . . I can't . . . tell."

Papá raps the tip of his cane on the floor. Frankie jumps. "So you're going to protect the *culiao* who turned your face to a pulp?"

My fingers curl into fists. "We're trying to help you, Frankie. Like you asked me to."

"Even though three broken ribs, liver and kidney damage"—Papá takes a shallow breath—"and some bad memories of a motorcycle and mountains haven't put me in a forgiving mood." He turns toward me and flashes his crooked smile. Despite what he just said, it's the happiest I've seen him since I arrived a month ago.

After a long moment, Frankie says, "All right."

Papá motions with his head. I step forward, one sweaty hand fingering the knife in my sweatshirt pocket, the other holding the screwdrivers. "What's in the bedroom, Frankie?"

"Stuff," Frankie mumbles.

"What kind of stuff?" I ask. "Guns?"

"Yeah."

"Drugs?"

Frankie shakes his head this time. "The cocaine was given to someone else."

"Like the punk cops that beat the shit out of me," Papá says.

"I'd say that's a pretty good guess, Mr. Aguilar." Frankie blows his breath through the space between his teeth, making a whistling sound.

Papá nods. "Anything else in there we might like to know about?"

Frankie lowers his head but doesn't answer.

I squeeze Frankie's bare upper arm. "We'll get you to safety if you tell us. Papá knows people in other countries."

"Tapes," Frankie whispers.

I hand him the box of screwdrivers. "Take off the lock."

Papá calls on the walkie-talkie for Rafael to come upstairs and repost outside the door, to keep Frankie from trying anything with the screwdriver. I don't think Papá realizes I grabbed the switchblade. He lights a cigarette, takes a puff, and gags.

"You want it?" He hands the cigarette to Frankie.

Frankie inhales. "Thank you, sir." Smoke comes out with his words.

Papá steps back. "Take the whole pack. They taste like rotting fish."

After fifteen minutes and another cigarette, Frankie has the entire doorknob disassembled. We enter.

There is no bed. No night table. No dresser with old-lady clothes. Only a desk, with shelves and a chair behind it and several chairs in front. One shelf holds a reel-to-reel tape player, with about a dozen boxes of tapes on the shelf below.

"Are those the tapes you're talking about?" I ask Frankie.

"That's how he keeps track of assignments. He doesn't write down much."

"Who?"

"My uncle."

"Your own uncle beat you? The one you admire so much?" I ask. It must have been right before I called yesterday.

"Yes." Frankie doesn't lift his gaze from the parquet floor.

I pull the boxes from the shelf. When I turn to set them on the desk, my father is holding a pistol, glancing from it to Frankie's face. I break into a sweat. "Put that down!"

My father starts to laugh. Then he stops, hands me the gun, and grabs his stomach, in obvious pain but still smiling. "Scared you, didn't I?" he rasps.

"Not funny," I say.

"Worse than that," Frankie says, unfolding himself from his fetal position under a chair. "Maybe you shouldn't listen to those tapes."

Papá spits onto the floor. "Maybe I should."

The pistol feels heavy. Its black grip is oily, and I have to hold it with both hands so I don't drop it. I point the barrel toward the floor.

Papá opens the desk drawers, one by one, pulls out a few papers, pens, a wad of cash, and passports. He counts eight passports, which he leafs through before stuffing them into the back pocket of his borrowed jeans.

"Pack up the evidence," he orders. "And Mr. Heider Villalobos, get your clothes together. You're coming with us."

"I am?"

"Don't be a *pendejo*," Papá says. "You think I'm going to let these guys kill you? Look what they did already."

"Thank you, sir."

With his weak left hand Papá picks up a pen, twirls it back and forth. "When we take you, will anyone report you missing?"

Frankie blinks rapidly. "Probably not."

He turns and leaves the room, and when he comes back with a duffel bag and wearing a threadbare sweater, his eyelids are red. Dirty clothes stick out of the bag. He drops a tissue onto the floor and with his sneaker wipes the spot where Papá spat. Half of the tissue turns green.

Frankie shakes his head and says, "Not good," under his breath.

He goes into the bathroom. I follow, gun in my right hand. He sweeps his toothbrush, toothpaste, deodorant, shaving cream, and aftershave into the duffel but leaves behind the unopened box of condoms. In the office Papá examines the framed pictures on the wall, writing notes from time to time. I arrange the tapes in the duffel.

We wait for Papá to finish. He covers the tape boxes with papers, notes, documents, and one of the framed pictures. His gaze falls on the pistol, still in my hand. A shudder runs through him. He nods twice.

"Leave the gun," he tells me. Then he takes another piece of paper from the drawer, grips the pen in his bruised fingers, and writes,

Romeo defected to the Capulets.

—Guillermo Shakespeare

CHAPTER 29

On the way to the car, Ernesto and Rafael hold Frankie's arms. Papá shuffles behind them with me on his weak side as lookout. When no one's watching, I slide the switchblade out of my pocket and drop it through a street grate.

In the crowded backseat, I'm the buffer zone between Frankie and Rafael. I repeat to myself, "Guillermo Shakespeare," as if it were a calming mantra, pronouncing the last name the Spanish way, *Shock-es-PEAR-ay*.

"Hey, Nino, what do you want me to do with the *facho*?" Rafael asks. I turn away from him—forty-five minutes standing guard haven't improved his breath. Slumped in his seat, Frankie hugs the duffel bag to his chest.

"Nothing. I'll take care of him."

I can't wait to get out, with Rafael glaring at Frankie and me like we're a pair of stinkbugs, Frankie's dirty laundry right under my nose, and Rafael's holster and gun digging into my ribs every time we take a right turn. In the front seat, Papá leafs through a stack of papers. Nobody else says a word until Ernesto stops by

the radio station to pick up a reel-to-reel tape player.
I'm the one who gets to hold it on my lap.

"We don't have much time," Papá says. "Guns, drugs,
other documents—whatever evidence they have
they'll destroy."

"But we can't go to the *carabineros*. Look what they did
to you," I say.

"Those two are gang members. Rogues. Their passports were in his uncle's collection. But you're right—
I'm not sure who we can trust." He glances up from the
papers. "Ernesto."

Ernesto keeps his gaze on the slow-moving Sunday
morning traffic, people on their way to or from Mass.
"Yes, boss."

"I'm going live with the story tonight."

///////////////////////

Tía Ileana and Berta are baking a cake when the three
of us burst in, lugging all our stuff. Berta drops her
wooden spoon. "Not another one, damn it!"

My aunt marches into the living room, a spatula still
in her hand. "Chelo, this is not safe for Berta and me."

Papá clears his throat. "You were the one that met him."

"Because you were working. Instead of looking after
your daughter like you should have." She points the
spatula at him. "*Your* daughter."

Frankie starts for the door, duffel slung over his

shoulder. "I'm out of here. I'm not staying with a bunch of *mari*—"

"Frankie, shut up!" I grab the other end of his bag and pull him all the way into the guest bedroom. He's too shocked to fight back—or maybe he thinks I still have his knife. I slam the door behind me and trap him between the door and me. "Want to be safe here? Or out on the street with everyone trying to kill you?"

"You heard her. They're kicking us out," he says.

"I'll take care of it."

I help him take off his leather jacket and make him sit on the bed. Then I sit next to him and trace the sharp edge of the bruise with my finger. He shrinks backward. "Does it hurt?" I ask.

"A little. I put ice on it last night."

"Okay, don't move until I come back for you. And keep your mouth shut."

I walk back into the living room—to Tía Ileana holding the phone. "Who're you calling?" I ask.

"Your mother. That boy's the last straw. I'm sending you home before there's any more trouble."

"No!" I cry. "We can't give up. You said so yourself." I look at Papá, who's seated on the sofa, eyes focused somewhere beyond the window. "Tell her to let me stay, Papá. It's your decision."

Tía Ileana speaks up next. "Your father has a special report to finish by this evening. No matter that he belongs in the hospital right now, not running around Santiago to round up hired killers."

"Papá?" I wave my hand in front of his face to get his attention. Then I crouch beside him, blocking his view of the window. I stare into his eyes behind his glasses— the whites a dull yellow, and dark circles underneath. Above his gray and brown stubble, his face is ashen. "You promised we'd help Frankie get out of the country. Remember?"

He shakes his head slowly, like he doesn't remember. Like he doesn't intend to keep his promise. Bracing himself against my body, he stands, grabs his cane, and limps out of the room.

I take Papá's place on the sofa. Where he sat is still warm. If they send me home, where will Frankie go? Will Rafael and his goons kill him? Will his gang kill Papá? I know one thing: This endless war between families will go on without me. And if half of me is Papá and his world, it's a half I'll have to cut away forever.

Somewhere behind me and over the hum of the kitchen fan I hear a gurgling noise, like water flowing through a clogged drain. Doors open and slam shut, followed by a high-pitched moan. And then Frankie's voice.

¡Qué carajo!

"Excuse me. I need to check on Frankie." *Make sure he's not climbing out the window to escape.* I stand and straighten my sweatshirt.

I pass the closed door to Berta's bedroom, where Papá must be resting. The door to the guest room is ajar. And the voice isn't coming from there but from the bathroom.

"Frankie?"

"In here. I need an ice pack, now."

"Are you all right?"

"Hurry!" he shouts. I hear another moan, a retch, a splash. "Easy, Mr. Aguilar."

I run to the kitchen, dump an ice tray into a fresh towel, and run the towel under the faucet. "What's going on?" Tía Ileana blocks my path into the hallway.

"Papá's sick!"

She steps out of the way. I open the bathroom door and hand the ice pack to Frankie, who bends over my father. Papá is on his knees beside the toilet, Frankie's arm around his chest. Frankie has pushed the sleeves of his sweater above his elbows, and he presses the ice pack to the back of my father's neck.

"Frankie!" My legs buckle. I grip the doorframe.

He looks up at me. "Withdrawal, Tina. I'm trying to keep him from having a seizure."

"Just bring me a drink, kid," Papá chokes out. His voice echoes inside the bowl.

"No, Papá!" I scream. "Your liver will explode."

"Already did."

Frankie speaks up next. "Come on, man. You can quit. I've seen you. You're not weak, like . . ."

Your father?

I feel Tía Ileana's presence behind me. I turn my head. She and Berta stand next to each other, their eyes wide.

Papá lifts his head, squints, and glances around. Sweat runs down his face. "How nice. A crowd to watch me vomit."

"That boy," my aunt sputters.

"I'm not hurting him, ma'am," Frankie says. "I know what I'm doing. I helped my father detox, like, five times. And at home, too. No money for—"

Tía Ileana interrupts. "Chelo, you're going back to the hospital."

"No." Papá swallows, gags. "Must . . . finish . . . report." He dives for the bowl. My insides tighten.

Frankie raises his voice above Papá's heaves. "He can't go back. They'll kill him. Nine thirty tonight. This guy Rambo—he and I are supposed to pull him out of the hospital bed and carry him off to some secret location. My uncle is going to meet them there to find out what he knows—"

"About all the bad stuff your gang has done?" I ask. I reach for my father's glasses, sitting next to the sink, and hand them to Tía Ileana. She wipes them off with a tissue she takes from the front pocket of her chinos.

"And everything else my uncle and his friends have done over the years."

"I bet your uncle has a lot of friends." Like the customs officials that hassled me. And maybe whoever gave Papá that bottle at the demonstration.

"And then they plan to kill him in a way that it looks like a suicide." Frankie lowers his head, looks into Papá's face, into his gaping mouth. "You done, sir?"

Breathing hard, my father turns toward Frankie. Frankie wipes Papá's face with a damp washcloth. "Can you repeat what you just said? I missed it," Papá rasps.

Frankie lifts my father to the edge of the bathtub, flushes the toilet, and lowers the lid. While he describes the plot again, Tía Ileana and Berta step away. I hear their raised voices in the kitchen.

"It's all on the tapes," Frankie says. "And something else I should tell you now before you hear it there. I didn't mean to say some of those things about Tina. I couldn't let my uncle know that I cared about . . . that I'd fallen—"

Papá cuts him off. "I'm a guy. I know how that works."

"Yes, but"—Frankie scrapes the top of his head—"I told him about you wanting to get a gun. I was going to put it in your drawer next to the bottle you hid there."

Papá doubles over, retching. Frankie holds the washcloth to his mouth. One side turns pale green. "So she really did tell you," my father says. "It wasn't just a bad dream." He glares at me through the open door.

"Don't blame her, Mr. Aguilar. She was worried about you," Frankie says while he pats Papá's face and lips with the washcloth's clean edge. "She doesn't want you to die. No one in your family does." He throws the washcloth into the bathtub.

A door slams on the other side of the apartment. Moments later Tía Ileana returns with a lemon wedge. She hands it over my head to Frankie, who gives it to Papá.

"So your uncle wanted to get me to talk." Papá touches the lemon to his tongue and squeezes his eyes shut. "How was he planning to do that?"

"Whiskey. All you can drink and then some."

"Had me figured out." Papá's cheeks hollow out as he sucks the lemon.

Frankie adjusts the ice pack at the back of Papá's neck. Despite the lingering odor, I step inside the tiny bathroom and sit on the closed lid facing Papá and Frankie. "And you were supposed to go with that Rambo guy."

Frankie nods.

"To help my father drink himself to death." I guess they were supposed to work as a team—first beating people up and then kidnapping them for the professionals to kill.

"I should save people for once in my life. Not let them shoot themselves or die drunk in a pile of garbage."

Papá coughs and clears his throat. "How did you get involved with these guys?"

"Two years ago." Frankie licks his lower lip. "The government built some houses in our *comuna*, and my father applied for one. He got turned down. He was barely working then, selling soft drinks at the bus station—when he wasn't passed out or too hung over."

"So you have plenty of experience with hopeless alcoholics," Papá says.

Frankie's eyes lock on Papá. "You're not hopeless, sir. You have a job."

"One that pissed your uncle off immensely." Papá drops the lemon, holds a trembling hand to his mouth, and burps. I rub his back, between his shoulder blades.

A worried expression crosses Frankie's face. He motions for me to stand and get out of the way. "You need to—?"

Papá shakes his head. "Go on, kid."

"My mother told me to ask my uncle for help because he had connections in the government. He said he wouldn't help my family get the house, but he'd help me. He set me up with jobs, gave me money, paid for my sisters' school, and bought me the motorcycle when I was old enough to get my license."

"Jorge Heider Bustos," Papá says. "Army officer. Retired to start a courier service but kept on contract for special operations."

"How do you know this?" I ask.

"The pictures on the walls. The papers I took out." Papá raises his head, in the general direction of Tía Ileana. "Your office uses Speedy Couriers, right?"

"Sometimes," Tía Ileana answers.

"Better find a new service tomorrow."

CHAPTER 30

Berta leaves alone with the cake. Promising to wake him up in time to finish his report, Tía Ileana gives Papá his pills and convinces him to lie down on my bed. Frankie and I stand outside in the hallway and listen.

"Ooh, your poor bed." Frankie gives me a half smile. "He doesn't smell so good."

"I can deal with it." I don't tell Frankie this used to be one of Papá's places to crash when he returned to Chile illegally and lived underground. He probably showed up plenty of times in not such great shape.

"But your aunt's cool. I never met a . . . a . . ."

"Lesbian."

"Yeah." He looks relieved.

"You probably have and don't know it," I tell him.

Frankie scratches his head. "That's the weird thing. You have a subversive family. My family's for the government."

"For now."

"Right. For now." Frankie pauses. "But when I was holding your father and he was sick. It was like all the times with my father trying to quit."

I lean against the wall, hands in my sweatshirt pockets. "You knew exactly what to do."

"I hope he beats this thing."

"Me, too. But he was tortured. He has terrible nightmares. And flashbacks."

"My father, he did it to people. And he had the same thing." Frankie bounces his back against the wall. "But my uncle, he interrogated people and nothing like that happened to him."

I slide one hand out and touch Frankie's upper arm, the way I still do with Max when we talk about the craziness in each other's lives. "I never met your father," I say. "But, deep down, he must have a good heart like you have."

"Yeah, maybe, once upon a time." Frankie taps the nose his father broke twice. "He was weak but pretended to be strong. Now my uncle—he's strong."

"Is that supposed to be a good thing? To want to be like him?"

Frankie squeezes my hand—almost too tight, like he doesn't know his own strength. "I always thought it was. And I hated myself for being weak. My uncle always said you could pick out a person's weakness and use it to destroy him."

"Like he tried to do to Papá?"

"But your father was stronger than we thought."

"Because you helped him in the end," I say. *Maybe love is stronger than all our strength.*

Frankie doesn't speak for a long time, and then he asks, "Do you still love me, after all this?"

I will never forget how he refused to carry out his uncle's orders, and how he took such good care of Papá this morning. "I still care about you. Wherever you go, I want you to have a good life."

"Good enough." He kisses the top of my head.

"What are you thinking?" I ask him.

"It sounds really strange." Frankie hesitates. "I'd like to watch your father sleep."

"To make sure he's okay?" I recall the nights he slept on our sofa, after my parents' big fight in Madison that was the beginning of the end for them. I always kept a safe distance and looked away whenever I passed him, because he reeked of alcohol and cursed and writhed in his sleep.

I turn the door handle slowly, trying not to make a sound. Sitting in the desk chair reading a book, Tía Ileana shushes me. Papá lies curled up on his uninjured side under the sheet and blanket, his dark gray hair spread across the pillow. His mouth is slack and there's a damp spot on the pillowcase next to his face. I hold my breath and listen to his steady, shallow breathing. I hope he's dreaming of something nice, like playing soccer or wading in the ocean and letting the waves chase him back to shore.

"I have to get some stuff," I whisper to my aunt.

"And him?" She eyes Frankie suspiciously.

"He wants to check on Papá. Because of his father."

Frankie nods. "Is this his first detox?"

"Yes," Tía Ileana says.

"The first one's the easiest. Each time my *papá* tried to quit, it got worse." Frankie pushes up the sleeves of his sweater. "Got to get it right the first time."

He steps toward the bed. I extend my arm to keep him from coming too close. "He might hit you if you startle him."

Frankie crouches and rests his bare elbows on his thighs. "He looks so peaceful." He lowers his voice to nearly inaudible. "I've never seen a subversive sleep."

I shrug. "No different from anyone else." I'm glad Tía Ileana didn't hear what he said.

Frankie scoots forward, still in a crouch. His fingers brush Papá's cheek. Papá's mustache twitches, and Frankie steps back. "No fever."

I scrunch up my face. "Why would he have a fever?"

"Sometimes without alcohol, they lose the ability to regulate their body temperature. We had to pack my father in ice once so he wouldn't bake."

A cry escapes from Tía Ileana. "Did he recover from that?" she asks.

Frankie shakes his head. I think it must have been terrifying for him. But what's worse: the damage someone else does to a person you love, or the damage that person does to himself?

"He didn't wake up for two days. Or recognize us for a week," Frankie finally says.

"You said it wouldn't be that bad for Papá. Because it's his first time quitting."

"Still want to be careful."

I nod and lean against the wall. The room seems to rock back and forth like a cradle.

"Let's go." I struggle not to yawn.

"In a minute." Crouched again, Frankie stares at my sleeping father—both of them completely still. After a while, Frankie stands and follows me out of the room. "I sure hope he helps me like he promised," he says in the hallway.

"He will," I answer, though I don't know exactly what Papá plans to do. I drop to the sofa, and Frankie sits beside me.

"You look tired," he says.

"I didn't get any sleep last night."

"I got an hour, maybe." He covers a yawn. "You can have the sofa. I'll take the floor."

I stretch out on the sofa, while he tries to make himself comfortable on the rug using his sweater as a pillow. Even though I still have on all my clothes, I feel cold. I listen to Frankie roll from side to side, trying to protect his beat-up face. Then I hear whispers, followed by silence.

When I awaken, it's dark outside. Light shines from the kitchen and from underneath the door to the guest room, and as my eyes adjust I realize I'm the only one in the living room. I tiptoe to the bathroom. Someone must have taken a shower recently, because water drips from the shower curtain and the mirror is damp. I wipe the mirror with the sleeve of my sweatshirt and pull my hair into a ponytail.

When I come out of the bathroom, Tía Ileana meets me. "How's Papá?" I ask.

"Working on his report." She frowns. In one hand are a cup and saucer with a soggy tea bag hanging from the saucer's edge. "I let your boy rest in our bedroom. He didn't look very comfortable here."

I knock on the door to her and Berta's bedroom. There's a shuffling, and Frankie opens the door. In the dim light his entire face looks bruised.

"Sleep well?" I ask.

"Yes. Nice of your aunt to let me have the bed."

A total educational experience for Frankie—first watching a subversive sleep, and then napping on the bed of two women who love each other. I grin. "You're never going to be the same after today, Frankie."

"Probably not." His face turns serious. "What did you decide about me?"

"I don't know. I'll ask my father."

Frankie tucks his T-shirt into his jeans and follows me into the guest room. Papá sits at the desk. He wears a rust-colored sweater I've never seen before. His damp hair hangs straight to his shoulders. Headphones cover his ears, and he writes notes in a spiral notebook while listening to the tape player. I stand next to the desk, where he can see me. Eventually, he glances up. I wave. He lifts off his headphones.

"How're you feeling?" I ask.

"Better. Ileana fixed me two empanadas and a bowl of soup. I kept it all down." He pats his stomach. "I'm almost done with the report, and Ernesto's picking me up in half an hour."

"Frankie's here."

"Good. I have some news for him."

I sit at the foot of the rumpled bed and Frankie takes a spot in the middle. Papá turns his chair around and straddles it.

"Okay, kid," he says. "I took care of you as I promised. Booked you on a flight to San José, Costa Rica, at eleven twenty-five tomorrow morning, changing planes in Panama City. You arrive in San José at seven in the evening."

Frankie presses himself against the wall. "Costa Rica?" he repeats. I wonder if he even knows where Costa Rica is. And when he gets there, he'll know no one and have nothing to do. No school, no job, no home. No family—not even the terrible one he has now.

Papá slides his chair closer to the bed, leaving a scrape mark on the wood floor. "That's right, José Francisco."

"Frankie. Call me Frankie, sir."

"I have a friend, a lawyer, who's going to meet you at the

airport and help you get settled. You might want to get his laundry done tonight, Tina. Machine's in the basement."

"Excuse me?" I cut in.

Papá smirks. "Okay, Frankie, that's her way of saying she's a liberated gringa so do your own fucking laundry."

I laugh. Frankie still looks too stunned to speak—or to appreciate my father's humor. Papá hands Frankie a passport, and he flips through the pages, staring at each blank one. I lean toward him. The picture looks like a younger Frankie, one with a smooth face, longer hair, and an innocent gap-toothed smile. His teeth appear larger in his smaller face—and so does his crooked nose. His uncle must have taken the picture years ago and then used it when he got passports for the entire gang.

"Costa Rica doesn't have an army," Papá says. "I think that will be good for you."

"Yes, sir," Frankie says. "And I'm sorry for all that stuff I said on the tapes. About you and Tina."

Papá runs his hand through his hair. "Starting tomorrow, when I turn copies of the tapes over to the authorities, my insides are going to be splattered on every newspaper in Chile."

Behind me, from the direction of the kitchen, the teapot whistles.

Papá continues over the clatter of my aunt making more tea. "Ironic, though. Your *capo* wanted to beat out of me whatever information I had on your group so he could cover it up. But I had nothing but guesswork until you showed up. And now I have all I need. Including proof of the attack on Rodolfo Guerra and who did it."

Frankie stares at his hands—hands that beat up a musician two months ago, made me feel so good last week, and this morning saved my father from a seizure.

Papá raps the back of the chair. Frankie's head jerks up. "What are you going to do about your uncle?"

"Nothing. Nothing I can do."

"Forget about him. Help the rest of your family—in whatever way you can." He flips the chair around, rests his elbows on the desk, and glances at the door. "Now get out of here, you two. I need to finish this."

I go to the kitchen to help Tía Ileana. Frankie follows me. When we get there, Tía Ileana hands me the mint tea she made for Papá, with two aspirin tablets on the saucer. "Please bring this to your father, *amorcita*. I've seen enough of him for today," she says.

"Sure." I have no idea what else went on between them while I was napping, but she clearly needs a break. I grab a couple of gingersnaps from the pantry to help soothe his stomach from all the aspirin and leave the cup and saucer on the desk next to him. He doesn't say anything, but before I leave, he gives my wrist a quick squeeze.

Back in the kitchen, Frankie says, "The tapes. He's never going to forgive me."

I spot Tía Ileana drinking her tea in the living room. "You spared his life up in the mountains. And risked yours to do it." I pour steaming water into two more cups for Frankie and me. "And you helped him this morning so he could finish the report—even if the report gets you and your family in trouble."

"I've seen what those seizures can do to a person. I couldn't let your father go through that."

"I'm sure he appreciates it, even if he can't say it." I touch my wrist where Papá squeezed it.

"Don't let him give up on himself, Tina." Frankie's dark brown eyes meet mine.

"I won't." *Why does he care so much?*

"At first I thought you were crazy, to protect him like you did. But then you two made me see . . . we're all just people."

We lean against the kitchen counter, facing each other as we drink our tea. And I realize that for all the time I spent with him, wanting to know about his dying father and what it meant for Papá's future, it all comes down to one thing: *don't let him give up on himself.* Something Frankie's father must have done long ago.

But I can't make Papá love himself. All I can do is show him how much I love him, even if he can't love me back. Even if sometimes it seems as if my love and everyone else's love isn't enough to save him.

"Hey, you two, where's Ileana?" Papá stands in the doorway, leaning on his cane. Behind him, there's no one in the living room. Tía Ileana must have finished her tea and taken a well-deserved nap.

Beneath Papá's sweater, one side of his shirttail hangs lower than the other.

"*Chuta*, you buttoned your shirt crooked again," I say.

"It's radio, not television."

I bend down and rebutton his shirt from the bottom up. After the second button I push up his sweater and see the shirt pulled tight over the swollen, hard upper right side of his belly. I leave the next two buttons open, fix the remaining ones, straighten his sweater, and finally, tie the laces of his boots. Stepping backward, I gaze at his shaggy hair, stubble, and sallow complexion, then gently pat his stomach. "You look pregnant."

"Don't even say that word. Your mother will kill me." He winks at me.

I smile back. "She'll have to get in line to do it."

"Forget it," Frankie says. "His kind, you can't kill."

"What, the cockroach?" Papá sets the cup in the sink. "And by the way, I'm not coming back here tonight. Ileana's driving you to the airport."

"Why not?" Disappointment dulls my voice. Is Papá still avoiding me? Does he still blame me?

"After this report airs, I'm not taking any chances on someone following me here and putting you guys in danger. Besides, a couple of birds and I need to talk about this feather-plucking problem. Because—"

A long buzz interrupts Papá. He presses the intercom switch next to the phone. I hear a string of letters and numbers—a secret code?—Ernesto's voice recognizable through the intercom. My father buzzes him in.

Less than a minute later, there's a knock at the door. When Papá opens it, Ernesto steps inside, panting as if he ran all the way up the stairs. Papá slaps Ernesto's back like old friends who haven't seen each other in months instead of eight hours. "Ready, Nino?"

"Yes." Papá rests his bruised right fist on Ernesto's shoulder. "One of these days, I should cover the news and not be the news."

"Super idea. It's a lot healthier." Ernesto steps back from Papá and stretches.

Papá nudges Ernesto toward the room with the tape recorder. Then he puts his arms around me, and I hug him back, careful not to squeeze his right side. He smells of mint tea and soap. I bury my face in the stiff wool of the sweater. And I hang on for a while, no longer *La Coneja*. Hoping that he's forgiven me and we can start all over again.

I know what he was going to say before the buzzer interrupted him. He needs to heal, and even then he won't be the same person he was so long ago. But I'm not the same person, either. I can wade into the ocean by myself now, and I can drag someone else out who looks like he's going to drown. I mouth into Papá's sweater, *I love you*, before letting him go, taking the world of José Francisco Heider Villalobos with him.

CHAPTER 31

Monday, August 14: 7 days until I go home

After a few weeks feathers grow back pale and soft in the spots where the birds plucked them out. Papá says they'll eventually blend in with the rest. When I stroke the soft new growth, Pablo bites my finger.

"Ow!" The bird hops onto Papá's shoulder. I shake my stinging hand. "Why'd he do that?"

Papá lifts Pablo onto his finger. "Because we don't want to go back to that place, ever. Right, Pablo?" He stares into the little parrot's eyes.

"Did I hurt him?"

My father shakes his head. "It's more like an irritation. They live with a certain amount of pain. So any unusual sensation upsets the balance."

A chilly wind blows Papá's hair aloft, revealing a downy gray undercoat at his temple along with the crisscrossed scars that will never fade and that I'll never touch. Víctor circles us and settles on a branch above my father's head. Papá and I have figured out that Víctor can only settle on the tree's firm branches. Our fingers and shoulders are not stable enough for a one-legged bird to balance himself.

The secrets of crippled birds take their place among my memories of my new *papá*.

///////////////

A week before I'm supposed to return to the United States, Frankie phones the house. I've spoken to him several times since the day he left for the airport, hidden under a blanket in the backseat of Tía Ileana's car. I know that he arrived safely in Costa Rica. And that he's taking classes to become a doctor's assistant, and English classes so that one day he can come to the United States. But after he moved from the lawyer's home into a room in a boarding house, he hasn't had a phone of his own or the money to call.

As soon as he says hello, I can tell something happened. "What's wrong?" I ask.

"My father. He died a week ago. I got a letter from my sister today."

"I'm sorry." But not surprised. And I can tell from Frankie's tone that he expected the news as well.

"I wasn't there." For a few seconds, Frankie doesn't say anything. Then, "I ran away."

"That's what you always wanted—to have a better life. One day you'll be able to help other people. The rest of your family, too."

"They need me now."

Not doing the things he did. Sometimes running away is the right thing to do. And sometimes staying is hard, but right. "They can wait," I say, echoing the words my aunt told me. "You need to save yourself first." She said it's a lesson she too has to learn.

"Is your father there?"

"He's asleep."

"Still sleeping a lot?"

"It's all the exercise I make him do."

"Can you wake him?" Frankie sighs. "He knows where my uncle went."

I pull the phone into the living room where Papá lies on the sofa. I lift the blanket and gently squeeze his shoulder. He stirs. I hand him the receiver and tell him Frankie needs to speak with him.

"What's going on, Frankie?" Papá motions for me to help him sit. His body is warm from sleep. If changing positions still hurts him, he doesn't show it.

I make out every other word of Frankie's tinny voice, telling Papá about his father's death and asking if there's any way his family can get in touch with Jorge Heider Bustos to let him know about his brother.

"He and his business partner fled to Paraguay," Papá says. "There are warrants for their arrest for drug trafficking and bribery. He probably wouldn't come back even if he found out."

Frankie's response is too muffled for me to understand. Then Papá says, "I don't recommend it. They've charged you with beating up that musician. The two *carabineros* and three other gang members in custody will pin other attacks on you for a deal on their drug charges." He clears his throat. "It's best you stay where you are."

I snuggle next to Papá, close enough to hear Frankie all the way in Costa Rica and to smell the aroma of smoke that clings to my father. Wood smoke rather than tobacco. One of the other things we've done together is build a fire in the living room fireplace. And he says cigarettes still taste strange, which, according to Tía Ileana, means his damaged liver is taking its time to heal.

People feathers don't grow back so fast, she said. *His body is showing us all how to be patient.*

Frankie tells Papá about the last time he saw his father, when he didn't stand up to the cops and his father called him a coward.

"Trust me. He wouldn't have remembered it the next day. What happened to him or whatever he said to you," Papá says. He maneuvers his clumsy left arm across my shoulders.

"But I let the cops humiliate him." A pause. "And those were his last words to me."

"Listen, Frankie. If it had been me"—*and it really could have been him*—"I would have wanted you to take me home, clean me up if I needed it, and put me to bed. Salvage what dignity I had left." I feel Papá's chest expand and contract. "Because you're not responsible for his decisions."

"Thank you, sir," Frankie says.

"How old was your father?" Papá asks.

"Forty-one."

"He lost a tough battle. I'm sorry."

After Papá hangs up, he slumps. His body trembles, his breath comes in rapid gasps, and his heart hammers against my right side, the way it did two days ago when he tried to climb the Cerro Santa Lucía with me and only made it halfway. The guy who was euphoric at breaking into an apartment rented by the leader of a murderous gang is about to lose it because some alcoholic he never knew drank himself to death and they were the same age.

I grip his shoulder with one hand, clutch his wrist with the other, and place his hand on his no-longer-swollen belly. "Breathe when I tell you. Don't think of anything else." I move my hand from his shoulder to his back, to the space between his shoulder blades so he can feel each breath against my hand.

It's what you do for family.

My father's heartbeat slows. His breaths synchronize with mine. He sits up straight and blinks a few times, as if waking from a deep sleep. Then he hugs me and says the words I've waited far too long to hear: "I love you."

"I love you, too, Papá." And with those words I have another good memory of my new *papá*.

////////////////////////

That evening as soon as Papá leaves with Tía Ileana for his meeting of *Alcohólicos Anónimos*, I dial home. Evan picks up.

After our usual hellos, I ask him how the house is coming along.

"Kitchen cabinets went in today. They're delivering the stove tomorrow."

"What color did you decide on for the house?" It feels strange, speaking only English.

"Yellow."

"'Mellow Yellow,' huh?" I hum the opening bars. "I guess Petra was doomed the minute you guys played that song at the wedding."

"She tried her best."

"So when do we move in?"

Evan names the things that still need to be done: sand and seal the floorboards, tile the bathroom walls, hang curtains, carpet the stairs. I want him to say the house won't be ready for a while. It will make the next part easier.

"Is my mother around? I need to ask her something."

"Vicky!" Evan calls. "It's Tina." He says good-bye and my mother comes to the phone.

First, she thanks me for calling. She's the one who's phoned every time so far—despite all the times I almost called or wrote to beg her for a ticket home.

I gulp a mouthful of air. "I'd like to stay here an extra couple weeks. Until the start of school. Papá and Tía Ileana said it's okay."

"Don't you want to help with the house? And pack your things?" She's surprised. I expected her to be.

"I don't have so much stuff. There's something I have to do here."

"Something you have to *do*?" She doesn't sound pleased, and I wonder what she's thinking. She knows Frankie is in Costa Rica. I told her he'd gone there to study as a high school exchange student for the year. Maybe she thinks I have another boyfriend already. That life in upside-down-land has made me totally boy-crazy.

"Yeah. It's kind of like the house. My project."

"Marcelo's house is new. It can't be falling apart yet."

I glance at the clock. Seven fifteen. Tía Ileana will be back soon from dropping Papá off. And if I don't quit stalling, their phone bill will be huge.

Papá, Tía Ileana, and I had agreed not to tell my mother about what happened last month. So she wouldn't think that I misbehaved, Papá went out and did something dangerous when he should have been watching me, Tía Ileana couldn't manage her family, and Frankie came from a family of killers. But Papá still isn't strong enough to return to work full-time, and it's not fair for Tía Ileana to take vacation days from her job because of him and me.

"It's, uh, Papá. He's . . . not doing too good."

"If it's his drinking, you need to come home. You can't change him."

"It's not." I listen to the static on the line. "He got hurt. In an accident."

"What? What kind of accident?"

"He doesn't want to talk about it." Tía Ileana says he needs to talk about it if he wants the nightmares and panic attacks to stop, and she and his doctors are looking for a psychologist that he'll agree to see. But we can't force him.

"Let me speak to him," Mamá says.

"He's not here."

"Where is he?" Her voice breaks.

"At a meeting. He had to give up alcohol. Because of the"—I twist a strand of hair around my finger until the circulation cuts off—"the accident."

"When's he getting home?"

"No, Mamá," I say. "Whenever you two talk, he ends up getting drunk and you end up crying. That won't work anymore."

She doesn't answer—I think she's too shocked to say anything.

"Frankie's father died last week of liver failure. Papá will, too, if he doesn't take care of himself. And what's Evan going to say if you keep crying over the husband you divorced?"

Mamá sniffles. "He was my first love. You never forget your first love."

"It's over, Mamá. From now on, talk to me only. Papá, too, when he calls. None of this, '*Hola*, Tina, how's school? I need to talk to your mother.'"

That gets a little laugh out of her. Good. In our tiny apartment Evan won't be able to eavesdrop and think I'm acting like a jerk to my mother.

"How bad is he?" she asks.

"Some broken ribs. Liver and a kidney messed up. He was pretty sick for a while, and he gets tired." I shake out my hand, where the circulation still hasn't returned to my index finger. "The doctor thinks he'll be well enough to ride a zip line in two weeks. There's one where Tío Claudio just moved, and I want to ride it, too."

"Claudio? My brother?"

"We talked about it when I went to Las Condes." And we've made him swear not to tell her what really happened to Papá.

"How does he get to sleep at night, without . . . ?"

"Warm milk. And lots of exercise."

"That's super." She sounds genuinely happy. "So are you taking care of him?"

"When he's not working. He still has his show."

"I'm sure he's a terrible patient."

I grin, though she can't see me. "I'm up to the job."

At home I'd be sanding floors and hanging curtains. I have no skill at tiling bathrooms or carpeting stairs.

And I can't solve all of Papá's problems, either. But I can help him climb to the top of the *cerro* without collapsing and bake treats to fatten him up before he gets stuck forever with the nickname *El Esqueleto*, the skeleton. And we can have some more good times together that we'll always remember—good times the way we are now and not the way we used to be.

Author's Note

Tina's story came to me in the course of revising *Gringolandia* after it had been accepted for publication. I had been reading some of the testimonies in the *Informe Rettig* (the first of two major human rights investigations of General Augusto Pinochet's seventeen-year military dictatorship in Chile) about Rodrigo Rojas, a Chilean-born teenager living in the United States who died after soldiers set him on fire at a demonstration in Santiago in 1986. The investigation revealed the efforts of paramilitary groups—right-wing groups allied with the military but not under its direct leadership—to silence potential witnesses of this and other atrocities through threats, abductions, and beatings. Officials of the regime went to great lengths to cover up their human rights abuses and at times enlisted people who were not formally in the military but associated with it—like Frankie's uncle—to intimidate or wreak revenge.

Surviving Santiago takes place in June and July of 1989, nine months before the end of the dictatorship. The Pinochet dictatorship came to power following a bloody coup on September 11, 1973, that toppled the elected socialist government of Salvador Allende. In the days and years after the coup, more than 3,000 Chileans were killed or "disappeared," and more than 38,000 were imprisoned and tortured. Like Tina's family, nearly a tenth of the country's population emigrated for political or economic reasons between 1973 and 1990.

Economic policies implemented during the 1980s led to the kind of commercial development—including modern high-rise apartment buildings and enclosed shopping malls—that Tía Ileana's company represented. But while the wealthy and well educated prospered, poor and working-class Chileans endured the brunt of the repression and saw little improvement in their standard of living. By the 1990s, Chile had one of the most unequal distributions of wealth in the world.

In 1980 Chile's constitution was revised to give more power to Pinochet and the military. Under its provisions, a plebiscite (an election in which the only options are yes or no) held in October 1988 would determine whether Pinochet would rule for another ten years, or leave office after the election of a new government the following year. Even if he lost, Pinochet would remain a senator for life and the military would retain its funding and privileges. Despite years of repression and press censorship that was only somewhat loosened to allow the electoral campaign to proceed, the Chilean people voted "no" to their dictator's continued rule. In October 1989, the people voted again, and in a rebuke to the dictatorship, the opposition Concertación soundly defeated the right-wing National Alliance. The Concertación's parties have continued to win a majority of the Presidential elections ever since.

Although the 1988 plebiscite represented the victory of nonviolence and democracy, the events leading up to it were far from peaceful. On September 7, 1986, urban guerrilla fighters from the Manuel Rodríguez Patriotic Front ambushed the general's caravan. While Pinochet and his ten-year-old grandson escaped uninjured, five of his guards were killed. Over the next few days, four well-known leftist activists were kidnapped and murdered in retaliation, including an editor of the magazine *Análisis*, José Carrasco.

The extreme left engaged in revenge killings as well. In April 1991, a little more than a year after the elected government took power, a splinter group of the Manuel Rodríguez Patriotic Front assassinated right-wing senator Jaime Guzmán, a former Pinochet speechwriter and co-author of the 1980 constitution.

These kinds of deadly attacks were spectacular and designed to instill fear, but they were also rare in comparison to other countries in Latin American and to Chile itself a decade earlier. By 1989, politically active Chileans normally did not travel with an entourage or take other security measures, such as varying their route to work. However, many former political prisoners who had endured torture like Marcelo continued to suffer from post-traumatic stress disorder and physical ailments related to their brutal treatment in prison; the danger of suicide far exceeded that of homicide. According to the *Informe Valech* (the most recent human rights investigation), the life expectancy of former political prisoners is 60 to 65 years; the average life expectancy in Chile nears 80 years.

Pinochet and military officials demanded silence and freedom from prosecution as a condition for handing over power to an elected civilian government. However, the courageous efforts of Catholic Church officials, journalists like Marcelo, and lawyers and judges to reveal the truth and, ultimately, to prosecute the perpetrators and compensate the victims played a major role in reducing violence motivated by revenge. Beginning in the late 1980s, those on both sides who perpetrated acts of violence and terrorism found themselves increasingly on the margins. Chileans across the political spectrum worked together to rebuild strong democratic institutions and a prosperous economy.

———

I was in Chile at the beginning of 1990 and witnessed personally the transition from dictatorship to democracy. I consider it the most inspiring experience of my life, and I am grateful to the Society of Children's Book Writers and Illustrators, which funded my trip through a Work-in-Progress grant, and to the many Chileans who showed me their country and told me their stories. Franca Monteverde and her late husband, Nelson Schwenke, opened their home to my husband and me for the three and a half weeks we spent there. Nelson and I took a roll of photos of Valparaíso at night, competing to see who could hold the camera with a steadier hand. Eduardo Peralta gave me a tour of the Vicaría de la Solidaridad, the Catholic Church's human rights organization. (I also saw the McDonald's in the Plaza de Armas, but being a vegetarian, I didn't eat there.) Marcelo Nilo, Manuela Bunster, and Jaime Barría guided me through their neighborhoods and introduced me to their families and their lives. Dozens of Chileans shared their often painful experiences with me in the hope that I would tell people in the United States what happened to them, and to prevent the same thing from happening again, anywhere in the world.

A note on names: In Spanish-speaking countries, people usually have two surnames (last names). The first of those is the father's name, and the second comes from the mother. The principal surname is that of the father, which is the one used for alphabetical order and carried through to the next generation. Thus, Tina's father is

Marcelo Aguilar Gaetani, and he is generally referred to as Marcelo Aguilar. His print byline sometimes reads "Marcelo Aguilar G." Tina's name, Cristina Aguilar Fuentes, comes from her father's principal surname, and then her mother's. (A woman keeps her maiden name but traditionally adds the *de* after marriage.) In both the United States and Chile, Tina uses the surname Aguilar rather than Fuentes. The strictness of these naming conventions varies from country to country, but in Chile during this era people tended to observe them seriously.

Surviving Santiago is a work of fiction, and, as such, it features invented characters. The radio station Radio Colectiva, La Pizza Pellegrino, and Speedy Couriers are fictional as well, and any resemblance to real enterprises by the same or similar names is purely coincidental.

For further reading:

Ackerman, Peter and DuVall, Jack. *A Force More Powerful: A Century of Nonviolent Conflict*. New York: St. Martin's Press, 2000.

Agosín, Marjorie. *I Lived on Butterfly Hill*. New York: Simon & Schuster, 2014.

Allende, Isabel. *My Invented Country*. New York: HarperCollins, 2003.

Bolaño, Roberto. *Distant Star*. New York: New Directions, 2005.

Constable, Pamela and Valenzuela, Arturo. *A Nation of Enemies: Chile under Pinochet*. New York: W.W. Norton, 1991.

Muñoz, Heraldo. *The Dictator's Shadow: Life Under Augusto Pinochet*. New York: Basic Books, 2008.

No. New York: Sony Pictures, 2013. (feature film)

Acknowledgments

Surviving Santiago traveled a long and circuitous road to publication and received much help along the way. My editor at Curbstone Press, the late Alexander "Sandy" Taylor, suggested I write Tina's story when he accepted my manuscript of *Gringolandia* in 2007. My daughter, Madeleine, who was sixteen at the time, was my first reader and contributed to several chapters that, sadly, did not make the final version. Still, we had a lot of fun discussing the story and writing the first draft as we traveled through Spain in the summer of 2007, and I hope these memories are as wonderful for her as they are for me.

After the closing of Curbstone Press at the end of 2009, Ellen Geiger of Frances Goldin Literary Agency took me on and stood by me through rounds of rewrites. My breakthrough revision occurred as a result of my second semester workshop at Vermont College of Fine Arts, led by Jane Kurtz and Rita Williams-Garcia. Jane became my advisor and shepherded me through the rewrite of my first two chapters. Another student in the workshop, Cori McCarthy, read the full draft and connected me with the editor of her powerful and original debut novel (which she also submitted to our VCFA workshop), *The Color of Rain*.

That editor was Lisa Cheng of Running Press Kids,

and I cannot thank her enough for giving my unusual story—and me—a publishing home where I feel part of a family. I am so thrilled to be working with her talented team that includes my VCFA classmate Val Howlett, designer/illustrator Teresa Bonaddio, and copy editor Susan Hom. The sales and marketing team at Perseus Books Group remembered me from Curbstone Press and *Gringolandia*, and I appreciate their enthusiasm and support. I really do feel that this is my homecoming.

I thank the beta readers and members of my various critique groups over the years: Elizabeth Janicek, Beverly Slapin, Gene Damm, Brett Hartman, Lynn Jerabek, Laura Kinney, Mary Nicotera, Lisa Rubilar, Linda Elovitz Marshall, Deb Picker, Anita Sanchez, Kate Hosford, Shelley Saposnik, Heather Strickland, and Kathleen Wilson. I also thank Barbara Seuling and the other members of her summer 2009 Novel Revision workshop for guiding me to my story's ending. As with *Gringolandia*, Mario Nelson helped me with the Chilean *castellano* and kept me up to date on ongoing investigations into the human rights abuses of the Pinochet dictatorship.

In the Author's Note I recognize the Chileans who helped me with my research and shared their stories with me. On this page, I'd like to thank all the readers of *Gringolandia*, who came to love the Aguilar family as much as I do and who wanted to know what happened to Tina and her father. In the twenty years it took for me to write *Gringolandia*, I never thought I would write a companion. I appreciate above all else the opportunity to revisit the lives and world of my fictional family and to remember the courage and generosity of the real people who were their inspiration.